EAST BOUND

NANA MALONE

EAST BOUND
Copyright 2021 by Nana Malone

Cover Art by Najla Qamber

Photography by Wander Aguiar

Model: Lucas Loyola

Edited by Angie Ramey

Proof Editing by Michele Ficht

Published in the United States of America

CHAPTER 1

East

An ice-cold sensation washed over me, leaching all heat, warmth, and affection from my body. Leaving behind a shell.

What the hell had she done?

Spasms gripped my gut and held my breath hostage as I tried to think through any rational explanation.

But there wasn't any rational explanation.

Nyla had betrayed me. The first time I had let anyone truly get close to me in years and this was what happened. I had actually let myself care about someone, and she was still investigating us. Had she ever stopped?

In the beginning, I'd thought I was playing her. Keeping her occupied and away from what the London Lords were doing. But she was the one playing me.

Fuuuck.

I placed a frantic call to Ben as I exited the flat.

He answered in the middle of the second ring. "What's up, mate?"

"We have a fucking problem."

He could hear the tension in my voice, and his tone changed entirely. "Is someone dead?"

"Nyla didn't stop investigating us."

"What do you mean, she didn't stop?"

"You heard me. She didn't fucking stop. I'm looking at the fucking murder board of everything we've done. She knows it all. And if she doesn't know it yet, she's trying to make the connections. Someone's feeding her information. Right now, she has a list of at least ten of our Elite members, and she obviously plans to keep going."

His long drawn out, "Fuuuuck," on the other end was a reassurance that he understood the seriousness of the situation. "Come back to my house."

"Yup. I'm on my way in. Just need to make a quick detour."

"I'll call Bridge and Drew." He sighed. "Fuck, mate, I thought you'd handled her."

"Yeah. Motherfucker, I thought I had too."

For years, I employed limits. I had boundaries. I had lines I would not cross.

Not anymore. Those lines were specifically set for people I cared about.

That list no longer included Nyla.

Are you sure about that?

I shoved aside the worry and the voice of reason that attempted to surface. That voice wasn't real. *She* wasn't real. I'd thought I was falling for her. I'd thought I was becoming less closed off than I'd always been. But I'd only been fooling myself. Any relationship with her was a pure fabrication on my part.

Yes, it was real.

The fuck it was. And since it wasn't real, I was going to do what I should have done with her from the very beginning.

I strode out of the building, turning toward where I'd parked my car.

Charlie Cox, general manager of the Soho London Lords, wasn't used to getting calls on a Sunday from me, but he still answered cheerily.

"Hey, Charlie. Sorry to interrupt your weekend, but I need a lockdown protocol on an Agent Nyla Kincade. I don't want her anywhere near the premises or any hotel we own anywhere. You got me?"

He didn't even hesitate. "Yes, sir. I'll make it happen straightaway."

I knew if she still had her badge it would have negated me barring her from London Lords hotels. But she *didn't* have a badge anymore, so she was going to be shit out of luck.

I thanked Charlie and then made a call to my assistant, Belinda. She didn't answer, but I left her a terse message. "Belinda, I have a no-access protocol on Agent Nyla Kincade. If she attempts to contact our offices in any way, shape, or form, call me immediately."

When I was done with that, I had to stop and lean against a post box. My blood was roaring, making me weak. That sinking feeling in my gut left me dizzy.

My inability to breathe felt like a goddamn elephant had parked itself on my chest.

I leaned over slightly and forced a deep breath into my lungs. Long, deep, sharp pulls. Why the fuck did I feel this way?

This was Nyla. She was always clear and direct. I knew that about her. So how had I not realized she was lying? Speaking the truth was at her very core, so what had I missed? She wouldn't have told an outright lie, but fuck, there could have been a million little evasions. Half-truths I didn't see.

You were the idiot who was thinking with your cock.

Fuck me.

I forced myself to stand up straight. I wasn't going to be a

3

pussy about this. I was going to make her pay. I was due a pound of flesh.

I forced myself to slide into the leather seat of my BMW. I cranked up Stormzy, needing some good old grime to get me through what I had to do.

Up until that point, I had treated her with kid gloves. But those kid gloves had only put everyone in danger, and I didn't plan to make that mistake again.

On my phone, I pulled up my security folder, tapped in my code, and opened the app I'd programmed myself then engaged Bird's Eye Protocol.

Bird's Eye Protocol was my full surveillance package. Anything and everything I needed to see, I could. It wasn't something I did lightly as it was a gross breach of privacy. I didn't have it on the lads or my sister.

I'd set the cameras when I hadn't known her just in case of a situation like this. I'd never turned them on inside her flat though. Only the ones outside.

It was the most invasive form of surveillance. Normally, I would have cameras inside her home and at her work, but I only had the one in her laptop and in her office. I needed more cameras in her flat. The one across the road was the only security system that I tapped into.

I had at least downloaded the software onto her phone before we'd spent much time together. Before I'd started to catch a case of feelings.

I'd mostly forgotten about it afterward, but I needed it now.

Or you could just talk to her.

What the hell was that bullshit about? No. If I talked to her, she would know she'd been caught out and formulate a lie. This was all because I had to get my cock wet.

Fuck. Of all the daft things.

You can bitch, or you can fix it.

Oh, I was going to fix it, all right. And Nyla was going to regret ever crossing me.

All she did was make you love her.

And that was bad enough.

Once my Bird's Eye Protocols were engaged, screens popped up on my app about everything Nyla. Her phone gave me her location. She was headed back toward the tube.

I leaned forward into my glove compartment and pulled out several surveillance cameras. It was a matter of quick work and tricky placement. But I was back in ten minutes after bugging their whole lair, or whatever the hell she and Amelia called that place.

Checking my phone, I smiled when I saw she was headed toward London Lords. That would give me time to properly place cameras in her flat. I'd want eyes on her bedroom, loo, the living room, and her kitchen. I already had her desk at work, the main conference room at Interpol, though she wouldn't be using those for a while. And now her makeshift lair.

You're a sick freak.

Nyla wouldn't make a single move without me knowing. No way in hell was I getting caught unaware again. We'd risked too much. Come too far. When this was over with Jameson, I'd walk away from her. But for the foreseeable future, I had to keep an eye on her, and I would.

She'd already shattered my heart. No way in hell could that happen again.

Nyla

WHAT A SHIT SHOW.

I scurried out of the tube and practically ran to the London Lords Hotel in Soho. *Christ.*

I needed to see East. I had called him twice, but he hadn't answered. I knew he had a meeting, but what if he hadn't gone to the office? Where else could he be?

Panic had my heart pounding into my ribs. The normal *thump, thump* steady rhythm going *taka-taka-taka.* Amelia was good. She was *very* good. I couldn't believe how much work she'd already done.

I hadn't known she was *that* invested.

Weren't you the one who compelled her? Fed the interest?

What the hell was I going to do? She was my partner. My best mate. I had dragged her down this rabbit hole, and now, she'd given it a life of its own. I needed to warn East. At least let him know what was going on.

The bellhop met me with a smile. "Good morning, ma'am. Do you have any luggage?"

I shook my head. "No thanks."

Before he could question me further, I shuffled inside. My trainers made a *squeak, squeak, squeak* sound as I hustled on the sleek marble floor with the chandelier's light refracting across the striations.

The concierge found me next. "Agent Kincade, it's a pleasure to see you again."

I frowned. "Have we met?"

"We did, briefly. How can I help you today?"

I pointed to the lift. "I'm just going to see Mr. Hale. It's urgent."

He gave me a warm smile and clasped his hands behind his back before giving me a slight bow. "I'm so sorry, but Mr. Hale is not available at the moment."

"Well, do you mind if I just go up and wait? This is really important."

"I'm so sorry, Agent Kincade. You won't be allowed to go up and wait."

A fissure of unease crept up my spine. "I don't understand. What's going on? Is there a reason you won't let me upstairs? I know he put me on his permit list."

"Well, as you understand, Mr. Hale resides in the penthouse loft. Unless he specifically has you on his access list or you have a warrant, then I can't let you up."

From the periphery, I noticed two large men dressed in suits inching their way toward me. Then I knew. "What's happening here?"

Thomas, the concierge, or at least that's what his badge said, gave me another soft smile. "Perhaps if you can come back at another time something will change?"

I blinked at him. How was this happening? I had just *left* East. We'd shagged this morning. He'd looked at me like he adored me.

Did he say the words?

I shoved the thought aside.

"There must be some kind of mistake, Thomas. Check again. Call him. I was just here a few days ago. Surely, nothing has changed."

How the hell had he kissed me goodbye like that then banned me from the hotel? What had happened?

My brain kept trying to offer a myriad of unhelpful scenarios. But I refused to believe them. He did care about me. No way he could fake that. Hell, I'd met his friends. They'd enveloped me as part of their team. Part of the plans.

There was no way this was happening. No way in hell. I *knew* him.

Are you sure about that?

He wouldn't have given me that kind of access to the people he loved the most in the world. He trusted me. *We* trusted *each other*. I believed him when he told me about the Elite and what had happened in the past. This was a mistake. It had to be.

When I realized that security was, in fact, coming for me, I sighed. "There is no need for all of that. I'll just keep calling him."

They formed a lose semi-circle around me. Not too tight as to alarm me or to draw attention, but enough so I could see them positioned strategically in case I decided to cause harm or do damage.

Whiskey. Tango. Foxtrot.

Something was wrong. Something was very, very wrong.

I put my hands up. "Fine. I'm leaving."

The concierge gave me that tight smile again, bowing even lower. "Madam."

His effusive smile irritated me. "So, just out of curiosity, if I was staying here, could you boot me?"

His smile was easy enough. "Oh, I'm so sorry, Agent Kincade, but we're all booked for the evening. If you prefer, you can try and make an online reservation."

I shook my head. "Nope, it won't be necessary. I understand."

This was a mistake. It had to be. As I frantically staggered back out onto the streets of Soho and into the crowd of people bustling around me, the sounds of the car horns, the din of the city fading into the background, a numb, icy silence overtook my body. He'd done this on purpose. He'd blocked me. Between last night and this morning, something had changed. What the hell could have happened?

Or everything he's told you was a lie. He doesn't actually care about you. He told you what you needed to hear to get what he wanted.

I leaned against the stone exterior of the hotel. I had no choice since I felt as though my legs were about to buckle and I couldn't breathe. There was no way East would cut me off like this. There was no way he wouldn't talk to me.

Well, he did. So, what are you going to do now?

My head swam. My brain refused to believe what was right in front of it. Refused to acknowledge that not only had I been cast aside, but in the most painful way possible.

East was done with me. But instead of talking to me this morning when he'd kissed me and told me how much he cared for me, all along, he knew what he was planning to do. He knew that he was done. He knew that I was blindly falling for him.

My automatic reaction was to fight back. Hurt him just as much as he'd hurt me. Hurt him the way every other man in my life had hurt me. I wanted to. I wanted to make him bleed. But some voice inside me which had been quiet before spoke even louder in the numbness.

Think. This doesn't make sense. Follow your instincts. Your gut will lead you.

But my gut was wrong.

Figure out the pattern. Apply logic. This isn't right. Something else happened.

I ran my hands through my hair as I tried to piece it together. We'd kissed goodbye. The way he'd woken me up this morning, all sexy, lazy smiles and let-me-feed-you breakfast, and 'Oh wait, here's my cock instead.' Kissing goodbye at his car. The way he watched me go down the stairs at the tube. And then I'd gone to Amelia's secret flat. What could possibly have happened between then and now?

Nothing. You just got fucked and fucked over by the billionaire. You weren't the first, and you certainly won't be the last.

CHAPTER 2

East

IT DIDN'T MATTER what I told myself. Nothing prepared me for walking into her townhouse. Traces of her honeysuckle scent still clung in the air. Every surface was a reminder of somewhere I'd had her or somewhere I wanted to have her again.

Something in my gut tightened. God, why did she have to be such a duplicitous bitch?

Or why can't you choose the right woman?

That was a question for another time. And one I didn't really care to answer.

Breaking into her flat was easy. When I'd taken care of security because of Denning's unannounced visit, I'd made myself a copy of her keys, but I'd never used them until now. All vestiges of giving her privacy or of me somehow being a good guy were long gone. I'd be coming back here to check on things, move cameras around in case it seemed likely she might be onto the surveillance.

Do you even care? Do you want her to know you're watching?

That idea tightened something else. I did, in fact, want her to know I was watching her. Would that make her hot? Would that make her breasts heavy and her nipples tight... knowing I was watching? I muttered a curse as my cock throbbed.

Christ. I did not have fucking time for this. Forcing my mind away from thoughts of her touching herself to the idea of me watching her, I focused on the job at hand.

Setting up the cameras was easy. Kitchen, bedroom. I told myself it was necessary. Not that I *wanted* to spy on her.

Who are you kidding?

When this bomb exploded in my face, and it would, neither of us would back down. And what the fuck would I do if she brought some dodgy bloke back here? Would I watch it?

Yeah, you will, you naughty boy.

I ground my teeth at that. The idea of someone else touching her was enough to set me on edge. I wanted to mark her, to make it clear to all interlopers that they were unwelcome. Particularly in the bedroom.

I'd have to curb my murderous impulses toward the unforeseen future bloke who wouldn't even know I existed. When I hid the camera, just behind her mirror and motion activated of course, I noticed one of her drawers was open. A bright set of fuchsia knickers stuck out. I went to close it, my fingertips lightly tracing the satin. I groaned as my fingers traced over the lace.

You really are a sick fuck.

Goddammit. I hated her so much.

No you don't. You want her. And you're feeling betrayed. So you think a pair of knickers is going to solve your problem, but it's not. You've been down this road before.

Her scarf. I groaned. I'd wanked off with the scarf more often than I cared to think about, and that had been a poor facsimile.

But that didn't stop me from shoving the knickers into the pocket of my trousers.

I set a camera by her bedside as well as in her alarm clock. Just so every time she woke up, I would see her face.

Are you sure this is the healthiest route, mate?

I lied and told myself I was just doing a thorough job.

Sure you are, mate.

God, why her? Why had she done this?

I had trusted in her honesty, but I should have known better. But I'd *wanted* to believe her, and it had worked.

A text came in, and I pulled my phone out, frowning.

Theroux: *We need to meet.*

I tapped out a quick reply.

East: *When?*

Theroux: *Friday. I will text you the location.*

I wasn't going to worry about what he wanted from me. I'd deal with him later. Right then I had Nyla to finish dealing with.

I finished up in the bedroom, leaving everything except her dresser drawer exactly as I'd found it, including the door that wasn't quite closed. In the kitchen, I set up more cameras and another one in the telly. That was easy enough. Then I glanced around and said goodbye to a place that had come to feel homier to me than was absolutely safe.

This is for the best, really. You were getting too close anyway.

As I shut the door of the flat and wiped down the handle, I vowed it was the last time I would step foot in her flat.

Even then, I knew it was a lie.

East

LATER THAT NIGHT, my team watched as I paced the length of Ben and Livy's sitting room, my oxfords making clipping sounds on their marble floor. My tie was askew and my sleeves rolled up. Essentially, I was a disheveled mess.

I could feel the sets of eyes on me. Ben, Bridge, Drew, Livy, Telly. Even Lucas and Bryna eyed me like I was a ticking bomb about to go off. My only saving grace was that Roone and Jessa's flight had been delayed, so they weren't there to witness me slowly losing my shit.

Drew ventured to say something first, although tentatively. "Mate, it's all right. We can fix this. It's not the end of the world. It's not like she knows the inner workings of the Elite. There's not much damage she can *actually* do."

My gaze snapped to his. "Are you fucking serious? This is the fucking end of the world. At least for her it is."

Drew held up his hands and eased back in his seat like I was breathing actual fire.

Bridge opened his mouth, but then I pinned him with a glare, and he snapped it shut again. Were they really trying to lecture me on worst-case scenarios? Twice I'd fucked up now, and it was going to cost us. I'd let an actual viper into our nest, and there was no telling how much damage she'd already done.

Livy was the bravest. "East," she ventured. "Look, we all met her. At worst, she fooled us, but at best, maybe this is a huge misunderstanding. Have you considered that?"

I crossed my arms and glowered at her. Under normal circumstances, I would give her whatever she wanted. I normally thought she was a goddamn delight. She was bright, and funny, and smart. And if Ben hadn't called bagsies, I might have gone for her myself. But now... Now I felt like she was betraying me. Like somehow, she deliberately couldn't see what Nyla had put me through. "Oh please, do keep talking."

She arched a delicate brow, that small gesture managing to

beat back my inner dragon some. "Okay. I get it. You got your feelings hurt. But what is wrong with you? Yes, maybe there was a room with a bunch of photos in it."

"No, not maybe, Liv. Absolutely. And I promise you, your photo was right there. Every single one of us in this room is going down if she has her way."

"Well, she'll have to prove it first, and she can't. So she can dog us, she can come at us, but there is no proof. And she has to deliver it. That's how Interpol works. So relax for a moment. She knows that. She's not daft; she's smart. So stop and think. This doesn't sound like Nyla. The woman that I met the other night was direct, and she was clear. There was no pretense. She's the kind of woman that accidentally steps in it, because she's *too* direct and says the wrong thing. No way would she have been shagging you if she didn't actually *want* to be with you."

I hated the flare of hope in my chest. I hated that my brain so easily latched onto the most unlikely scenario. I hated that I was so desperate to have this be an option that I let Livy talk some more.

Instead, I needed to let my hatred speak for me because at least that was rational. I'd been thinking with my dick for too long. Following my heart for too long. "Liv, I appreciate it, but that's really naive. She's coming for us. And we've got to do something about it. It's my job to protect the team, and I failed. Wishing it wasn't so isn't going to change anything."

She sighed. "Easy does it. I'm not naive. You're overreacting. Where is the cool logic? Where is the calculation? You're jumping to burn this woman, and you don't even know what was going on. Maybe that's her coworker's vision. What was her name, Amelia Jansen? Did you ever consider that?"

I'd provided the team with full dossiers on Nyla and her

partner before I'd brought her around. I didn't think anyone actually read those.

Apparently, Livy does.

My brows snapped down. "What is it with you? Why are you opting to believe her? She's coming after us. Your *fiancé*, you, the rest of us. None of us will be unscathed. Why don't you understand that?"

Ben pushed to his feet. "Mate, calm down."

"Of course, you'd come to Livy's defense," I spat.

"Yeah, well, she's my fiancée, isn't she? Look, I get it, mate. This is a problem. But we're all here, and we'll figure it out."

I knew what he was doing. Trying to diffuse me. Like letting a kettle sing for a bit after you turned off the stove to let the pressure dissipate. "Fuck, you make it sound so easy. She's fucking Interpol, and I told her about the Elite, like a wanker." The center of my chest tightened. Fuck, why was it so tight? I tried to breathe through the constriction and found I was only able to take short breaths. Then the room started to spin.

Fucking hell. I was having a goddamned panic attack. I hadn't had one since I was a kid.

Stop it. Your panic isn't real. Control the situation. There is enough air.

I forced three deep breaths which brought my temperature down.

Bridge, usually my partner in rationality, eased back in the couch, spreading his long legs out, trying to get comfort and space. "So what are you going to do? You can't put that cat back in the bag. So she knows about the Elite. Does that matter?"

"What are you fucking on about, mate? Of course, it matters." Why couldn't they see it? "I have employed Bird's Eye Protocol. She won't be able to breathe without me knowing about it."

Telly, uncharacteristically quiet for most of this argument, perked her brow. "What the fuck is Bird's Eye Protocol?"

Livy didn't seem to know either. But Lucas, Lucas had a clue.

The prince pushed to his feet as well. "Dude, that path is fucked. I get it. I have no intention of going to prison. I'm too pretty to be someone's bitch. But, bro, this isn't the way. When she finds out, it's going to be open fucking season."

That was only *if* she found out. "She won't find out. I am that good."

From her chair, Telly asked again, "What in the fuck is Bird's Eye Protocol?"

Ben shrugged, familiar with my security protocols. "It's full surveillance. Cameras everywhere. In her home, in her office, her car. The full monty."

Telly turned her gaze to me then. "You think that's wise? Poking our noses into things we probably shouldn't even know about half the time?"

"Yeah, because we have to see what's coming. Theroux already got to us."

She threw up her hands. "How the fuck were you supposed to know to look to the sky? You took out the cameras, every last one of them on the CCTV. We were literally untraceable with that diamond. How were you supposed to know Theroux had a drone in the sky? You're not God."

I was supposed to be pretty damn close. "It's my fucking job to know."

She sighed. "One man can't know everything. And sooner or later, you're going to have to see that. You have no control over this. I get that. And it is terrifying. I get that too. But this whole person-of-interest angle you've got going on, it's a problem. She's law enforcement. And when she finds out you've been watching where you shouldn't be, we'll have bigger problems than we do now. In the meantime, why don't we focus on something we *can* actually control or at least get a handle on?"

I rolled my neck. The tension knots had been there all fucking day, and there was no easing them.

You could ease them by talking to her.

Fuck. It's like no matter what I did, my rallying point was always her. Like my body was fighting me not to go to her.

Drew sat forward again. "All right, if you don't want to talk about Nyla, we won't. Just a reminder that you gave your word. No Bird's Eye Protocol on any of us."

I scowled at him. "Oi, mate. First of all, the last thing I need to see is your naked arse. I saw plenty of that when we were at Eton. Secondly, you know I have a moral compass. I don't spy on my mates."

Livy grumbled in the corner, saying something along the lines of, "You love her, you idiot, and she won't forgive this."

I didn't give a fuck if she forgave it or not. Even if I had feelings for her, I would show her no quarter.

"Good thing I don't need her to forgive me." I pinched the bridge of my nose. I needed to get them back on track. "Okay, so Theroux. He's asking for a meet on Friday. I think Ben and I should go and meet with him."

Bridge laughed. "Mate, if we decide to do this, you'll be in the van. Coms guy. You're obviously not thinking clearly. Drew gets to come."

I shook my head. "No, if we're meeting with him, I go."

Bridge calmly continued. "Mate, Ben and I are both better at hand-to-hand combat. Drew is an excellent negotiator. You're the tech guy."

"Which means I can at least scan the property, check out the perimeter, see what kind of security he has."

Ben spoke slowly to me, as if I was an idiot. "Mate, there is no way he is going to actually take us to one of his safe houses.

There won't be anything to examine. You're the lookout and driver."

He had to be kidding me. "Oh, hell no. I'm security. I go in with you, or we don't go at all."

Ben scowled at me. "What is with you? There is nothing to prove here. We've all made mistakes. Remember that time I had to trust a woman I didn't know with sensitive information? She's my fiancée now."

Livy beamed at him. "More like you foisted your contraband on me and almost sent me to jail, but that's really beside the point."

"Are you two done playing loving and happy families?"

Surprisingly, it wasn't Ben who took a piece of me. It was Telly. She slowly leaned forward in her seat. "Oi, mate, you think you fucked up. And even then, none of us think you fucked up because we all met her. It's unlikely that *all* of us would be wrong. So maybe you should talk to her. Maybe you clear the angle of 'we're coming at it head on,' but don't take a piece out of my best friend's happiness just because you're full of piss and vinegar right now. As for Theroux, I'll go. *I'll* be in the van. Pretty boy here gets to go inside with you. You four are the London Lords. You're the faces."

Lucas perked up. "Can I come too?"

We all shook our heads, and Ben outright denied him. "No, your face is too public, and we're not giving Theroux the satisfaction. You're benched for now until we figure out what the fuck he wants."

Lucas grumbled. But with Bryna holding his hands, he didn't argue too much. He was a prince by title, but a con man by birth. And before he'd ever found his way to his family, he'd been one of the best thieves in North America. I hated to think that we'd need him again, but we most probably would. But first things first. We had to deal with Theroux. And then we'd deal with Nyla. I wasn't going to let anything distract me from that ultimate goal, which was to protect my mates by any means necessary.

———

East

W ELL, *that went well.*

So far, I'd managed to put my team in danger, then I'd exposed them to Interpol, and now I'd pissed them off. Fuck, I knew I'd been bang out of order with Liv. None of this was her fault. The blame belonged squarely at my feet, and I was having a hell of a time with that knowledge.

If before I had been England's best striker, I was now in the position to be sacked and traded at any moment. I really needed to get my shit together or this was going to go very, *very* badly for everyone.

Easier said than done.

A prickle of unease tripped down my spine as I left Ben's house in Belgravia. It lingered on my skin like a hoard of gnats set on annoying me to death. As I pulled down the drive and out the security gate, I couldn't explain it or understand it, but I knew I was being followed.

That was the last shit I needed. Already things hadn't gone exactly according to plan. This uneasy, unsettled feeling was determined to follow me around

Was it Theroux? Was it his men? Hell, could it be Garreth Jameson? Did he know we were coming for him?

I pulled over outside of the square and parked my car, wanting to see just what I was dealing with. The little voice at the back of my head told me that was a bad idea and that I was making a mistake. But then, this other little voice that was full of fury, anger, disappointment, and pain wanted to fight.

I locked my BMW and started to walk. Despite how obnoxious and gaudy it was, it didn't stand out in this part of London. I walked with no real aim.

I might not live in Belgravia, but I was familiar enough in that part of London to know it like the back of my hand. I made a left, and then a right, conscious that I had a shadow following me. Conscious that my instincts were screaming that something wasn't quite right.

I nodded to passersby walking their dogs. It was late in the evening, nearly eleven, but I saw a young couple pushing a baby pram, looking exhausted.

Parenthood.

Please, God, never set me up for that bullshit. Because guaranteed, even if they tried not to, they would fuck that kid up. And then they'd have to think about things like protection. And God help them if that baby was a girl, because they would never ever be able to keep her safe from twats like me. I shuddered.

Across the street, I made a quick right and then ducked into the shadows and waited. It didn't take long. At first, I heard the clip-clop of what sounded like high heeled shoes. A fast, clipped run as if some woman hammered about having the wrong bloody address. And then I heard a steady, soft footfall that turned into a rapid pace. Faster than the woman in heels.

It was accompanied by panting. A jogger maybe? Less than five seconds later, I watched as he ran by. And then it was quiet. Almost like someone was *trying* to be silent. There was the odd rustle of leaves and then utter stillness, and I knew. Someone had come for me. As I stilled, ready to do what I had to do, there was a brief prickle of warmth as I wondered, what if it's Nyla coming for me?

That brief lapse of focus caused my awareness to falter when one of the shadows stepped into the alley.

Only the moonlight glinting on the metal barrel of the gun snapped me to attention just in time.

With a twist to my right, I used my left hand to jam against the metal, deflecting the gun. And then with my right, I brought up a hook under the arm, hitting my opponent. And then we began to grapple for dominance, for control, for the gun.

He tried to jerk on my grip, but I pulled him even farther back into the darkness, well aware that there were trash barrels and bins in the alley. The last thing I needed was noise to bring someone in search of what was happening.

I took an elbow to the gut and doubled over forward, but I didn't let go. Instead, I dragged him even farther back and whipped our bodies around, whacking his shoulder, and unfortunately mine, into the brick wall. He grunted, and the gun clattered out of his grip.

Now, we had a party. He twisted in the opposite direction, sending his left elbow backward. I ducked and planted my face between his shoulder blades, mainly to avoid getting clocked in the temple.

I delivered a kidney shot with my left fist, twisted my body and twerked it just the way I'd been shown in all my MMA classes. He yowled. His knees buckled from the pain. I let him fall and then delivered a knee to the back of his head. As he fell forward, I released him, aiming to pull him up by his shirt. But the fucker was strong. He swung his legs around in a pin wheel. The move caught one of my ankles, sending me onto my back.

I rolled, briefly cataloging the pain of my spine hitting the pavement but brushing it off. I didn't have time to dwell on that. Quickly, I rolled to my left, keeping my eyes on my attacker. Doing a reverse push up, I shoved back up with my feet, and he pushed back up to his. My eyes were now adjusted to the darkness, and the motherfucker smiled at me evilly.

"I can kill you just as easily with my hands as with a gun."

"Well, mate, I mean, at least show some respect. If you're coming after me, then you know who I am. And don't you think you owe me the courtesy of realizing that I'm not going to make it easy?"

His voice was gravelly when he spoke. "You're a pussy. You didn't even know you were being watched."

I grinned at him then. "Are you sure I didn't? What, you thought I ambled on into this dark alleyway for shits and giggles? You're an eejit."

And then I saw it in his face as it dawned on him that he'd been the one pulled into the trap.

"Just one question though; who the fuck sent you?"

"Fuck. You."

"I'm not sure you understand. I asked you a direct question, and you didn't answer. It's quite rude. Who sent you?"

He shrugged then. "Your mum."

"So, now we're trading mum jokes. Okay, I have one," I said as we turned, circling each other with our fists up. "Your mum is so ugly that all she could do was produce a baby who is the spitting image of her."

The bloke was about six feet tall, wide though. Stocky. Big meaty fists. If I got hit by one of those, it was going to hurt. *A lot.* His upper lip curled in a sneer. "Was that your best attempt?"

I stopped moving then and planted my feet. "No. I know it was a little weak. But I needed to distract you."

The fucker had the good sense to scope out his surroundings.

"Yeah, fucker, we're not the only ones out here."

Then he staggered toward me. The brunt of the hit on

the back of his head shook him, making him crumble in front of me. Anger and irritation flashed in his eyes before he fell.

I dragged in shuddering breaths "What the fuck took you so long?"

"Well, excuse me for having faith in you to handle that." Drew stepped out of the shadows. "I mean, I was kind of enjoying your jokes back and forth. But he was right. Your joke was weak."

I breathed a sigh of relief as we rolled the twat over on his back. "I wasn't making a joke though. It's just a statement of a fact. He is ugly. And thank you for not making me ruin this suit. It's one of my favorites."

Drew just rolled his eyes and leaned over. "Why am I the one who put him down?"

"I was playing with my food. Working out my frustrations."

"Yeah, fair enough. Do you know who he is?"

I shook my head. "No, but we're going to find out."

I quickly searched his pockets but came up empty. Then I took out my phone and the case I had for it from my back pocket. I always kept a piece of sticky film just for these situations, should I ever need to lift a print.

I peeled back the covering of one of the film sheets and took an imprint of both thumbs and then resealed it. Then I took a photo of him. "Let's find out who he is. Maybe who he works for."

Drew panted. "Yeah, anytime you want to say thanks, I'm just sitting here waiting."

"Oh, come on, all you had to do was stand in the dark and knock the guy out. I did the hard work. I actually did some fighting there. I almost tore my suit. This is a Boateng, dammit."

Drew rolled his eyes. "God, why are you such a princess?"

I blinked at him owlishly. "Because I like to look good."

He laughed. "So ugly, yet so lame."

I scoffed. "Please, we all know that I'm the prettiest of us."

Drew rolled his eyes. "I'm pretty sure that's Ben."

I rubbed my jaw. "I am insulted. You know what? Let's ask your mum."

Drew made a gagging sound. "You wish."

I turned to the eejit on the ground. "So, what the fuck are we going to do with him?"

"Call housekeeping. Then you get to find out who's coming after you."

CHAPTER 3

Nyla

Talk about sad.

No, screw sad, this was an intervention waiting to happen. After being humiliated at London Lords, I was dragging my sorry arse back home.

Where else was I going to go? It was bloody Sunday. And perhaps, I'd spent a concerted amount of time at the off-license searching out the best wine on my way home. Not that it really mattered what kind of wine I chose to consume.

So you're just going to sit there feeling sorry for yourself?

I tried to tell myself that wasn't what was happening. That I was just drinking some wine after a shitty breakup where I didn't exactly know what I'd done wrong or why I was being broken up with. But this was fine. Everything was *fine.*

Seriously, when did you get so pathetic?

My argument with myself was not helping my mood.

In the end, I bought one bottle of red, one bottle of white, a bottle of rosé, and snacks. Several kinds of biscuits. And even American Cheetos. I'd missed American Cheetos. When I was a child, I consumed copious amounts of Cheetos, getting cheese dust smeared everywhere in the back of Mum's car.

My father would insist that they were bad for me. And all said and done, I was inclined to agree with him. But still, that cheesy, powdery goodness, artificial all the way, was comforting. And in moments like this, when I was under stress and duress, that was what I needed.

With my double-fisted bags of shame and glory, I stepped outside the store and brought up my hood, hoping none of my neighbors saw me in my sad joggers and jumper.

This was breakup food. I already had pints of ice cream at home. This was only to tide me over until I could do real grocery shopping. But the idea of perusing Sainsbury's, even online, was too much to bear. I could make do with wine and Cheetos.

Okay, Maltesers too. Because one needed chocolate in moments like this.

How in the world was this my life? I had once been a badass with a great job and good friends.

But then I'd had the not-so-bright idea of leaving MI5 to come and work for my father at Interpol. Why had I done that? From the moment I made that painful decision three years earlier, I'd only been unhappy. Any effort to get my father to notice me was met with disdain. Because, as he said, I shouldn't be chasing approval.

But he was my bloody father.

Although, if I was being honest, I didn't so much chase his approval as want him to notice that I was *fantastic* at my job. All on my own. And I couldn't really give up a good fight, which, you know, was probably a detriment from his point of view.

With a sigh, I hefted my bags, wishing I'd brought my trolley along, but my townhouse was only a few short blocks, and I would survive.

I turned a corner and started to get that prickly heat sensation along my neck. The same kind of heat I'd listened to on more than one occasion. The same kind of instinct that said, 'even though the man approaching you walking his dog is smiling and looks friendly, like somebody you might meet in a pub, doesn't mean you can trust him.'

That heat slithered along the back of my neck. I switched my bags to my left hand and reached inside my pocket for my set of keys.

We weren't even supposed to have Mace. It was illegal in Britain. But there was a little puffer tab that was created by MI5. It looked like a key fob. But one press in the direction of whoever was trying to attack you, and it would puff out a fine mist and powder. One that would act like Mace, stinging the attacker's eyes and giving them boils. It was temporary of course, nothing permanent. But it was enough to allow time to get away.

In the name of safety, every single MI5 agent had one. Sadly, it was a one-time use situation.

I'd never had to use mine, and didn't turn it in when I left the organization. It was on my key chain. And unfortunately, it seemed like I might have to use it.

Up ahead, the guy was turning onto my street. Unfortunately, I had to pass a darkened alley to get to my home. I scowled. Why the hell wasn't the off-license on a better marked road?

Also, why did you have to stop at the off-license? That's pathetic.

It wasn't pathetic. I got dumped. I had a right to wine. At least it wasn't bourbon.

I'd had a bourbon stint once while in uni. That had ended poorly, and I'd never done it again. I tried to assess if there was a possibility of me making it around the alley, but that would involve having to turn around and go back.

No. I could do this. All I had to do was make sure my hands were free. I could make this happen.

When I passed the alley, it was a feat to ignore the screaming whine of my instincts beckoning me to do something. To fight. Or run. Do something other than walk steadily forward. My instincts begged me to pull out a bottle of wine and be ready to use it as a weapon. But I was rational and stayed calm. I knew that my puffer tab was the best defense I had. And home was close. Home was *so* close.

And then I had a wayward thought. *Who are you going to call if this goes south?*

I wasn't calling East. That was for damn sure. I wasn't calling Denning. I supposed I could call my father. That's *if* he would answer.

I settled on Amelia. But how had I gone from having a whole crew, a whole team of people behind me who would come at a moment's notice if needed, to having only one person I could rely on? There was no one to call except Amelia. I would absolutely rely on her if I had to, but, God, my life had certainly gone tits-up in the last few weeks.

Once in the alleyway, I marched with purpose. Slapping forward, head up, eyes alert. Ready for anything. But sadly, nothing happened. All that anticipation, all that tension for nothing. What the hell was wrong with me?

Maybe this whole East thing had messed me up more than I thought.

I stepped one foot in front of the other, step after step, and managed it through the darkness, the broken streetlamp up ahead flickering dimly. Once I passed it, knowing that I was halfway through made me breathe slightly easier. It also made me even more aware of my surroundings, the rustling of footsteps behind me, the voices and laughs from a club or a bar up ahead.

All somewhat familiar.

At the end of the alley, just when I was breathing a sigh of relief, someone called my name. "Nyla."

I coughed and jumped. "Jesus fucking Christ."

It was Hazel, Denning's girlfriend, and I walked right into her.

"Hey. Are you okay?"

"Jesus Christ, what are you doing here?"

She held up two bottles of wine. "I have a party on the next block over. I just walked from the tube." She pointed back at the brightly lit tube station.

"Oh, right."

"What are you doing here?" she asked.

I held up my packages, and because I had no excuse save to admit that I might now have a drinking problem, I said, "Uh, yeah. I also have a party."

She laughed. " We should have you over again."

"Oh yeah, like it went so swimmingly last time?"

She laughed. "Well, okay, it could have gone better, true. But, you know, I think you had a point. Denning can be an arsehole."

My eyes went wide. "What?"

"Look, I know who I'm marrying. I do. There's nothing you could tell me about him that I don't know. He can be the worst, but when he has moments of kindness and vulnerability, it's amazing. And that is the Denning I know. I'm sorry you had a different experience."

"Yeah, if he makes you happy, it's none of my business."

"Right. But are you okay? You looked a little scared."

The furrow of her brow, her wide blinking eyes, did say concern. But there was something just, I don't know, off about her being there.

"Why would say that?" I didn't know her that well. It was

entirely possible she knew someone over here. After all, the flats in this neighborhood were high-end, fancy. All kinds of people lived in them. People who might even buy her art, after all.

"You're sure you're okay?"

"Yeah. I'm fine."

She hesitated. "Do you want me to walk you to your party?"

What, and discover that it was a party of one? A pity party for myself? Hell no. "No, it's all good. I'm just going to head upstairs."

"Well, great. I'm glad to see you, Nyla. You have a good night, okay?"

I nodded and gave her a wan smile. Honestly, she was very nice, but her choice of Denning made her suspect, so I knew I couldn't trust her and would never be able to.

But, poor thing, she was definitely too good for him. And she had no idea.

———

Nyla

MY GLASS BOTTLES clinked as I placed my bags on the counter. I pulled out the white and the rosé, placing them in my refrigerator. The red I uncorked and let sit for a moment.

For several long beats I forced myself to take soothing deep breaths to try to calm my racing heart. I was fucking losing it. Three years ago, I'd had an ideal life. Why the fuck had I ever left MI5? I'd been happy. Rising. Doing well. My father respected me. I'd had friends, so many friends.

But now? God. My life had shrunk to this Interpol job, which I'd recently lost when I was suspended by my own father, an ex I hated who had ruined my soul, my one friend I saw regularly whom I'd also worked with, and a man who no longer wanted me.

To make matters worse, I was actually pining for it all. I wasn't used to being a loser. I was a badass who took charge of things.

Oh yeah... You're such a badass that you're going to drink that entire bottle of wine without a glass, aren't you?

I eyed the bottle curiously. Wasn't I doing the environment a favor if I drank it straight from the bottle? For the first time in my life, I had nothing to do, nowhere to go, no case to follow up on, nothing. I should be relieved. I hadn't had a vacation in, God, how long? An honest to God vacation, relaxing and shit. At a beach. I should go to the beach, not in the UK, but somewhere sunny.

Some time away would certainly do me good. Everything was upside down, and I needed to figure out how to get back on equal footing. But how? I didn't even know how I'd gotten off the right footing in the first place.

You know how. You trusted East Hale.

I grabbed the bottle, sans glass might I add, and headed for the living room. But before I passed the threshold, I tripped on something pink and frilly. Upon further inspection, said pink and frilly thing appeared to be my panties.

What. The. Hell?

We'd made love all over the flat the night before, but he'd gotten me naked in the living room, not the kitchen. So where had these come from?

Frowning I held them up. It was a fresh pair. They still had the faint scent of my detergent.

Maybe, they'd stuck to me when I'd gotten dressed this morning?

Or he knew he was leaving and tried to take a souvenir.

No. That was creep city.

But just the kind of shit he would do.

Unable to help myself, with bottle in hand, I searched my flat. If he'd been there, he had to have left some evidence.

I knew I wasn't being rational. But with every sip of wine, logic flew out the window. Who needed rationality when I had wine?

I told myself I was being crazy, that I'd find no evidence. But in my bedroom, the hint of musky aftershave lingered in the air. And there was a divot on my duvet. I could see the faintest hint of an impression.

You're grasping at straws.

No. I wasn't. He'd been there. But the question was, why?

I might've been angry with him. I might've thought that he was being a juvenile prick. And he might've even scared me just a little, but I still trusted him. I knew he'd been telling the truth about the London Lords. If I was being honest with myself, I'd known before I even started chasing them. What had irritated me the most about the Lords was that I didn't like to lose.

I fell back onto my bed, careful of my half-empty bottle of wine. How had my life gone from what I'd always wanted to this? Running around my flat, swearing I could smell the man who dumped me. If I hadn't started talking to East, started falling for him, my life would have been normal. Sure, I might have hated being under the constant torture of Denning Sinclair, but at least it would be mine. At least I'd have cases, a purpose.

You'd be making your father proud.

Instead, this was my life. Lying about on my duvet with a half-empty bottle of wine.

I wasn't pathetic. I just needed my job.

Ever since I could remember, I'd wanted to be an Interpol agent just like my Dad. I thought it was so cool when he went skipping off to different countries, working with law enforcement. I'd thought there was a whole lot more of chasing the bad guys, but it was mostly bureaucratic except for the occasional case where I was tracking down jewel thieves. But even then, tracking them down was mostly following paper trails, investigatory stuff. There was very little actual chasing of the bad guys. When the time for that came, I called in local law enforcement. But still, I needed that chase. My brain needed to work. Without it, who was I? That was the problem when your job was your whole life.

It had given me meaning. A purpose. A way to connect with my father even after years of not being able to really communicate with him. Oh, I knew my father loved me. I didn't have the usual daddy complex that most girls did, but I felt like I was always disappointing him. I knew, that in so many ways, I wasn't exactly what he wanted in a child. The worst part was, Denning the Dick had exploited that. And now I was paying the price.

No more thinking about Denning.

My brain gave me a replacement. *East.*

The way he'd hovered over me last night, one arm braced, his hips bracketing mine. His other hand cupping my cheek as he held my gaze.

My bed smelled of him... of something woody and expensive. He'd come back today. For what though? His things? I was unable to find any evidence that he had been there, but everything in my cells told me he had been. Like his presence had cast a shadow in my flat on everything he'd touched.

And don't forget the knickers. They hadn't been there this morning. I'd done a mental sweep of the place as we'd left. I hadn't seen them. He'd been back.

Or maybe that's wishful thinking.

It was. Wishful. I wanted him back so I could rail at him for doing this to me, for turning me into this weak, needy person.

You're not needy. You're heartbroken. It's different.

My mind wouldn't let it go. The possibility that he'd been there. But why?

Did he want something from me?

Was he... watching me?

My skin flushed hot at the thought, and I throbbed between my thighs. Missing him. I was so fucked. I'd been had and discarded by the billionaire. I needed to get over it as quickly as possible.

But the idea that he couldn't let go stuck with me. He'd watched me before from cameras across the street at the parking tower. I'd kept my blinds lowered after that. But if he was going to torture me, then maybe a little payback was in order.

My phone buzzed, and I forgot all thoughts of revenge as I dove for it, praying that somehow on the other end of the line would be a new purpose, a new intention. Ooh, even better, a new job, though I hadn't exactly applied for one. Or better than that... East with a fucking apology.

"Hello?"

I hadn't even checked the number. What if it was Denning, bugging me like the dick that he was?

But the voice on the phone wasn't familiar. It was mostly British but slightly accented with something else. French? Maybe Italian? No. Definitely, French. "Agent Kincade, this is Francois Theroux."

I bolted upright. "Excuse me?"

"Francois Theroux," he repeated, as if I could have possibly missed it the first time.

"Oh, I didn't know we were phone buddies."

"You are a joy, Agent Kincade."

"Hardly. Try telling that to my father. I am pretty sure he sees me as the bane of his existence, but you didn't call to talk about my daddy issues. What exactly do you need from me, Mr.

Theroux? Because I have been trying to figure it out, and I still don't know. So I think I need you to explain."

"You don't trust easily, do you?"

"Nope, sure don't. I learned that the hard way. What do you need, Mr. Theroux? And why are you willing to throw away your freedom and your livelihood because of it?"

"Who says I'm throwing away my freedom?"

I coughed out a laugh. "I'm sorry, but aren't you the man who told me that you would turn yourself in to me?"

"Oh, I actually intend to turn myself in to you. I make a habit of keeping my word, Agent Kincade."

My head started to hurt. I should have made it clear that I wasn't dealing with him anymore. I should have told him no. I should have made him go away. But no, instead I stayed on the phone with him, entertaining whatever the hell he had in mind for me. "If you turn yourself in, you somehow think that means freedom?"

"Agent Kincade, just because I turn myself in to you, that doesn't mean I will stay incarcerated."

"And you just told me your plan."

"You don't know the half of it. So, what say you? Do you want to hear what I need from you, Nyla Kincade?"

"And if I'm not ready? If I don't want to hear it?"

"That is, of course, your choice. But I wouldn't bite off your nose to spite your face if I were you, especially not when you can have everything you've ever wanted. Are you willing to take that risk? Are you willing to think outside the box for once? You have to trust someone."

"How about we just say that I don't trust anyone? And I will be watching you."

"That's a fair arrangement."

"So, what do you want exactly?"

"You can relax, Agent Kincade. There's nothing nefarious

about what I want. I'm merely asking for your assistance in finding someone."

"My assistance?"

"Yes, I want you to help me."

"And what's going to happen to this *someone* when I find him?"

"That, my dear, is not your concern."

"See, that's the thing. I don't want to help anyone if their intention is to end someone's life."

"Would you like me to promise you that I'm not going to kill him?"

"Well, considering I don't trust anyone, I wouldn't believe your promise anyway. How about you tell me who you want me to find, and I'll determine if I turn him over or not?"

"And how does that bring me any guarantee, Agent Kincade?"

"Oh, it doesn't. But weren't you just talking to me about trust?"

He chuckled. "My, you are a handful, aren't you? Well, even though my word apparently isn't worth much to you, I still give it. No one is going to die. At least not by my hand."

"What's he done?"

"Suffice it to say that he took something from me, and I want it back."

"You do realize I don't work for you, right? You can't make me make me do things I don't want to. I have zero intention of doing anything illegal."

"Agent Kincade, I am wounded that you think I would ask you to do such a thing. I recognize that your integrity matters to you. It's important. Sadly, I have to inform you that I am not the villain you think I am. Not everything is as black and white as it seems."

"Now, that's just the thing. I do believe in black and white, not shades of gray. I think black and white is safe."

"It might be safe, but you'll find that you end up very disappointed, because not all men can be heroes. Not all men see things as black and white. Not all men can be exactly what you want them to be. So what do you say? Will you help me or not? The choice is yours."

The move was mine. I didn't think I'd ever wanted anything so badly. A chance to show my father that I wasn't a disappointment, that I could close the biggest open case of his career. "I would do it, except we have a little problem. I am no longer an Interpol agent. As of a couple of days ago, I've been suspended."

The cursing on the line was so inventive I wasn't sure I'd heard some of those words before. "Agent Kincade, now is not the time to play games. You will go back to Interpol, because my plan does not work if you do not. Without your access, you're useless to me. And something tells me that you would very much still like to be the apple of your father's eye."

That stinging burn in the dead center of my chest told me he had my number. He knew exactly who I was, what motivated me, and why I needed it. I hated that I was that transparent. I hated that the stranger who knew my father so well could read me without ever having met me. "What do you want me to do? I've been suspended."

"If you've been suspended, then find a way back. Because at the end of the day, all your father has ever wanted was you by his side."

"Clearly, you don't know him as well as you think you do if you think that's what he wants."

"Sometimes your parents can surprise you. What you *think* they want is not what they actually want. Go back. Talk to him. Be contrite. Apologize or do whatever it is you need to do. If you do that, I swear to you, you'll be back in. And I need you back in for this. Besides, how else would you show your father that he made the mistake of a lifetime if you're not back at Interpol?"

"What you're asking is impossible."

"No, nothing is impossible given enough time and resources. Unfortunately for you, Agent Kincade, you don't have much time. So if I were you, I'd figure out a way to make that work."

CHAPTER 4

East

THERE WAS NO AVOIDING HER.

Nyla had infiltrated my mind. As much as I wanted to cut her out, in a few short weeks she'd become so intertwined in my world that I couldn't extricate her. She was more than under my skin. She'd woven herself down to a cellular level. But she was the enemy.

Or maybe you have it wrong.

I didn't have it fucking wrong. I knew I didn't.

What was worse, what pissed me off even more, was that after everything we'd been through, what happened in Monaco, all the shit with her father, she knew she had to be careful.

Her boss was obsessed with her. She wasn't taking care of herself. She wasn't sleeping. She wasn't paying attention, wasn't watching to see if she was being followed. And she was.

By me.

Bird's Eye was more than cameras and phone tapping and computer hacking. It was actual, physical surveillance... by me.

You know this makes you a creeper, right?

I was not a creeper. She was coming for us, so I was going for her. She deserved everything that she got. Hadn't I taught her? Hadn't I asked her to be more careful? But there she was, running around the world like she hadn't been attacked. Like she hadn't found her fucking boss inside her flat. Why didn't she give a shit?

She's not your problem anymore.

That was true. Still, I rubbed at the ache in the center of my chest. This was my own fault. I'd let her get too close. My phone chimed, and I pulled it out of my pocket as I watched her flat from above the parking tower. It had been a matter of a few keystrokes to purchase the small flat above the parking levels that looked directly into her townhouse. And then it had been a simple phone call to have a decorator come in with some simple comforts. A couch, a desk, somewhere for my laptop and computers. Just so I could keep an eye on her.

Are you protecting her? Or are you protecting yourself?

With that ache in the middle of my chest, the one that I couldn't rub away, I wasn't sure which it was. If she wasn't going to protect herself, she certainly needed protecting. And this way, I would know what she was planning. While I'd been at Ben's, I'd tracked her by phone. Like a compulsion.

As much as I hated it, as much as I didn't want to believe it, I'd trusted the wrong person. I had made that mistake. And now, it was coming back to haunt me.

My phone chimed again, and I glowered as I pulled it out of my pocket. When I saw Nyla's name flash next to the messages, my thumb hovered over it. I tried to talk myself out of doing what I knew I shouldn't. My thumb hovered over her name and I wanted to press it. I wanted to see what other lies she could spout.

Don't do it mate. Slide and hit delete. Ignore it. Like you have all the others.

Instead, I slid it to read her message.

Nyla: *Are you watching me?*

Instant fucking hard on.

Christ. Did she know I was there?

I glanced down to her flat. The lights dimmed and she strolled out from the bedroom.

Another text.

Nyla: *I can feel you watching me.*

Fuuuck. Beads of sweat popped on my brow. Could she feel my gaze now as it licked over her skin?

Nyla: *Matter of fact, since you won't talk to me, I'm going to just go ahead and remind you of what you're missing by not hearing me out.*

Jesus Christ, she thought this was some kind of joke? I'd trusted her. I brought her in to meet my family. I'd let her behind the shield. She knew more about the Elite than any non-member who wasn't married to a member. That could hurt us. And while we wanted to hurt the Elite, or rather specific numbers of them, it had to happen on our timeline and in the way that we deemed proper and necessary. I didn't want Nyla poking her head in because she would seek and destroy. Her cuts would not be surgical, and the blowback would land on Ben, Bridge, myself, and Drew. I didn't care what happened to me, but the lads, they had lives... families.

In the low light, I could see that she'd dragged over her loveseat so that it was in my direct view. She knew I was here. Fuck my life. How did she know?

Because you're unoriginal, you knob. You've done this before.

Jesus fucking Christ, *anyone* could be watching. I quickly ran to my laptop, opened it, and with a few keystrokes, I was into that camera and shut it down. Even if only temporarily. I didn't need anyone else hacking into CCTV and seeing whatever the hell she was about to do. It was going to be my own private torture. *My own private hell.*

Nyla: *Since you're not going to talk to me and just watch me, I want you to know that I still want you. But since you walked out on me, sometime real soon, someone else is going to make me feel good. And you won't be able not to watch. And it will hurt. No less than when you walked away from me with no explanation.*

My dick begged to be touched. Licked. Fucked. By her. Only her.

Too bad. He couldn't have her.

She was on the loveseat now, and she was... Oh hell, was she dancing? There was a suggestive sway of her hips as she turned to face the loveseat and bent over. I swallowed hard as I watched her arse sashay back and forth, and then her thumbs hooked into those tight boy shorts as if to tug them down.

Oh, fuck me. I eased into the high-backed chair that I'd had brought into the flat. Why was she doing this?

She must know you're not strong enough.

Jesus Christ.

My gut knotted as my erection throbbed. I wanted her. I was so desperate for her. I could still taste her. Less than twenty-four hours without her, and I was jonesing like an addict.

I watched her arse sway, back and forth. Back and forth. I ached to slide those shorts down, so I could see her full curves and that delectable arse. I wanted to bite it. To slide my tongue through her lips and bury my whole face into her. Or even better, slide my dick home. Fuck, she was killing me. And she knew it. She gave a little sexy swish of her hips and turned. The subtle movement sent her hair swinging over her shoulders, cascading down. All I wanted to do was fist my hands in the lush fullness and tug it as I owned her.

She eased down onto the edge of the loveseat and then wrapped her hands around her waist and gently pulled up the camisole she was wearing just enough to show the undersides of her heavy breasts, and then she stopped.

Fuck me. Come on, show me what I need.

But she didn't. Instead, she opened her legs, showing me her secrets. Laying back on the loveseat, with one hand, she pinched one of her nipples, and my mouth watered. Her other hand slid down between the valley of her breasts, over her belly, to the juncture of her thighs.

I could see her mouth moving, dictating a message that pinged on my phone.

Nyla: *I've got my hands full. If only you were here to help me.*

Oh fuck.

I was at a crossroad. I knew what I needed to do and what I should absolutely, categorically *not* do. But Nyla Kincade was giving me a show. She knew what I liked. She knew what I *needed*, and she was giving it to me. With jerking motions, I reached for my belt. I yanked down the zipper on my trousers none too gently as I gripped my cock and yanked it out. He was bursting beneath my palm, screaming for freedom. I wrapped my hand around and slid up and down as I cursed, "Fuck you, Nyla."

Nyla: *You want to fuck me, East? You want my fingers to be yours? Or maybe you want to use your mouth instead of your fingers.*

"Yes. Yes, I fucking want to."

My voice was raw and guttural. It was like she could hear me, could hear what I wanted, what I needed. On the monitor, I used my camera to zero in on what she was doing. And it was like I was in the room with her. Her middle finger gently rubbed over her clit in easy, circular strokes before dipping down, down, into her center. Then she pulled it back, repeating the motion. With every dip inside her center, her back arched and her camisole threatened to show me those pretty tits that I wanted to suck on.

Fuck my life. The tingling at the base of my cock was quick to start, and I had to grip tight on the base to stop it.

"No. I'm not doing this." I tried to reason with myself.

Too late. You are already doing this. This is happening. Go with the flow and let it happen. There is no stopping this.

Nyla: *Are you desperate yet? Are you dying to remember what this feels like?*

"Yes. God, yes."

I watched her, and I had no choice. My gaze was fixed on her as she played with herself. As her fingers became mine, as I pretended my mouth was on hers, I couldn't help it. I knew we were locked in this game, and there would be one loser. It would be me. Because I was torn between the people I was sworn by oaths and family to protect and the woman who I couldn't stop staring at. My hands swept over my dick, and the sensitive tip wept for her. A shudder went up my spine, and I knew I was close. So fucking close.

Nyla: *Are you watching me? I'm close. Sooo close.*

And I could tell the exact moment she broke apart. The way her back arched and her teeth bit down on her bottom lip as she buried her fingers inside of her sweet cleft. Then the electricity shot up my spine, and I was coming. An explosion of need, and frustration, and anger.

I don't know how long I sat there, my fist on my dick, my head thrown back, panting. When I lifted my head and reached for some tissues, there was another message.

Nyla: *I miss you. Talk to me.*

And I knew. I knew there was no way I could hold out

forever. I needed to decide what to do with her. I needed to learn how to walk away from her.

———

East

As FAR AS I was concerned, I was winning the day. I'd managed not to creepily stroke myself as I watched her from across the street for a whole seven hours.

You deserve a goddamn medal.

The night before, it had been all I could do to not physically walk over to her flat and replace her fingers with mine.

My cock thickened in my trousers. An irritated twitch meant to chastise my heart for refusing to speak to her. I had to shake my head to clear the image.

I pinched the bridge of my nose as I lay my elbows on my desk. I didn't know how to make this hell stop. I needed to focus on our damn financials meeting. Livy needed budget approval to move forward.

Drew as our financial advisor, was giving us projections on our future projects and was droning on about liquidity and debt to income ratios. I think it was good. Ben wasn't frowning, so that had to be good, right? I needed to get my head in the game.

"Okay, so we'll be able to continue the Dubai build?"

The room went silent. I lifted my head to find my mates eyeing me like I'd lost my mind.

Bridge tried to ease the pain of chastisement. "Mate, we talked about that twenty minutes ago. You agreed to cut spending by ten percent."

My eyes popped. "The fuck I did!" They'd been trying to cut my budget for two years now. I wasn't pulling back from the design. Building was just taking so long. Apparently a floating hotel was a complicated endeavor. But I had a vision, and I wasn't giving it up. "No way in hell I said that."

"Then fucking pay attention," Bridge threw back.

"Look, can we fucking drop it?"

I could hear Ben practically growl from my couch. "Oi, mate. Easy does it."

From the peanut gallery, Drew offered, "He's just sad because he got his arse kicked the other night after leaving Ben's."

"What the fuck? I didn't get my arse kicked. I was lying in wait for the fucker."

Bridge opened his mouth to offer something, but I pointed a finger in his direction. "Nothing from you, arsehole."

He shrugged. "Oh? I see you're still in a fantastic mood. Are we going to talk about the idiot who thought you might be up for a little game of cricket? You know, using your head as the ball?"

"Did you get anything on him?"

Bridge shook his head. "No, our contacts with the police said he wasn't talking. They only have him for the assault, so we don't have much. Just your statement."

Fuck. "The fingerprint analysis came back with nothing. He's not in any databases anywhere."

Drew pinned me with a look. "So is this the time when we ask if Nyla could check databases that you can't access?"

He was trying to goad me. "I can access them all. Her systems are just faster because she actually has the password and doesn't have to hack in."

He held up his hands. "You know, maybe if you actually talk to her. Clearly, you want to keep shagging her. It's making you tetchy not to. So why don't you just keep shagging her but keep her at a distance?"

Ben shook his head and turned to glare at our friend. "Mate, I don't think that's helping."

Drew shrugged and looked up from checking his phone. "What? She's fit. And look, he's clearly wound up tight. He needs it. He was so busy thinking about all that prime arse he isn't getting that he got jumped."

"For the love of Christ. I didn't get jumped."

Yeah, you did mate.

And what this lot didn't know was that without even touching me, without even being in the same room, she'd given me an orgasm strong enough to knock me out for at least thirty minutes.

You could have her. In person. Touch her. Lick her. Fuck her like you want to do.

Fuck me.

Ben stretched his legs. "Since East clearly can't focus on financials, can we discuss Theroux for a moment? He wants to meet, but I'm not sure it's in our best interests to go. What are our options?"

I crossed my arms. "I don't like it. But I've made my position clear."

Drew shrugged. "I don't like it either. But do we have any fucking choice?"

Ben shook his head. "I don't think we do. He's got imagery of us. So if he wants to meet, we need to meet. We just need to pick a location we can both be happy with." He rubbed his jaw. "East, what are the chances that we'll be able to surveil him using any of your special toys?"

"We can try it, but I promise you, he'll want to meet us at a location with no CCTV. We'll be searched and scanned. He's been careful and able to evade capture for thirty years, mate. There are new advancements, but short of actually taking police in with us, we might be out of luck."

For the next thirty minutes we all tried to come up with

plans that could work. Ones that wouldn't get us killed in the process.

Bridge offered up, "Oh, why don't we just have him meet us here?"

I frowned. "What, in the office? He's going to come with men that will attract attention, and I'd rather we weren't connected with a renowned thief, if you don't mind."

He rubbed his chin. "You could scrub the cameras. Meet downstairs."

Ben sat forward. "There's no way he's going to join us in public."

"I don't know." Livy shrugged, leaning forward. "Look, you told me that he's a master of disguises and has evaded capture for thirty years, which means he has repeatedly been out in public. Obviously, he does it with armed guards or a protection detail. That makes sense. But there's got to be an element where he disguises himself. You know, hiding in plain sight. Why don't we just ask? It's our home turf. Cameras will be on. And from what I have read about him, he likes the prestige of staying out of reach. He likes the challenge. He wants a way to do something flashy."

I watched as Drew checked his phone again, a tight frown forming between his brows.

What the hell was he looking at? I'd meant to talk to him the night before after I'd been attacked, but there hadn't been time after making police statements. There was something going on with him. I didn't like it.

Bridge leaned forward, rubbing the dark stubble on his jaw. "Actually, it's not a bad idea. We control the location. He wants our help, so he has to agree to our terms. He's already threatened us. So I want a demonstration of good faith."

I frowned. Bridge was right. I designed the systems. There were cameras everywhere. I had it all wired for sound, the whole hotel. "Okay, let's do it. He's supposed to call in the morning for a meet location. Are we sure we want to do this?"

I glanced around at my mates, more than a little worried about just how in over our heads we were. But I knew there was nothing I could do to stop them. They knew what was at stake. To be able to continue, we needed to meet with Theroux. He had the key to bringing down Garreth Jameson. And since he had the key and had us on tape, we had to deal with him, whether we liked it or not.

Bridge gave me a clap on the shoulder and a head nod, and then he walked out, followed closely by Ben and Livy. Drew was the last to leave. Before he did, I asked, "Mate, everything okay?"

He flashed me that typical Drew grin. The one that said, 'Everything's great. I'm fine.' The one I didn't believe. "Yeah. Are *you* okay? You're short with everyone. What's going on?"

"Stop deflecting, what's up?"

Another mask slid over his face. One I'd seen a lot of late. As if he was assessing his angles. "Nothing, just family stuff."

"Well, doesn't that include us?"

He sighed. "It's just shit with my father. I'll deal with it. I'll tell you lads about it when I figure out what I'm going to do."

"Mate, you know if you need us..." I let my voice trail.

"I know. I'm just trying to deal with it on my own." Drew's lips quirked into a brief smile. "You know, maybe you should talk to Agent Kincade, because there are too many balls in the game right now. You can't afford to piss off Interpol."

"Not going to happen. I've already made enough mistakes with her. I'm not going to keep making them. Besides, she lost her badge, remember?"

"Suit yourself. We're about to embark on some real daft nonsense. It wouldn't hurt having someone with connections in our corner."

All I wanted was Nyla Kincade in my corner, preferably stripped naked, thighs spread for me so I could watch.

I cleared my throat. "I hear you. But honestly, we've got this. We don't need her."

I only wished that was true.

CHAPTER 5

Nyla

I'D ALLOWED a whole drunken night to feel sorry for myself and woke up with the cottonmouth and regrets to match. I knew my show and tell display for East had been a mistake. Hell, anyone could have seen me. But I'd drunkenly pleasured myself in front of an open window in the hope that he'd gotten my texts and had been watching.

That was a real low point. All day, when I'd been feeling kind to myself, I told myself it had been because of the copious amounts of wine I'd consumed.

But tonight, I was taking my life back. Okay fine, I was at least getting out so I wouldn't repeat the night before. Also, I still had to fix the whole *Amelia was going after the London Lords* thing. I might be well ticked off with him, but I knew that Amelia was barking up the wrong tree. And I was the reason she'd noticed the tree in the first place.

I had to give it to Amelia. She was thorough. Always had been. It's what made her a good agent. She might not be flashy or quick with the quips, but the one thing she had going for her was her sheer tenacity.

Since East wasn't taking my calls and I wasn't allowed to see him, as if I'd been wiped from his party invitation list, I didn't really have any choice. If he wouldn't talk to me, I had to try and fix things with Amelia. I had to try and do something.

I headed back to Amelia's secret flat, and I could see all of her connections. I knew what she was trying to do, and she wasn't far off. She was smart. It was well thought out. She had every note I'd ever mentioned with some other connections maybe I hadn't made. But the number one connection at the center of it all was Bram Van Linsted, the man I'd put away for corruption, embezzlement, and fraud. I had also put away his father for human trafficking, along with several of his associates.

I hadn't been able to link Bram to the human trafficking, but there was no way the father had that kind of business going on that his son didn't know about. The funny thing was I hadn't even been looking for them. I'd been after jewel thieves. But I had run across these breadcrumbs and hadn't been able to leave them alone, and I'd been derailed. But as I studied the suspect board, I wondered if I'd been derailed on purpose.

You were. But still, you caught a human trafficker. A ring of them. Is that bad?

It wasn't. East had told me everything, and my instincts told me he was telling the truth. They had derailed me but for a reason. And it was a reason I could get behind. From the research I had done on Tobias Varma, he had died in a mysterious accident. It was tragic, really. So young. So full of hope. A scholar, winning all kinds of academic awards and achievements. An athlete who'd been in several charity runs and an Iron Man before he was nineteen. And then just like that, he was gone because of a sudden heart attack, which led me to believe that East was right. It had been covered up. And if everything about the London Lords he told me was true, and I had a feeling it was, then Amelia was on the verge of finding out everything about them. That organization, the secret society known as the Elite, had covered it up. So the London Lords had a good reason for going after a man like Bram Van Linsted.

I heard the key rattling in the lock, and I turned to face Amelia. In her hands, she had bags of take-aways and wine. "Hey, you're here. I'm glad. When you texted me, I figured I'd feed us so we could go over the evidence."

I studied her dark cocoa skin and her vibrant dark eyes, and she had that look about her. The one where she had a fish on a hook with no plans to let it go. But I still had to try, because Amelia was no fool, and I had given my word to try and protect East.

Even if he's cut you out of his life?

Whether he was speaking to me or not, I'd still given him my word. "Hey yourself. Let me help you."

I grabbed the take-aways and could smell the fresh dumplings inside. My stomach chose that moment to roar.

"I see you're hungry." She studied me. "Let me guess, you've been staring at this while trying to piece it together, and you didn't have time to eat?"

"Well, not exactly."

"So, what do you think? I mean, you were kind of quiet before, but the key piece is speaking to Bram Van Linsted. I'm sure he's got an ax to grind."

I swallowed hard. "You think he'll have something for us?"

"I do. I mean, this is it. He's the piece. He, of course, is asking for the moon. His freedom. The fraud charges are clearly substantiated, he will do time. But I might be able to get him a reduced sentence. Better accommodations even."

I stared at her. "Absolutely not, Amelia."

"Well, it may just depend on what he gives us. We have him

on corruption. Embezzlement, sure. We know he'll do some time, but we can get that greatly reduced. But whatever information he'll give us, if he'll lead us to bigger crimes, which you know they're involved with, we might get his sentence reduced."

"You forget, we also put away his father for human trafficking. We're not going to let any Van Linsted out."

"We couldn't make a case against the younger one."

"Yeah, but just because we didn't make a case doesn't mean he didn't know."

Amelia's brow furrowed. "Look, I know that you and East Hale have a thing, but never once have I ever seen you let any emotion get in the way of doing your job. Hell, you're worse than I am. Remember that bloke from three years ago? The Chutney case?"

I groaned as I opened up the moo shu pork and the scent of ginger hit my nose. "God, he really was stupid good looking."

"I know. And the way he eyed you and up and down and flirted with you, I mean... From the body language alone, you were like, 'Hello, man, I would very much like to shag.' But you smiled and flirted as you put handcuffs on him. Nothing touches you. Why are you even hesitating now?"

I sighed. "Listen, let's say Bram Van Linsted *can* tell us something. Whatever it is, it's not worth letting him out. It's just not. I'm not trading alliances here. I'm not going to get in bed with someone horrible just to get to them. There's got to be a better way to do this."

"What other way? You've been dogging them since you met them. If you think that they're somehow involved with the case, which, again, I agree, it doesn't really make sense when we don't have a case against them for the trafficking. But they're involved in other dirty dealings, and if we could uncover them, this is a career making case, and you wouldn't have to work under Denning anymore. I'll be a lead investigator instead of just a regular agent. So come on, strap up. Let's do this."

"I agree with you. This is a career making case." I left out the part about it possibly being a career ender too. "I just want to do this right." *And protect East.* "I just don't think getting in bed with Bram Van Linsted is the way to do it."

She rolled her eyes. "Look, I hear you, but all I'm saying is that we interview him. That's all. If he gives us something, great. If not, we'll cross that bridge when we come to it. But it doesn't cost us anything to speak to him."

"He won't talk to us unless we come with something on the table. And let's be real, we have nothing. I'm not even an active agent anymore."

Amelia sighed. "Let's just call you a consultant. I *am* an active agent. I can get us in there to talk to him."

"Amelia, listen to yourself. You're excited, and you have done so much work on this. I get that. But we need to be careful. And look, maybe this organization actually exists but it's not what we think it is."

Amelia put down her honey-glazed shrimp and then crossed her arms and stared at me. "He's gotten to you, hasn't he?"

I blinked at her. "What do you mean?"

"The venerable Lord East Hale. He's gotten to you."

I swallowed hard. "No, he hasn't. I'm just trying to be smart. Find the truth of things. That's our job."

She shook her head. "No, something's changed. A little over two weeks ago, you couldn't wait to get your hands on them. You questioned anybody and everybody who was willing to tell us anything about them. You even infiltrated a dinner they had. Went in disguised, mind you, and then had to run for your bloody life. And you're now telling me that we should back off? What else could this be besides they've gotten to you. *He's* gotten to you. What, just because you shagged him?"

The heat crept up my neck, and I was thankful that I was wearing a buttoned-up blouse over my camisole and that there was low lighting in the flat. "That's not what this is about. My attraction to him has no bearing on my ability to do my job. Well, I guess it's not my job anymore, right?"

Amelia winced. "Mate, you know that's only temporary. All you've got to do is talk to your father."

"He's the one who suspended me. There's no talking. But look, I don't want to argue about this. This is great work, but I think there's more under the surface. And I don't think us offering deals to Bram Van Linsted is the right course of action just now."

"Why are you so dead set against it? Wouldn't you love knowing the truth? No matter where it leads you?"

She knew how to get to me. And I did love to know the truth. I had to know.

But you already know.

If this was the only way to satisfy Amelia, I knew I'd do what had to be done. Besides, one conversation with Bram Van Linsted and she would see what I saw. That we couldn't let a monster like him run around free and clear. It didn't matter what he could offer us on the London Lords. And there was no believing a word he said. Besides, from what East had told me, they had a currency of secrets. There was no way in hell Van Linsted was going to tell us anything, especially not without a deal on the table. So maybe I didn't have to worry about anything at all. I believed East was telling me the truth, and even if he didn't want my protection, he was still going to get it.

CHAPTER 6

East

Between Nyla and Theroux, I hadn't taken the proper time to deal with Belinda's fuck twat husband.

Seeing as I wasn't going anywhere near Nyla and the team had come up with a plan for Theroux, I needed to deal with this particular twat of a loose end named Jack Lloyd.

Belinda had come to work as usual, alert, ready to go. But there was an all too familiar sadness in her eyes. Watching Nyla every night was going to be bad for my sanity, so Belinda and her problems were a good distraction.

Taking up my old activity was the comfort I needed. Walking through the London streets, following the people who thought they were hidden, I felt like my old self.

We had a deal, Jack and I. He didn't put his hands on Belinda, and I didn't call in his gambling markers. Now I *was* going to call in his markers because he clearly hadn't listened. But before I did that, he and I were going to have a visit.

And as an added bonus, I was in Walthamstow, completely

on the opposite side of Victoria, so there was no chance of seeing Nyla in that dank dodgy hell.

I took the steps down into the basement of the off-book gambling house, Lynn's. I'd only been in places like this once or twice. I wasn't really one for poker. I'd wager on buildings, commerce, things like that. I might even wager my mates for a car or something frivolous. But I didn't wager money over things that weren't important.

At the doorway, I nodded to the bouncer, pressed my hundred quid into his palm, and kept on walking as if he wasn't there.

I found that it was easier to let money do the talking for the most part. No one ever asked any questions if you let money do the talking.

I found Jack just where I'd expected to. It took him a moment before he noticed me. When he did, he stood up from his table as nonchalantly as possible. And then ran.

I shook my head. Fucking hell, I hated it when they ran.

But apparently the bouncer was grateful for the hundred quid, and he told someone on the radio to stop him. I nodded my thanks and proceeded with a smile as the man at the back of the room handed him off.

With my hands on his lapels, I shoved him out the back door where the bracing fall chill greeted us. "Mate, I thought we had a deal."

"I'm not your fucking mate." He struggled against my hold.

"It's odd that you say that, because I have noticed my mates don't like to hit women. That's kind of a rule we have. Overall, don't be a twat."

He tried to shake loose of my grip, but I just tightened it and threw him against the wall. "Now, now. We have discussed Belinda. I told you not to put your hands on her. But you can't seem to help yourself."

He struggled in my hold, but I let some of that fury out. The rage I'd been holding so tightly. I let just enough of it loose to let him know that I could kill him right there and not give a fuck. "She's lying. I haven't touched her."

"I told you, I don't like you putting your hands on women. My assistant in particular. You don't listen. So I'm going to teach you a lesson."

His eyes went wide.

"You see, I've been feeling very frustrated in the last several days, so you're going to help me work some of that out."

"You can't do that. I haven't done anything to you."

"Yeah, see my assistant comes into my office every bloody day looking haunted. No woman should have that look. And she's constantly in fear. But she does her job with a smile. She's really excellent you know. My life would be a lot easier if I was shagging *her*. But alas, she seems to prefer losers. Like you. So we're going to try this again. It's called aversion therapy." His eyes went wide. "Every time you think about hitting something, I'm going to knee you in the nuts. How's that work for you?"

He coughed and struggled some more.

"Oh, good. I do want you to struggle. It'll make this much more worthwhile."

I hit him then, relishing the sting in my hand. The reminder that despite how I felt, I was, in fact, still alive.

I didn't relish kneeing another man in the nuts, making his eyes water as he bent over, weeping. I didn't get my rocks off like that. But seeing as I didn't consider him a man, I did it.

I hauled him back against the wall. And he still cupped himself. "See? You don't like that."

"Y-y-you don't know anything."

"I read the police report."

"B-b-but they told me those were sealed since she didn't press charges."

"Not sealed from my people. I know what you did to her. One time you hit her so hard in the stomach that she went into shock. The report said blunt force trauma to the reproductive organs. Did you kick her?"

I kneed him again. All my disgust, my loathing coming out with force. And this time all he did was wheeze as he sank to his knees. That's when the sobbing began.

"You're filth. Disgusting. You don't deserve to walk this earth. People like you, the bullies who torture and torment women. God, if I could eradicate you, I would find the most painfully long, excruciating way to do it. People like you practically ruined my sister. People like you roam around thinking you're God's fucking gift and loving it. But I like hurting you."

He writhed on the ground, but I hauled him up easily. This time I left his nuts alone and went for his face. "You see, I read the report." *Pop.* I didn't even feel the hit on my knuckles as I broke skin. "She told the police that she made the mistake of picking a handsome man." I popped him again. "So perhaps if I make you less handsome, she'll make different choices." *Pop.*

"Stop. God, please, don't kill me."

I blinked down at him. "Oh no. Did you think I was going to kill you?"

"Y-you're not?" His brow furrowed in confusion as he looked up at me.

"Oh no, no. I'm going to leave you in a heap. And then, I'm going to go inside and tell those blokes in there that you're a nonce. After that I'm going to walk out the front door."

He struggled and tried to scramble away. "N-no. It's not true. Why would you do that?"

"What do you think that lot will do to you for diddling children?" My smile was more than a little evil.

"But I'm not. I've never touched my kids."

"Yeah, well, I don't care. You told Belinda if she reported

you to the police you'd take the children. That was a mistake. By the time I'm done with you, you won't be allowed within a hundred feet of them."

He let the mask of simpering fear slip and spat, "I hate you. "

I smiled at him. "Yes. Excellent. That's how you should feel. That's how I wish Belinda felt, but mostly she's afraid of you. I'd like to change that paradigm. I want *you* to be afraid every time you see her. I want you to know real fear in your life. Do you understand me?"

By the time my hand went numb, he was a bloody pulp of a mess. And I knew I was going too far, but I couldn't tamp back that fury, that rage.

You have to. You're angry and frustrated because the woman you love, isn't here. As for this asshole, leave him standing. Because you have a moral center. Most people don't. He'll get what's coming to him in the end. Use your best resources and burn him.

I could burn him, but I only had one burn, and I wasn't wasting it on him. But there were other ways.

Make sure you're doing this for the right reason, not because you can't take out your anger on Nyla.

I was doing this for the right reasons. Nyla had distracted me from all the other things I had going on. But no more. I was back on track. And I was going to be just fine without her.

Nyla

AS IT TURNED OUT, once Amelia made up her mind, there was no changing it.

We were going to see Bram Van Linsted if it was the last thing in the world we did.

His father, Marcus, and several of his friends and acquaintances had been arrested for human trafficking.

Bram, while seemingly innocent on the human trafficking charges, was arrested for fraud, corruption, and embezzlement. He'd claimed a priceless piece of jewelry was missing. However, authentication showed that his family had only ever owned replicas. He'd covered that up and tried to collect on the insurance.

His own mother had been the one to give him up. She had also outlined an extensive set of financial schemes, all designed to cheat the family company and line his personal coffers.

Nice family.

He was absolutely the last person on earth I wanted to see. Even though I hadn't been able to pin him on the human trafficking, I kept thinking that surely, I had missed something. Somewhere.

Something told me I better get used to that kind of disappointment.

Like now. I wasn't into making deals with arseholes. But I wasn't in charge. This wasn't my show.

To put it bluntly, I was there as backup. I had no badge, and I wasn't willing to compromise myself to get mine back, so second fiddle it was.

What does that say about you?

Amelia led the way to her car. And I could tell that she was unsure if she should let me drive or not. Normally, she drove. Would it be different now? It was a new feeling having no place.

But I was glad she still did. Amelia was more than capable. She was exceptional, really. I had put her up for promotion to lead her own team three times in the last year and a half. But somehow budget cuts never seemed to let that happen. Amelia paused at the driver's side door of the Shelby. "This is weird, isn't it?"

"I'm so glad you said that because it's very strange."

"Look, I'm sorry it has turned out this way. Are you sure you won't come back?" she asked in a pleading tone.

"Not now. But look, I'm happy for you. Just because my father, Denning, and I don't see eye to eye doesn't mean I don't have respect for Interpol. I just can't be there right now. But you are going to be amazing."

"Thanks love, but I don't want it to be because of you losing everything. The way Denning has acted is so bullshit. And you recognize that anyone in the building who has ever maybe witnessed Denning being a complete dick to you has been reassigned."

"What?"

"Oh yeah, remember the Toolsit mission? When he called you a dizzy flake in front of the whole team and screamed at you for nearly twenty minutes about how you'd entered the wrong coordinates?"

"Jesus Christ, how could I forget?" It was later discovered that I'd given the right coordinates and his special two-man team overlooked something, so we lost our lead. Afterward, there had been no apology, nothing. Just a brief acknowledgement from my father that I hadn't in fact fucked up, then nothing.

"All those agents are on different teams now."

I shook my head. "I will never understand it. Of all the things I miss, Denning Sinclair isn't one of them."

"He's a proper twat."

"Well, I appreciate you saying it."

"It's the truth, and I mean every word of it. Now, let's go talk to Bram Van Linsted." Amelia hesitated. "Look, I know you're not enthused to talk to him, but it's a solid lead."

"This is your team. I follow you now. That's what's important."

"Thanks, it's nice to have your support."

"Of course. Regardless of what else is going on, you kick arse. Now, let's go."

Amelia gave me a nod, her eyes glassing over and shimmering slightly with unshed tears. "All right, let's go."

Nearly an hour later, we were pulling into Belmarsh Correctional Facility in Thamesmead. There was a whole series of badge identification checkpoints and checking of all weapons as well, keeping them in lockboxes, the whole nine. Then we were led down the hall to the right and into an interrogation room.

We took the two seats on one side of the bare table and waited for Bram Van Linsted to show up. I hadn't seen him since his preliminary hearing. He hadn't been able to bail out since his family assets were frozen.

When he entered the room, his lawyer was also present, and she glowered at us. "To what do we owe this honor? I'm irritated that you did not present the matter to me directly before coming to see my client."

I thought Amelia would be rattled, but she wasn't. Not in the least. She was handling it like a total boss. "Mr. Van Linsted, you are well?"

"Well, it's not the bloody Four Seasons."

She lifted a brow. "No, I suppose it's not. But then, few things are." She leaned forward and hit record on her phone. She rattled off the date and the time before continuing. "Upon your arrest some time ago, you claimed that you have information that would be useful to us. Can you elaborate further?"

He shook his head. "No, I cannot." His gaze pinned on me. "I told you I'd come back. I told you that you would want to speak to me, but you didn't believe me then."

"Just answer the question, Van Linsted," I prompted.

Amelia scowled at him too. "We're here to listen. When you

were arrested, you said you could offer information. What was it?"

He sat back and crossed his arms even though his solicitor was prompting him with her eyes to respond.

"I don't think I will. I don't think you're ready to hear it."

Amelia frowned. "Enough jerking our chain. You either have information, or you don't."

I wondered how this man could have gone from refined and handsome to this. His skin was sallow. His nose looked like perhaps it had been broken. The exact opposite of refinement. It was then that Van Linsted looked between the two of us and started laughing. "Ah, I see. Something *has* changed." He glanced at me and grinned. "You are in the doghouse, which means you are now in charge." He pointed while looking at Amelia. "I find this shift intriguing."

Amelia tried to drag his focus back to the line of inquiry, but he wasn't having it. "Go on, tell us what you did."

"I'm not here to be interrogated," I said coolly.

"Oh, come on, I just want to know what you did wrong that would get you dethroned from the gilded towers. Tell me, did you fraternize with the enemy?" he asked while directing his eyes at me.

I didn't want to give him the satisfaction of being taken aback, so I tried my best to stay unaffected and smirked. But Amelia saved the day for me. "May I remind you, Mr. Van Linsted, we're supposed to ask the questions, not you. We don't have time for any of your crap."

"All right fine, I'll tell you what you want to know." He grinned at me evilly. "You are looking for an organization called the Elite. It's a secret society, but you know, since I'm in here and no one's done a goddamn thing to get me out, I don't give a shit about keeping their fucking secrets. Not anymore."

I made a point to show zero emotion. I wasn't going to get embroiled in this battle.

Amelia leaned forward. "Explain more please. Who are they?"

"The baddest, wealthiest men in the world. We *run* the world."

I couldn't help it. My mouth got away from me. Honestly, it wasn't my fault. "Well, not *we*, right? Because you are no longer master of anything."

He narrowed his gaze at me. And I could tell, I knew in that moment, he wished me dead.

"I can even tell you who's in it. But the most important thing you need to know, as you probably gathered from your work on my father's case, is that its members are powerful. They will do anything and everything within their power to avoid detention. They're involved in underworld activities, corruption, bribery, theft. This is not your ordinary secret society. This is something altogether different. These men are dangerous."

Amelia could sense it. She had him where she wanted him. "Unless you can give me names and a list of crimes, I don't buy any of it. So why don't we start with the names first?"

He laughed. "Ah, yes." He smiled at me then. "I seem to recall that you were snooping around some very specific members, Ben Covington and his mates."

I nodded. "That's not news."

"The list of their crimes is a mile long. You'll have a hard time proving it though. But one thing I could help you prove is the Canary Jewel. They stole it."

I smiled half-heartedly. "We're not here for conjecture. We're here for something you can prove. And unless you have proof, nothing you say can be of any use to us."

He turned to me then, his face a mask. "All right, you want something that you can use? I have proof. Ben Covington and his London lads, or whatever the fuck they call themselves, were working with my father on the human trafficking ring. The old man kept a ledger. I took it from him. It details his associates. You'll find the London Lords in there. A good mate of mine is holding onto it in his office for me. Rhys Mathison."

"And if you're lying?" I asked.

He smirked. "You're Interpol. I'm sure you'll check for authenticity and whatnot. You bring me a deal I can work with, and you can have it. The London Lords on a platter."

And just like that, a knife had been stabbed into my gut. I didn't hear anything else that happened in that interview. I *knew* he was lying. I knew I needed to warn East, and Ben, and Bridge. But I had no way of getting to them. No way to contact them. East wouldn't listen to me.

That's not true. You have ways in.

Olivia Ashong would listen. Jessa Ainsley too.

I needed to reach out to them, because if Bram Van Linsted had his way, he was coming for them, and he'd use Interpol to do his dirty work.

At the end of the interview, Amelia had a bounce to her step. "This is huge, Ny," she said as we waited for security to let us pass through the gates. She checked her watch and frowned. "Shit, I have to get back to the office since this is an unsanctioned fishing expedition. But listen, I need you to call some of your private investigator contacts and see if they can get us that ledger from Mathison. Maybe he's not a mate of Van Linsted after all. In the meantime, I'm going to try to get a warrant."

I turned to her. "You can't be serious. You don't believe him for a second, do you?"

"We have to look into it. And maybe I don't believe that they're part of the human trafficking ring, but he's told us what to look for. He can give us more access than we've ever had. And if he thinks that we're looking into them for the human traf-ficking thing, fine. But we are in. This is our way."

Out of the corner of my eye, I saw a familiar figure.

My brain stuttered as I tried to place him.

I couldn't remember where I'd seen him. He was tall and had dark hair, like East, but his was lighter, as was the stubble on his jaw line. He had a soft chin and jaw. Where had I seen him?

I narrowed my eyes and willed myself to remember. And then it clicked. Oh yes, that was Garreth Jameson. We'd met that night at the restaurant East had called The Hiding Spot, and he'd been very aggressive. So what was he doing here? As he signed in on the other side of security, my stomach rolled. I knew who he was here to see. Because someone like Garreth Jameson wouldn't be in a place like this unless he needed to be. So the question was, what were he and Bram Van Linsted plan-ning, and how badly was it going to hurt East?

Nyla

AMELIA and I parted ways at the office. When she headed upstairs, she gave me my marching orders to see if I could find a legal way into Rhys Mathison's office that wouldn't require a warrant. Staring up at her as she marched into the building, I tried to ignore the pang. I used to belong in there.

Now, well, I belonged nowhere.

And whose fault is that?

I started making some calls on my own then marched to the tube. When I reached my station, I paced in front of it as the phone rang and rang. Finally, Olivia Ashong's lilting voice picked up. "Hello? This is Olivia."

"Oh my God, Olivia. Please don't hang up."

There was a long pregnant pause. "Nyla, I'm sorry, but it's not really appropriate for us to talk."

I rushed to interrupt her before she hung up.

"I know, I know. Just listen for two minutes, okay? My partner, well, I guess ex-partner, because I'm not Interpol anymore, anyway, she's coming for you. She's coming for you hard. She's been speaking to Bram Van Linsted. We just left him."

Another long pause, but she finally said, "Why would I believe you?"

"I'm a lot of things Livy, but I'm not a liar. And you can check. Call Belmarsh prison and ask for the visitor's log. They'll tell you. We signed in. You will also want to know that he had another visitor today. One Garreth Jameson. But that's not the important thing. The important thing is he claims to have a ledger tucked away with some mate of his, Rhys Mathison."

Her voice went sharp. "What do they have?"

"He claims to have a ledger that points to the London Lords and the human trafficking ring. I know that's not true. But I don't know if he's had them doctored or if he's just deliberately yanking our chain. I don't know. But we need to get access to that ledger before my former partner does."

"Why would you help us?"

"Jesus fucking Christ. Well, for starters I went over the evidence with a fine-tooth comb, and there's no connection between the ring I split up and the London Lords. Other than the Elite. And even though I'm an idiot, I trust East. I do not trust Van Linsted. He's lying. I can feel it in my bones, and I know that it seems dumb to trust my intuition or my gut or whatever you want to call it, but I can't help it. I do. So, you need to do something."

"What do you suggest we do?"

"I don't know. All I have is the information. We likely won't make a run against Mathison until tomorrow. So between now and then, you lot need to figure something out. How to get the ledger, how to get a copy of it. Something. I don't know."

Livy's voice went quiet then. "You really do care about him, don't you?"

My gut knotted. "I did. But he tossed that aside, so you know, c'est la vie."

"He made a mistake. We can all see it, but he's... Well, you know him; he's stubborn. He's decided something, and he can't let it go."

"You know what? Right now I don't even care that he's stopped talking to me. Hell is coming."

"You said your partner is coming for us?"

"My *former* partner. Remember, I'm no longer Interpol. If we don't do something, Interpol is going to be after the lads in an official capacity, and there's not a damn thing either one of us can do to stop it. And even if he won't talk to me, he'll listen to you. So you need to warn him."

"Yeah, I'm on it." Before she hung up, she paused. "Nyla?"

"Yeah?" I asked.

"Thank you. You didn't have to stick out your neck to save us, but you are. That means a lot."

"I just hope I'm not too late. I don't know what you can do, but whatever it is, get it done.

I prayed to God I wasn't too late.

CHAPTER 7

East

"She said what?"

"She said that Van Linsted is trying to nail us with some kind of ledger."

I glanced around, my mind whirring. When Livy called this emergency meeting, I didn't know what kind of bomb she was going to drop on us. "I'm just telling you what she told me. Interpol went to speak to Bram for some reason. He's trying to negotiate a deal. Claims he has a ledger that ties you four to the human trafficking ring."

Bridge slapped the table. "That's a bunch of bullshit. We didn't have anything to do with it."

I shook my head. "Nah, mate. But whether we had something to do with it or not, these things can be doctored."

My mate ran his hands through his hair. "So, what? Interpol's just supposed to believe him?"

Livy shook her head. "I don't know. I don't know what's in the ledger, so I have no idea. All I'm telling you is what Nyla told me."

71

I was torn. I knew I shouldn't believe her, but I couldn't quite ignore that hopeful part of myself that wanted to believe she was trying to do something good by trying to help. But why? She started this ball rolling down the hill, so why would she help us now? Or was it a trap? Maybe to see if we'd steal it? "I don't like this. I don't like the fucked-up options it gives us."

Bridge shook his head. "I don't like it either."

Ben shoved his hands in his pockets and started pacing. "But what options do we have? At the very least, we need to see the ledger, figure out what it is, what it says, and then put it back. Or rather our own version of it."

Bridge asked, "Lucas, do you have a forger on standby? One that can do excellent work in not a lot of time?"

He smirked. "I have a couple of people who like a good challenge. They're not cheap though."

"Call them."

I stared at Ben. "Mate, we're taking hits from all sides here."

"Yeah, you think I'm not aware of that? This is most pressing for now though, and we're against the clock."

Drew finally spoke up from his corner of silence. "We have no choice. They're coming for us. We need to make sure we're not in that fucking ledger. Because even if Interpol eventually discovers that it's fake, it's a distraction from what's in front of us. We need to think about *why* Van Linsted's trying to distract us."

Drew had never been one for war games. He always preferred the negotiation. Finding a middle ground. Always a way out. That was him. But God, if he thought this was urgent, then we were in a tight spot.

Obviously, we all knew Rhys Mathison as he was a member of the Elite. He never really made any waves. Outside of a birthday or the occasional charity event, we didn't have much occasion to speak with him. I seemed to remember he liked golf, but I didn't know how to make golf leverageable.

His family was in publishing. He led a quiet life and had a solid bank account. Not flashy, but well respected. Why was he in bed with Bram? The Mathisons had been members of the elite for the last fifty years. His father had been the first one in his family selected. He had the right lineage, and Rhys was a legacy. We had no quarrel with him. Why would he do this?

I glanced over at Lucas. "Can you get in?"

Lucas shrugged. "Getting in isn't the problem. I can get in. Security will be a low threat. It's a publishing company. He probably doesn't even know what he has. Getting in and getting the ledger out is not our problem. The problem is getting the ledger back in. Because if they notice I've been there, security protocols will change, and it'll be much more difficult to put it back if someone realizes it's missing."

"It could be bait. Once it's taken, that points the finger at us. So we can't be anywhere near it. Unless, of course, we just ask Mathison for it."

Bridge peered at me. "You think there is leverage to press there?"

I shrugged. "He's not an enemy. I have nothing to push or pull on."

Bridge shook his head. "Well then, he's not an ally either."

"Solid point. But we don't have many choices here."

Lucas put his hands up. "Well, first, before anyone gets their knickers in a twist, let's do this. Let's see if we can get the ledger and either undoctor it or replace it. And then we'll figure out how to get it back in the building."

I shook my head. "This is bad. It's a credible threat."

Lucas clapped his hands together. "I've got my repelling equipment and my Gecko Tech glass climbing equipment ready. I can do this."

I rolled my eyes. "Or you can dress up as maintenance or cleaning crew and walk in through the front door."

He frowned. "Why are you always ruining things for me?"

"Because your fun is likely to get us killed, so I try to minimize that as much as possible." I glanced around. "They're coming for us. For *all* of us. So let's make them pay for it."

Even as the team threw itself into plans for getting in and getting out, I knew one universal truth; Nyla was front and center in my brain. But was she friend or foe?

East

WE WERE RISKING everything on Nyla's say-so.

I hadn't spoken to her. I hadn't seen her. I didn't trust her. A woman who I didn't, *couldn't* trust with my future and the future of my mates, had set us on this path. If we got caught there, that would lend credence to Van Linsted, and then there would be real trouble. There would be no justice for Toby, no justice for us, and frankly, I was worried about Ben because he was too pretty for prison.

Lucas startled me out of my mental ramblings. "You look worried, mate. I thought you wanted in on the stealing game?"

I glanced down at myself in my workman's jumper. "I look like an idiot."

"Yeah, but that's no different from how you normally look."

I rolled my eyes at Lucas. "Oh right, you're taking the piss out of me too?"

He shrugged. "Well, you do make it a little easy."

"You know what, I'm leaving you here. I'm going back to the van."

Lucas laughed and pulled me back. "Ah, mate. See, look at me using British slang and everything. Relax, I'm teasing. Just teasing. Come on. We'll get upstairs and get what we need. We look like we belong here. We are a cleaning crew."

I glanced down again at my navy-blue jumper. I looked like a knob, but if it got us where we needed to go, that was all that mattered. I pushed the cleaning cart into the employee lift, and we headed upstairs. I studied,Lucas, who looked like he was in hog heaven, and I said, "You know we're not going to steal anything else right?"

His face crumbled like a child who'd been told there was no ice cream. "But you didn't say that. You said we were breaking into a publishing house. I asked which publisher and realized that they published The Ruins of Valhalla series. Do you know how much I fucking love that series?"

I lifted my brows. "What?"

"Fantasy, dumbass. Fantasy with Vikings and Valkyrie. Whatever. Anyway, it's super popular, and they've been holding onto the final book. I want that manuscript."

I blinked at him. And then I blinked again. "You can't be serious."

"As a heart attack. You get what you need, and I get the last book in The Ruins of Valhalla a year before anyone else does. It's worth it."

"Will you just steal *anything?*"

Lucas smirked at me like I had asked a ridiculous question. "Sure, why not?"

"Would you steal a nuclear warhead?"

Lucas shrugged. "It depends on the scenario. If it was to keep it from a bad guy, then heck yeah. But then how does one dispose of that? That's the problem. And there's always going to be some idiot bad guy who thinks he should have it and he'd be trying to kill you for it. So that's a tough one, but I would steal it from a bad guy if there was a great way of getting rid of those things."

"You just like the thrill?"

"And now you sound like Bryna. Come on then. Let's do this."

The lift carried us up to the top floor. As we pushed our cleaning cart along, we noticed cubicles in the center section, and the office rows were steel and glass and had excellent views. Rhys's office was in the corner, with a commanding view of all of the South Bank.

I'd already handled the technology, shutting down the cameras, looping the imagery so that it would show recordings from the last hour. "Let's do this." I slid my glance to the prince, who would never quite be cured of his need to take things from people who were less deserving.

The security was fairly simple, easy decryption, and we were in the office in no time. Both of us had on comm units that looked like simple earbuds, and we bopped along as we listened to Stormzy blasting in our ears.

The laptop was easy enough to access. Simple firewalls and encryptions. Any teenager with half a mind could have gotten in. Only it was made slightly more difficult by Lucas leaning over my shoulder insisting I get the stupid Valhalla book for him. "I have it, are you satisfied?"

He simply held out his palm, and I placed the flash drive onto it. "You get to hold it for now, but I still need to decrypt what the fuck is on the rest of it."

He shrugged. "As long as I have it in my palm, I'm happy."

I rolled my eyes as I headed for the safe. "Stand over there, would you?" I pushed him out of the way of the main safe.

"What are you doing?"

I pulled a balaclava out of my back pocket, stretching it out before I put it on. "I have a feeling that with what's supposed to be in that ledger, Van Linsted would have asked for extra precautions. If I'm right, there's likely a camera in here. We certainly don't need our faces seen, so I'm taking a few precautious."

He nodded slowly. "You think about this shit all the time?"

"If there's a way to make things safer, more airtight, I do."

"I mean you really think through the rabbit hole. Who puts a camera inside of a safe?"

I chuckled softly as I let the decryption device do its work. "Someone who doesn't want something stolen."

To be even safer, as the decryption finished and the dial clicked into place I stepped out of sight, just in case. And sure enough, there was a tiny fucking pinhole camera. I reached up, putting a little piece of painter's tape over it just to be careful. I was still doing a double-check for anything else that might be in the safe. And then I found several ledgers. I wanted to take them all, but the chances that Mathison would miss them worried me. So I had to open them and look through them all to try and identify which ones contained Elite business.

There were two actually. One slim one, which looked like a series of accounts, but I wasn't sure what that meant. Then I found the other one. The one that Bram was talking about, and I could tell pages had been inserted. They looked like they were part of the original ledger, but when I checked the binding, the pages were off. And the paper stock was just a hair different than the originally bound paper.

"This is the one. It's been doctored. We have initials and dates of birth next to some line items. I don't even want to know what they are. Think your guy can fuck with this?"

"Let's hope so. We're headed straight there after we leave here."

I nodded. "Then let's get the fuck out of here. With any luck, we can return these tomorrow before he even knows they're gone."

"That will be trickier. And that's likely going to fall on you."

"Well, I think it's time I got to know Rhys Mathison anyway."

"Yeah. And why the fuck hasn't the Valhalla book released yet? That's what I really want to know."

"You're one of those crazies, aren't you? The ones who email the author demanding that they write to your will."

Lucas frowned. "That's just rude. I'm not rude. I mean, I did write him a letter telling him I was a huge fan and couldn't wait, and if he could at least just please respond back and tell me when to expect it, I would endeavor to be patient."

I blinked. "You see nothing wrong with that?"

He shook his head. "No, I was very nice. I told him I was willing to be patient. But I got no answer, and then the fucker hasn't released the book."

I closed the safe right after uncovering the pinhole camera, leaving everything as I found it, sans the ledger. Lucas was right. Getting in here again would be trickier, but it could be done. And thanks to Nyla, we had neutralized Bram.

Just as I tucked the ledger in to the damn jumpsuit, my phone buzzed with a text.

Theroux: *Change of plan. Meet new partner at Primrose Hill, tomorrow, 8 p.m.*

I glanced at the message and scowled. Why was he stalling? And the last thing we wanted was to bring someone else in. But I'd deal with Theroux later. One problem at a time.

So maybe you should hear Nyla out.

No. I couldn't. It didn't matter that I wanted to.

Or rather it mattered very much. The idea that I wanted her so much that I was willing to overlook everything was dangerous. She had already put us at risk.

I couldn't let her close again.

CHAPTER 8

Nyla

I HOPED to Christ that East had listened.

I hoped to God Livy had gotten through to them, because there was no avoiding it. Amelia was meeting me in an hour, and I hoped to have something to tell her. I was on my way to talk to Rhys Mathison myself and find out if he'd give me any information about the Elite or the London Lords. I fully expected to get nothing, but it was only a stall tactic while Amelia was working on the warrant.

He wasn't going to give me anything. But since I called myself an 'associate' of Amelia's and my MI5 five cover IDs still thankfully worked, one of those being a young intrepid reporter for *The London Gazette,* that would at least get me in the door and give me a chance to talk to him, a chance to poke around. But I knew it wouldn't get me very far, not without a badge.

You need that badge. You will have to go back.

No. I was not going to cave. I was not going to bend to the will of my father and Denning.

You might not have a choice.

The lifts were packed, and I saw several people circumventing them, going around to what I thought were backstairs. But it was another bank of lifts, smaller ones that were far to the left behind the guard station. Almost no one got in those, and the moment I saw the interior, I could see why. They amounted to not much more than a service lift. But they would do if I wanted to get upstairs quickly. Maybe I could poke around the office and say I'd arrived for my appointment early. At the very least, I could see if he had a safe.

Oh yeah, what are you going to do, break in? Steal the ledger yourself? You're basically stalling before Amelia can get a warrant.

And if I failed, East and his crew were out of luck. So I hoped to God Livy had gotten through to the guys. But no one had texted me. Not one word.

I stepped in the lift, and just as it was about to close, a hand slipped in and the doors slid back. At first all I could see was a shadow of someone tall, but when more was revealed, I gasped.

In front of me stood East, looking every bit as delicious as I remembered, his dark hair in messy disarray as if he'd been running his fingers through it. Or as if someone else had run their fingers through it. He looked fresh out of bed, except his clothes were impeccable.

Three-piece suit, that mint tie that brought out the green in his eyes, crisp white shirt. The suit was that houndstooth with a check that was so small the whole thing looked gray. And it was cut to fit his long lean frame, almost a little too slim. But that was the style. I recognized it as bespoke, and I wondered who the designer was.

"It's you," I breathed.

He froze for a long second. "Yeah, it's me."

And then he did the one thing I didn't expect him to do. He stepped inside.

I expected him to wait until the next one. I didn't even know what he was doing there. Was he there to stop me, or rather Interpol, from talking to Rhys? He was too late if he was only doing something about it today.

"What floor?" I asked. As if we were strangers. As if his cock hadn't been inside me, hitting that spot that made my eyes roll into the back of my head over and over and over again until I had naught else to do but arch my back, grip the pillows behind me, and hold on for the ride as he punishingly drew orgasm after orgasm after orgasm out of me.

Was I supposed to pretend that I didn't know about his habit of dipping his head, licking my nipples, and chuckling to himself as if the art of making me scream was a joke? It might have been a joke to him, but it had been all seriousness to me, because I'd believed him. Believed that he wanted me.

So no, I did not want to be trapped in a lift with him. I reached for the doors, but they closed too quickly, and the lift started moving. My question all but forgotten, he reached around me and pressed the button for the top floor.

He would be on this sixty-seven-floor journey with me. *Bloody fantastic.*

I just had to do this, didn't I? I'd wanted to avoid the crowds in the other lifts. If I'd just taken one of those, I'd be free, safe. Wouldn't be trapped with my enemy.

He's not your enemy. You care about him.

Because I was dumb enough to care about him, he felt like my enemy in that moment.

"I hope to God you're not too fucking late."

For a long moment, he didn't answer. And then he pulled something out of his pocket and tapped several buttons just as the lights dimmed in the lift. Then it stopped. I quickly grabbed the handrail behind us. "What the fuck?"

He turned to face me, taking a step into my space. "Why did you do it?"

I wanted to take a step back, but I wasn't going to give him the goddamn satisfaction, and I was already against the wall. "I didn't do anything. If that was you who stopped the lift, start it again. I don't do well with small spaces."

"I'll start it up again when you tell me why you fucking did it."

I just lifted my chin and glowered at him. "I don't know what you're talking about. I think we both have things to do."

"Why do you have to be like this? Why did you tell her?"

This time my brow did furrow. "I genuinely don't know what you're talking about. Honestly. So we can keep playing this cryptic game, or you can start the lift."

"We move when you answer my questions, Nyla. Why did you call Livy?"

My gaze searched his. "Are you serious right now? You could be in real fucking trouble. I called her to help. Hell, I guess I was too late."

It was his turn to frown. "What are you talking about?"

"Are you arriving now to take care of that ledger?"

The muscle in his jaw ticked. "I am."

"Then you're too late. Amelia's going to meet me here in less than an hour. I'm supposed to keep this guy distracted while she gets a warrant. Interpol's coming after him. If they get their hands on that ledger, you're so—"

He shook his head. "No, we got it yesterday. We've had the pages that were added re-altered. They point at those we know were involved in the human trafficking."

Relief flooded my veins, and I gripped the metal bar behind me to steady myself. "Jesus. You really got it?"

"I'd advise you not to ask how."

"No, I'm not going to do that. Because God knows what you'd tell me."

"I won't tell you anything. You can't be trusted."

Me? I couldn't be trusted? "And you know what, neither can you. You're a grade-A arsehole. All I have ever done is try to protect you. And this is how you repay me? Fuck you, East. Your dick's not that nice. Not nice enough to put up with this shit."

There would be times in the future that I'd look back on that moment and wonder why I'd used that particular phrasing. Because with us locked in this tiny lift, him so close, I did not need to be thinking about his dick and the silky-smooth perfection of it. The heavy length, how it hit all of those dark secret places inside me. I didn't need to think about that. Nope, not at all.

Except, I *did* know all those things. And he was standing so close I could smell him. I could practically smell the arousal, the need, the desperation. "Back off, East."

"No, I don't think I will. You're a naughty little girl."

"I'm not into playing your little games. So back the fuck off. If you got the ledger, I don't know how you're going to replace it. But whatever you have planned, I can't help you and I won't be involved."

But he made no move to make the lift start again. Instead, he stood so close, too close. Was he sniffing me?

He leaned closer angled his head just a little, leaning in so that his nose tickled the hairs along my neck. "You smell like honeysuckle, and I want to bury my face in your neck and to make you work those thighs as you straddle me. I dream of pounding into you until both of us are screaming. That's what I fucking want from you."

I stubbornly shook my head. "You can't have it. You tried to break me."

"If I wanted to break you, you'd be done already."

"Fuck off."

"I know you'd like to help me with that."

I shoved at his chest. "I hate you."

"Oh, the feeling's mutual, sweetheart. But ever since I watched you touch yourself and sink those delicate pretty fingers into your sweet wet pussy, all I've been thinking about is your taste and how I miss it."

"You're doing this because you miss my taste?"

He blinked as if he couldn't believe his own words. "Yes. I am." The furrow on his brow only grew deeper.

"Well, I'm not doing this. You broke me. You did it deliberately and did it coldly. So you don't get to shag me. Never again. I'm not letting you touch me."

He leaned in closer then, still sniffing, and a shiver ran through my body. And I knew I was weak. If he touched me, I was done for. Completely done.

"Are you sure about that? Because I think you miss me just as much as I miss you."

———

East

SNIFFING HER WAS A MISTAKE. An unmitigated, absolute catastrophe. Because now she was looking at me with her big hazel eyes, blinking, daring me, and there was nothing I could do except bloody give in.

I didn't wait for her permission; I didn't ask if she wanted this. I just crushed my lips to hers and moaned as her flavor hit my tongue.

I knew I was angry, too angry to do this gently. And so I waited. Waited for her to consent to being punished.

Oh yeah, sure, if that's what you think you're doing.

It was exactly what I was doing. I was punishing her and myself. Her for breaking me, me for letting her.

When her lips parted and her body molded against mine, I growled, dragging her against me, my hands over her ass, cupping her hard.

I didn't know how to find any gentleness within me. I didn't know how to find anything soft or easy. She had betrayed me. She had broken me. I had let her in, and she was a Trojan horse.

And for that she needed to pay.

Our kiss was all tongue and teeth and grunts and groans as her hands tugged at my shirt, my suit jacket, the tie, up to my hair, yanking. Every tug sent an electrical charge through my body, and I shook from the violence of it.

She wore this sexy cashmere gray sweater dress with tights. Damn thing came to her knees. And she was wearing those insane fuck-me boots that matched her dress color. They looked like some kind of soft gray suede.

I backed her up against the rail and the wall, and she clamped onto me. Then I dragged my lips from hers and chased them along her jaw. I muttered, "Now's the time to stop me, princess. If you don't say the word, I'm shagging you in this lift."

I held my breath, waiting for her to say no. When I pulled back to meet her gaze, I saw anger, fire, electric heat. She lifted her chin and glowered at me, and I gave her a cheeky grin. "Turn around," I growled, my blood thick with need. My brain overruled by my dick, closely followed by my heart.

"Fuck you."

My grin flashed again. "Oh, you're about to."

I spun her around before dragging both her hands over her head and clasping them in one of mine. Then I dragged up the skirt of her dress. "Hands here. Don't move them."

Her tight arse wiggled against my cock. "If you think I'm—"

With my free hand, I turned her head roughly and planted my lips over hers again before she could say anything else. I pulled my lips back. I muttered, "Shut up. You're ruining this. Isn't that what you said to me?"

"Fuck you."

"I see, you're repeating yourself."

The next several seconds were a blur of hands and teeth and the taste of her on my tongue, and I couldn't think.

Me, the thinker, the one concerned with safety and protocol, and yet I couldn't rub two brain cells together to stop this madness. She was doing this to me. This was *her* fault.

Oh yeah, it's her fault you don't have any bloody control.

It was her goddamn fault. Nonetheless, she held her hands on the wall like I'd told her to. Like a good girl.

Except she wasn't a good girl.

It was that thought, that memory, that betrayal that hovered just below my conscious thinking, that had me fisting the skirt of her dress, and I glanced down and nearly choked. Her tights were stockings, held in place by a gossamer yet hardworking garter belt.

"You're wearing this on purpose aren't you? To taunt me."

"I—I didn't even know I was going to see you. How could I—"

I nipped her ear with my teeth and treated her clit to a quick tap through the silk of her knickers.

She gasped and jerked her head to the side, presumably to tell me what for, but my lips were waiting for her. My tongue danced with hers even as my hand went to my buckle. I couldn't hear her voice, because if I heard it, I would believe. I would hear her lies and think they were real. And I couldn't. I just couldn't. I slid my thigh between both of hers, and kicked her stance wider. Her sharp inhale made me growl. "Wider, love."

"I'm not your love. Get this over with."

I chuckled softly as I dropped my trousers and boxers. "Ah, so we're pretending you don't like this?"

I was hard. Like a steel rod.

Could you die from a hard cock? Actual death from something being too good? At that point, I was willing to wager it could happen.

I didn't even take time to drag down her knickers. Instead I just slid my finger under that red thong that teased me, and I shoved it aside.

Without preamble, I lined myself up against her slick center, and I groaned. Her pussy was dripping. I bent my legs to get a better angle. "Why are you so wet?"

"Because I was thinking about my new boyfriend, not you."

With a muttered, "I hate you too, love," I sank home hard in one fluid thrust.

Electricity danced over my skin, and my vision went bleary. Holy Fuuuuck. I was lost.

Retreat. Slide. Retreat. Slide. She felt better than anything I could ever remember. Just the idea of her with someone else set my teeth on edge.

"You're a liar."

Her voice was breathy when she whispered, "And you're the devil."

Our movements were a torrent of thrusts and slapping flesh and whimpers and moans. With each thrust, her slick wetness clung to me like a silken sheath.

All it took was one quivering flutter from her pussy and just like that, my fingers intertwined with hers, my teeth were on her shoulder, and I broke my own oath to myself.

The oath I'd made to never feel anything for her again. That I was never going to touch her again. It was then that I realized my word meant nothing, because I was absolutely going to touch her again. I was absolutely going to break this oath again and again and again until I was nothing.

It didn't take long before she started to quiver around me, and I lost whatever hold I had on my sanity. In my own ears all I heard was the rush of my blood, her pants, the low murmurs of my name, and my grunting. And when she started to break apart, her little breathy moans and cries, the tightening of her hands on mine, I sank home deep one more time and was lost forever.

Maybe it was only a minute, but it felt like eons that I stayed inside her. Like a tenant refusing to leave upon receiving an eviction notice.

But then she pushed away from the wall and I had no choice but to release her.

The next several minutes were a blur of confusion, readjustments, and tacit denial of what we'd just done. Once her dress was down and my clothes were righted, I disengaged the stop button.

It's too late. This happened. You won't be able to forget it.

I prayed I was wrong about that.

CHAPTER 9

Nyla

EAST WASN'T the only one who could watch. I had just as many skills as he did in the surveillance arena. As I trained my binoculars on his penthouse from the building across the way, I took a sip of my coffee that helped to warm me from the chill.

What you two have going on right now is not love.

No, it certainly wasn't. It was mutual disdain. Was Van Linsted right? Despite what my gut told me, could it be that East had lied to me?

You certainly believed him when he told you he cared about you.

Granted, had he ever actually said those words, or had I just imagined them? Like in my own deranged mind, we were a thing. It wasn't his fault if I had chosen to believe what I wanted.

And there he was, marching around that penthouse like he owned the goddamn world.

This isn't healthy. First, you shag him in the lift, and now you're watching him?

I considered putting on a disguise and slipping inside the building, but getting up to the penthouse would have been tricky. This way, I wouldn't be in danger of running into him. Not that I cared.

Oh, you care.

And I did care. Who was I kidding? Now this idiot and his friends were in trouble. Bram Van Linsted had pointed the finger at them, and if he could provide any sort of evidence whatsoever, the London Lords were going to be up a creek.

It's not your job to protect them. They're grown men.

My gut just told me they were on the right side of this.

Oh, our infamous gut. Hasn't it gotten us into enough trouble?

My gut had, in fact, gotten me into more trouble than I wanted to think about. But sometimes you just had to follow a hunch. And as excited as Amelia was that we might have something on them, I didn't think she was thinking clearly.

Oh, and you are?

Okay, fair point. I picked up the phone and was about to dial East, even though I knew he wouldn't answer. Sure enough, he didn't. But I could see him reaching down to pick up the phone and look at it.

He could see I was calling. Jackass. What the hell was wrong with him?

Says the woman who's standing on a rooftop, watching her ex.

At least I wasn't behaving like Denning. I hadn't broken into his place yet.

The operative keyword was 'yet.' And to be fair, he liked to watch. That was on him.

From what he'd said in the lift, he'd really been into watching me the other night. And he'd started this little game.

Oh yeah, real mature.

I didn't bother leaving a voicemail. I'd already left so many. Asking for answers. Never begging though. Because God, that was just pathetic. I had told him to contact me because I was trying to protect him. But he didn't need my protection after all. He was a grown-arse man. Well, more like a grown-arse idiot.

As soon as I hung up, my phone rang, and I damn-near dropped my binoculars in my haste to answer. "Hello?"

"Agent Kincade, dare I ask what you're doing?"

Could he see me? Did Theroux know I was there watching East?

I certainly hoped not. After all, he'd likely be so disappointed that I was the one he picked to bring him in after all these years that he'd change his mind. "None of your business. What do you want?"

He chuckled then. "You remind me of someone. Always direct and to the point. Never any waste of words."

"What would be the point of wasting words? I'll ask again. What do you want, Theroux?"

"Testy, testy. You didn't have a good day?"

"If you're calling to find out if I'm back in Interpol, the answer is no. But I'm working on it. Can we get this show on the road? The sooner I help you, the sooner you help me. But again, I want some kind of guarantee."

"Ah, we're back to not trusting."

"If you were me, would you trust you?"

He chuckled then. "I learned a long time ago never to trust anyone. You probably need to learn that lesson."

"Noted. Thanks, Dad. Now tell me, what do you want already? This is the third time I've asked you that, and I won't ask again."

"Ah, fair enough. Agent Kincade, I am glad to hear that you are good at following orders, and I trust it won't be too difficult to get back into Interpol? Not letting your daddy issues get in the way?"

"My father and I are none of your business. Get on with it already, Theroux."

"The next step is going to bring you closer to me coming in, but you'll need to work with a partner."

"No. No partners. I'm not working with one of your low-life criminal buddies and giving them access to Interpol. Let me just be very clear. I don't need to do this, and I'm certainly not going to aid and abet any criminals."

He sighed. "Agent Kincade, you wound me. You would think you would know by now that when it comes to criminals, they come in all shapes and sizes. Those you call law-abiding citizens could be the worst of them all."

"Isn't that the truth."

"Besides, you already know your partner."

My breath caught in my throat. Amelia? Was she working for Theroux?

That sent my brain into a tailspin. But then he said the two words I most certainly didn't expect. "You will be working with East Hale."

I cursed under my breath. "What?"

"Yes. I understand you and Mr. Hale are already well acquainted."

"What the fuck?"

He sighed. "Young lady, I understand it might be a difficult partnership, but it's necessary. It has come to my attention that the task I have for you will be more difficult than I originally thought, but Mr. Hale has some avenues available that you might not be able to explore without him."

"You want me to work with him?"

"Why is this so difficult?"

It wasn't like the man knew that East and I were like fire

and ice, so it's no wonder he didn't get it. "I'm not working with him. Find someone else."

"I see you still don't understand, Agent Kincade. There is no one else. He is the other half of your team. You'll only be able to do this together. He'll have access into places that you'll never even imagine. So you can either have what you want, or stand by on the sidelines and watch someone else take the glory."

"I don't do this for glory. I do it because it's right."

"Again, spoken like someone else I know. You'll need to move quickly, and I'll need your decision by tomorrow night. I don't care how intimately acquainted you and Mr. Hale are. That's not what this is about. I'm not a matchmaker. I merely need a job done. Either you can do it, or you can't."

Just how the hell did know about me and East?

East

"ARE you sure you want to go through with this?"

I stared at Bridge in the bloody van, armed with my computers all around him. Ben and Drew were on coms at home. "You realize I can do this, right?"

Bridge frowned. "Lucas is out there somewhere in the dark, ready to give you an assist if you need one."

Lucas's voice chimed in the coms. "I'm just a beep in your pocket, mate."

I groaned. "Please stop saying mate."

"Hey, I'm British. Didn't you know?"

God, the prince was such a pain in the arse. "Look, it'll be fine. I'm just going to meet my new partner in crime. I pray that we don't get arrested or shot at. It will be good, right?"

Bridge mumbled something under his breath along the lines of, "God help us all. God save the queen."

"You don't even care about the queen."

He shrugged. "Yeah, but I care about your arse not getting shot, killed, or exposed. Any of those things really."

Ben's voice was sterner than usual over the coms. "Look, just be serious. Meet who you have to meet. Let's get this shit over with, shall we?"

Bridge once again patted me down, making sure I was ready. "Thanks, Mum. I got dressed all by myself."

He glowered. "Fine, make fun. But that thing there is probably going to save your life."

"Not if they stick a headshot, arsehole."

"If someone's angry enough to take a headshot, well, it was nice knowing you." He shrugged.

"I see. You're so concerned, aren't you?"

His grin flashed. "You're not that pretty. I won't miss you nearly as much as I'd miss Ben."

Ben's chuckle was rich. "I knew you thought I was pretty."

"Oi, would you lot shut it? I have to go out there and pretend I'm a badarse. So let me have my gun."

Bridge handed me a weapon warily.

"I see the look on your face. Might I remind you that I'm an excellent marksman, even if I do prefer computers to actual weaponry?"

"Yeah, yeah, except I haven't seen you on the range lately."

"Arsehole."

I slid the door of the van open, the chilly night air sneaking in and biting me in the joints. "Fuck me."

Lucas joined in. "No thanks. I'd rather fuck Bryna. She's cuter."

"Is everyone done with the jokes now?" I mumbled.

Ben chimed in. "Well, I didn't know that we were having a joke-off, but now that I do..."

"I swear to God, when this is over, I'm taking my position back in the van."

"Promises, promises." That was from Bridge.

I walked on the small path that was lined with perfectly trimmed hedges. Primrose Hill was a familiar neighborhood. I knew the ins and outs, and it was easy to hide, easy to mask yourself as someone who was just simply walking a dog or taking an evening stroll. At the massive statue, I took a left. Then another right, following the path, meandering as if I was out for my evening constitutional. And then I found the bench where I'd been told to wait. I checked my watch. Two minutes early. I'd be fine. Not like a sniper couldn't take an easy aim at me from here.

Relax, mate. Relax. It's fine.

I was just skittish because an international jewel thief was blackmailing me into helping him. What was there to be nervous about?

I heard the shuffle of feet on the gravel, and I turned my head at the noise. Fifteen meters away, I saw a woman walking briskly. She was dressed head to toe in black, including a woven cap on her head. Her march was familiar. Too familiar. I sat up even straighter. "Mates, are you getting this?"

It was Lucas who spoke. "Yup. A woman. Five foot eight. Could be Caucasian. Possibly Latin. Spanish, maybe? Long caramel colored hair pulled back in a braid. Big rack. Great arse."

Over the coms, Bridge muttered, "What was that all about Bryna?"

Lucas just laughed and quipped, "She has her own incredible arse too. I'm just not blind."

My stomach pitched because I knew who was walking toward me.

Fuck.

Was this some kind of Interpol thing? Had I walked into a trap? I stood before she even reached me. With ten yards to go, her step faltered when she saw me under the light. "East?"

"Fucking Nyla?"

Over the coms, everyone cursed. Ben, Bridge, Drew, even Lucas. "That's fucking Nyla?"

I shook my head. "I don't know what game you're playing, but turn right back around and go back where you came from." I pointed over her head to really emphasize she needed to go in the opposite direction.

"Quit your bitching. Theroux told me to meet you here. So I'm not going anywhere until we speak and outline what we're going to do."

"You're going to have to figure something else out because you and I are not speaking."

"What do you want to do, East? This is the deal. I'm who Theroux wants you to meet."

I shook my head. Even though I knew in my bones that I was there to meet *her*, I still refused to accept it. "No. Fuck that. And fuck you Theroux," I screamed to nobody in particular. "I'm not doing this. I'm not fucking working with you."

She crossed her arms over her ample chest. "I don't think you have any choice. I'm the only game in town. So it's either you work with me, or whatever situation you have going on with Theroux is over. And if you're like me, you have a reason for being here."

"Bullshit. I'm not stuck anywhere. I'm exactly where I want to be."

"Well then, so am I."

She had to stop this. She was going to get hurt. "I don't know what you're playing at, but this isn't fun and games. This isn't James Bond putting on a wax mask and running around being a spy. This is serious business. And you're not ready for it."

"*I'm* not ready for it says the guy who's usually in the van. I'm actually an Interpol agent. Trained to handle guns and catch bad guys. I have the experience for this."

"What the fuck do you want with Theroux?"

"That's none of your business. Just know that I'm here to do my part and move on. I'm not here for you."

On the line, Lucas muttered, "Ouch."

Ben, ever helpful, whispered, "Fuck, direct hit."

I heard clattering and moaning on the line, and then Bridge perked up with, "Yeah, that was me, after I got shot right in the heart."

And then there was Drew, ever the pragmatist, calling in from home. "Maybe you stop trying to antagonize her and get this done?"

Fucking Drew. He and I were going to have a conversation because I didn't know what was going on with him.

"You and I, Nyla, we're done. We have nothing to talk about."

"That's great, because I'm here to work. I have my reason for working with Theroux, and I'm sure you have yours. I just don't care about yours. And you shouldn't care about mine. What you *should* care about is getting the job done."

Fuck that. Such bullshit.

"I'm not working for Interpol, right now. As you know, I was suspended."

"Yeah, so you say."

"So I do. You're either going to trust me or not. That's entirely up to you." Nyla's gaze bore into mine. "What's it going to be, East?"

I knew what it was going to be. I had lost the moment she

walked up to me. I didn't know what kind of game Theroux was playing, but he was winning. He was an expert player and had moved the chess pieces just so. This job was designed to torture and torment me, and he was doing an excellent job of it.

"Fine. Whatever. I'm stuck with you for now, I suppose, but after this, we're done."

Her eyes slid over my body, making my skin feel prickly hot in every place she touched with her gaze. But then her eyes narrowed, and she said, "Yeah, well, someone should tell your dick that, because right now, you're hard."

And that was how Nyla Kincade dropped the mic on me.

———

Nyla

I KNEW his friends were listening because the fucking London Lords didn't do anything by themselves. *Ever.*

That's better than doing everything by yourself. Where is your goddamn backup?

Under normal circumstances, I would have had Amelia in the background somewhere. Watching. Recording. Sitting by with a gun just in case I was idiot enough to get shot. But now? Now there was no one. Just myself. Standing there, just a girl in front of a guy, begging him not to shoot her. Okay fine, also begging him to still love her. But even I knew that was a fallacy, because East Hale had never loved me.

He was able to just cut me out like that for no good reason. He ghosted me and then walked away. I had been a game to him. And unfortunately, I was not free of this game yet.

My phone rang in my back pocket, and as I pulled it out, it was again an unknown number. "Hello."

"Agent Kincade, I'm so thrilled that you are able to follow instructions. Could you put the phone on speaker, please?"

I scowled but did as I was told, all the while thinking to myself, *He vowed to turn himself in to you. You will be the one to bring him in. Just do as you're told.*

I hit speaker. "Now it's on speaker. We can both hear you."

East's eyes went wide, and he mouthed, "Theroux?" and I nodded.

"Well, I'm so pleased to see you two follow directions. Mr. Hale, before you get your knickers in a twist, I couldn't tell you Agent Kincade was one of mine. You never would have agreed, especially since your relationship busted up the way it did."

My gut twisted, because how the fuck did he know?

East looked as displeased as I did, with a deep scowl on his otherwise smooth and handsome face. The moonlight gave harsh slants, making his face far angrier than it already was. All ticking jaw muscle along that gorgeous bone.

"Just so you know, I've gone to quite a bit of trouble to make this happen, so please, do try and follow the rules. Mr. Hale, you know what I've got over you, and Agent Kincade, you know what's at stake. I thought you could just work together, so if you could try not to have a kerfuffle or two, that would be excellent."

I sniffed. "I don't think I've ever had a kerfuffle."

"Oh, so we won't count that one time in the park when you two had what we'll just call a 'dustup'? In full view of witnesses?"

How the hell did he know about that?

East's gaze met mine, and his expression was unreadable. There was no disdain. No anger. Maybe confusion? I wasn't sure.

"I trust the two of you can be adults and still work together even though your relationship is over?"

Way to slice home. I didn't deserve some random thief who

seemed to be one step ahead of me the whole time pointing out to me that my relationship was over. That the one person I'd trusted in years had walked away from me without a word. My gut knotted, and I felt like the bottom of my world fell out and I was in a free fall. He looked just the same. Handsome, with a beautifully chiseled jaw, full lips, dimples for days, and deep-set moss-green eyes. The wind ruffled his hair, making it look sex-disheveled. Fuck. I missed him. The pain was so tight and pinpoint accurate that I thought my heart was going to burst, and not in a good way. But instead, I tilted my chin. "I can stay professional if he can."

A muscle at East's jaw ticked. "I'm always professional."

I wanted to scream at him then. Scream, 'Oh yeah, is that why you fucked me and then left without a word? Used me and cast me aside?'

Instead, I said, "Fucking hell. You know what, this might not be worth it."

Theroux was quick to stop my retreat. "You know what's at stake. Now that the two of you have met and you know who your ally is, I'll tell you the target. Henry Warlow."

I frowned. "I don't know that name. Should I?"

East looked just as confused as I did.

"Henry Warlow," Theroux said, "is an old adversary of mine. And you can relax, Agent Kincade. I don't want you to kill him. I just want him found."

"When did you last see him?"

"Henry Warlow was last seen in Italy thirty years ago. That's all the information I have."

East crossed his arms, looking utterly displeased. And I knew why. A hunt for someone who hasn't surfaced in thirty years would be next to impossible.

"Okay, why do you need him?" I asked.

"That, my dear, is my business. Your job is just to find him."

"No, I want to know what you need him for, because as I said, I might not be Interpol anymore, but I don't kill people, and I don't break the law."

His chuckle was low and self-satisfied with a hint of amusement. "No, of course, you don't. Agent Kincade, I know that you don't trust anybody. But I assure you, my word is my bond. After all, what would be the point of doing business if you couldn't be trusted?"

"Said the thief," I muttered.

The corner of East's lips tipped up then. "You're counting on him to do something for you?"

"Mr. Hale, I would suggest that you mind your damn business. How you got here and how she got here are two different things." Theroux cleared his throat and returned to his more even tone of voice. "But I assure you, I'm not looking to kill him. The man owes me money. Actually, he stole something very valuable from me, and I would like it back. So, I have no desire to kill anyone. I need you to find him first, and then we need to locate what he stole from me."

"Jesus Christ, I'm helping a thief?"

"Think of it as you are finding a missing person."

East chuckled then. "Oh, so you think it'll be easy finding someone who hasn't been seen in thirty years? We don't know what alias he's using now. You probably don't have any of his last knowns, do you?"

"Yes, I do," Theroux said. "Look for a de Montague. I have been searching for both the Henry Warlow name and his other aliases for thirty years to no avail. I haven't found hide nor hair of them, but somehow, I think someone as connected as you, Mr. Hale, and someone as resourceful as you, Agent Kincade, will be the ones to make this happen. You'll be the ones to bring poor Henry Warlow home to answer for the things that he's done and to give back what he's taken."

My stomach didn't feel any better. "Let's just be very clear, Theroux. If we find Warlow, I'm not handing him over to you until you live up to your end of the bargain. Because you were right when you said I don't trust anybody."

I leveled a very direct gaze on East so he would know that I meant him. That he would know the depth of my rage toward him.

"Theroux, while I hate to agree with Agent Kincade, because she... Well, she doesn't trust anyone, and she's quite untrustworthy herself, I'd have to agree on this fact. So I'll need you in person, handing over my file, before I hand over the person you want."

"I knew the two of you would work very well together. See, you're already thinking alike. Excellent, you have a week to find him."

I laughed. "You haven't found him in thirty years, and you think we'll find him in a week? It'll take longer than that."

East agreed with me, shockingly. "She's right. Finding people takes time. It's like a puzzle you'll have to unravel. If he doesn't want to be found, he could stay hidden even longer."

"Fine, I'll check in after a week. Do find *something* of use to report."

And then Theroux was gone.

I glowered at East. "So, what does he have on you?"

"Nothing."

"I see. So, we're lying now? Well, to catch a thief, it takes a thief, right? So, you're definitely the right person for the job of finding this Henry Warlow character."

"I'm not a thief, Nyla."

"But you and I both know that's not entirely true."

"Still towing the line now, even though you're not Interpol now? I'm glad to hear you're not into killing people these days."

"What the fuck, East? You might not be who you pretended to be, but I was exactly who I said I was. I never lied to you."

"Sure, you haven't. You go and work alone, Nyla Kincade."

As he turned to leave, I called out after him. "Oh no you don't."

But he kept walking, forcing me to run after him, cutting off his path of escape. "We have to figure out a plan."

"The plan is, I'm going to find him, give him to Theroux, and be done with all this."

"You heard him. He wants us to work together."

"Fine. You look up whatever you can find and then let me know what you have."

"Oh no." I shook my head. "That's not how we're doing this. I'm not giving Theroux the chance to slip through my fingers. We either do this together, or we're not doing this at all. And I will do everything in my power to thwart your search. So you're stuck with me, which means revoking all your persona-non-grata bullshit at the hotel. And you actually have to answer your fucking phones now. But don't worry. I'm not going to be a stalker ex-girlfriend on you. You have nothing I want."

He stepped into my space then, and my breath caught. The night was chilly, but his heat seeped through me, making me soft and languid. "Let's not forget. I know exactly what you want."

"Like I said before, I'm not in this for you. I don't make the same mistakes twice. So let's get this thing done so we can *be* done. I'm getting tired of playing these games. I'd rather be with a fucking grown up."

"Sweetheart," he started.

"I'm not your bloody sweetheart."

"If you say so. But I should probably mention I've seen the name Henry Warlow before."

I lifted my brows. "Where?"

"Old photo of a boat race. In Lord Jameson's office."

"You didn't think to mention that to Theroux?"

"Not until I have a full understanding of what he wants with him. But look at me growing and sharing things. I'm so proud of myself."

"You're a wanker." He furrowed his brow at me, and then it was my turn to shift around and saunter away. I wasn't taking him on his say so. I wanted to do my own digging.

I'd text him in the fucking morning, and then we'd get to work. As soon as I was done with this though, I would be freaking clear of East Hale and would never have to see him again.

CHAPTER 10

Nyla

THE NIGHT FOLLOWING my meeting with my brand-new partner, Amelia invited me over. I genuinely thought we were going to have girl's time, but I was wrong.

She wanted to strategize. I arrived with wine and takeout, ready for some Netflix and chill with my bestie. But instead she brought our suspect board over from the other office.

"Oh, I thought we were, you know, maybe celebrating your promotion as it were."

She looked mildly chagrined. "Oh God, I'm sorry. I should have said. But honestly, I just want to get a head start on all of this. I mean, that was a wild meeting with Van Linsted earlier this week. We lost a few steps because the judge wouldn't approve the warrant and the crown prosecutor is still reviewing the proposed deal, but we're not shot out of the water yet."

I nodded, slowly trying to process that this was a working dinner when all I wanted to do was chill and complain about my ex.

But she continued on as if she couldn't see my disappointment. "So I'm thinking about what we can do for him if the ledger is good. I know the crown prosecutor is going to reject the original proposal, and he'll have to show good faith first. So these are the arguments we're going to present to him. We know that Van Linsted gave us some valuable information, and I'm not suggesting we release him, but—"

I wanted to pay attention. Hell, now I really needed to, but I just couldn't. "Amelia, I'm sorry. I just... Could we maybe just give it a rest for a night?"

Amelia frowned. "What is wrong with you?"

I didn't know what she meant by that. "Nothing's wrong with me."

"Well, something is definitely wrong with you, because the Nyla Kincade I know would be chomping at the bit over all of this. Van Linsted, for the first time since we arrested him, is willing to talk to us. To name names. We just have to figure out a deal for him. A reduction of sentence, something, and you're dragging your feet?"

I sighed and dropped the bag, already missing the mindless Netflix I wasn't going to be having. "Look, all I'm saying is pump the brakes a little bit and think."

She coughed a laugh. "Oh, that's rich. You *never* stop to think. Not once. And I have been your partner for a bloody long time. Not once have you ever stopped to think. Not once have you ever used caution. How come when I get to be lead, that's when you want to use caution? When I was able to convince that twat to talk, suddenly you lost interest in moving anything forward? Why is that?"

"Amelia, why are you being like this?"

"I'm not being like anything, Ny, I'm just making an observation."

My gut turned. Amelia and I were like scones and cream.

Always together. We'd solved some great cases together. Why was she being like this?

"All I'm saying is that maybe we should slow down and watch, because getting into bed with someone like Bram Van Linsted is not exactly in our best interest. It's not the safe route."

"I mean, honestly, just because I'm not doing it exactly how you would do it, doesn't mean I'm inept."

"Who's saying you're inept, Amelia? But don't you think it's at all interesting that Garreth Jameson was there to visit Van Linsted? That there's more at play here? We don't know anything for sure. There's a lot more investigating to be done still."

"What if I'm following my own hunch? You're notorious for doing that. Or maybe you're just not cooperating because it's not you leading? Maybe if it was you on the other side, you'd be more than happy to move things along."

I staggered back as if I'd been slapped. "Do you really think I would do that?"

"I don't know what I'm supposed to think. All I know is that Denning warned me that you'd be like this."

Fucking Denning. "Oh, did he?"

"Yeah, he made it pretty clear that things would change with you. That as affable and supportive as you've always been with me, the moment you weren't my boss that would change. It's like you're undermining me, just like you did him."

"And you believed him?"

"Well, what else am I supposed to think? I have a solid idea and a solid lead. One you're not going to follow up on because you're dick whipped or whatever."

"Wow, that is supremely unfair. And coming from someone who saw exactly what Denning did, how could you even say that to me?"

"Hey, I was the first one in your corner, not wanting to think that you had any hand in that whole Denning situation. I'm your best mate, but you're not at all happy for me that I'm in this position."

"I am happy. This is my fucking happy face."

She slapped her hands on her hips. "Yeah, I noticed."

I ran my hand through my hair, snagging it in the tangles. "Amelia, I couldn't be prouder of you. I have pitched for you to be made a senior agent for years."

"Funny how that turned out. You pitched for me for years, but the moment you leave, guess who's made the senior agent? Which tells me that maybe you're the one who held me up."

"Do you seriously believe that?"

"I don't know what I'm supposed to believe. Why won't you back me on this?"

"I'm telling you, it's not the right move."

"Now that I've made senior officer, I have some influence and more people listen to me. Why is it you of all people can't be on board with this? After I have backed you on everything."

I blinked at her. "Wow, so you want to pull that?"

"Yes, I do. How many times have you had some hair-brained scheme where things have been dubious? Where we've all but crossed the line, on nothing more than your say so. And now, I'm not even bending any rules. I'm going by the book."

"Look, I know this is your assignment, and I believe in you a hundred percent. I absolutely do. I don't know why you don't see that. But you have got to see there's something else at play here, and I don't think it has anything to do with the London Lords. You claim to have trusted my gut all this time. I'm asking you to trust it again. I just don't want you to fall on your face."

As soon as the words were out of my mouth, I knew I'd said the wrong thing. Her mouth hung open.

"Fall on my face, is it? All this time, you said Denning was a twat. I believed you. Denning is a twat. All this time, you go on and on about how he took your job. And I believed you. He took your job. It was a twat move. But I'm starting to think that maybe he deserved it. Maybe the reason you didn't get the job was because of you and your choices. You and your gut. Did your gut tell you to shag East Hale too?"

This time, my mouth hung open. "Wow, we're really going there?"

"You're the one who brought us here."

"Okay. I see. My personal life has nothing to do with any of this."

"I don't see it that way. You need to excuse yourself from this case."

"I'm not shagging East Hale. East Hale is nothing to me."

She frowned. "So what, he was just a mark?"

Jesus Christ, that sounded worse. No way was I telling her what had happened. Not now. "All you need to know is I'm not shagging him. Even though, let's be perfectly clear, you encouraged me too."

"I did no such—"

I shot her a look. "I think if you want to stay friends, maybe we shouldn't talk for a while."

"Easily achieved. I think some distance between you and me would be great right about now."

For some reason, the way she said that cut to the quick. As if I'd been bringing her down. "Wow, you've just been dying to say that, haven't you?"

Her shoulders sagged. "Actually, no. *Never*. I never wanted to be in this position, Nyla. I never wanted your job. Did I want my own team? Absofuckinglutely. Am I proud to have my own team? Yes. But I wanted a team that would support me. A team that I could grow and nurture. Not one that was under my thumb."

Was that how she looked at everything we'd done? All the time we'd spent together?

"Wow. So, that's how you feel?"

"That's how I feel."

I lost my appetite. My gut was churning. "Amelia, I love you. I want nothing but your success, but that doesn't mean I have to blindly follow you. When I think you're making a mistake, I'll tell you because I'm your friend."

"Oh, but I'll do that too. When you're being selfish, I'll tell you because I'm your friend."

"So now I'm selfish."

"Yeah, Nyla, you are. The world doesn't revolve around you. This isn't your play, where we're all just characters hoping for some stage time. I'm going to follow my own gut now and see how that feels."

"Amelia."

"I think it's time for you to go."

"Wow." The burning in my gut only spread. The sheer pain of knowing that I was completely and utterly alone hit me like a raw burn. My father wasn't exactly someone I could go talk to. East? Not an option. And Amelia, wow. She was on a path of her own. One that didn't have room for me.

Are you sure that's what she's saying?

I was in no mood for rational talk. It hurt too much. I left the food where it was, but I took the wine. At least I could have a drink. Even if it was all by my lonesome.

So this was what it was like to be absolutely, completely alone.

———

Nyla

Eᴀsᴛ ʜᴀᴅ ᴋᴇᴘᴛ ʜɪs ᴡᴏʀᴅ.

I was no longer persona non grata at the hotel, but I *was* escorted up, which meant East had given instructions that I was not to be left alone. Bloody fantastic.

When I was deposited at the penthouse and the bellhop rang the doorbell, it wasn't East who opened the door. Instead, it was a woman with dark curly hair, the petite one I'd met when East had introduced me to the gang. What was her name? Yes, Telly. "Hi, Telly."

She smiled. "Hi, Nyla. I'm glad to see you. You are here to save me from Captain I'm-a-grumpy-arsehole, right?"

"Oh, yes, I've met him. He's quite unpleasant, isn't he?"

"Yes, indeed. East, I really do like this one. Too bad you're a jackhole and didn't keep her."

I winced at that, but Telly took my hand and dragged me in. "God, you're so sexy. Hot too. Really honey, he's lost the plot, he has."

I followed Telly into the penthouse and found East looking as handsome as ever. His T-shirt was tight over his broad shoulders as he leaned over a laptop at the table. "Who is it, Tell?"

"The love of your life."

"Oh, Telly, you know full well I don't believe in love. Is it the stripper?"

"No, actually, it *is* the love of your life. I suppose we could ask her to strip though."

East whirled around and scowled when he saw me. "Oh, it's you."

Damn, that didn't sting at all. "Yes, in all my splendor. Should I do the striptease here, or should I wait?"

His gaze flickered over my body, and I could feel the pulsing heat of it. "That won't be necessary. I've seen it all."

"Yes, I know. It's absolutely bloody fantastic."

Telly plopped on the couch and gave me a wide grin.

"While I am a married lady now, I can still look, so feel free to do the striptease for me."

I laughed. "Maybe when we're alone. I don't want to offend anyone's sensibilities."

East ignored us both. "We have work to do. The sooner we can find Warlow, the sooner we are all free of Francois Theroux. So pull out a chair and get to work."

"Right, of course." I shucked my shoulder bag and pulled out my laptop before lowering myself onto his plush couch. I had to steel myself so I wouldn't think about what we'd last done on that couch. "Okay, so I already started a little background checking. I called some contacts at Immigration and had them do a search for me. There was a Henry Warlow who was studying at the University of Milan about thirty years ago. He was enrolled as a graduate student. There is, however, no evidence of him leaving school in the computer records, but so many of those records are still on paper. So they said they were going to look into it for me and let me know. But at least we know Henry Warlow was in Milan around that time."

East's brow furrowed at me, but he said nothing as he turned back around. Telly laughed. "That's his way of saying good work, because thus far, he hasn't been able to get that information. He's a little bit pissed because thirty years ago not everything was recorded on the internet, so East is having a difficult time with this particular assignment."

I nodded and joined them at the table. I worked better when I was alert and focused, so that meant not sitting on the couch, because I was bone tired. I hadn't been sleeping, and really, I honestly couldn't remember the last time I'd eaten, so, I would need to take care of that.

There was another knock on the door, and Telly sprang up again. "That would be the takeout. Now, while you two kids get to work, I actually need to go. Carmen just texted, and she misses me."

East whipped around. "You are not doing this."

"Sorry, mate, but she has already found more information than you or I were able to dig up, so she is a perfect partner. I'm going home. You two kids enjoy this Chinese."

East scowled at her. "You had this planned all along when you said you were going to help me. You set me up."

"Absolutely. I'm sorry." She looked alternately between the two of us. "Was that not clear? This *is* a set up. And since I knew that he was going to suggest that you search on your own and maybe just exchange information over a phone call, I was meant to be the glue. I have now glued you two together. Not sexually of course, because that would be awkward. So... enjoy."

She dropped the takeout on the table, and the ginger and garlic scents wafted up my nose, making my stomach grumble, and I knew that I would possibly kill someone for beef and broccoli. "We don't have to do this together. I can go home."

But there was a part of me, that lonely, crushing part, that prayed to God he would not send me home alone to my empty flat where I had no boyfriend, no best friend, and no job. The job thing. I could get it back, but like I'd told Theroux, that was going to involve eating a lot more crow, and I wasn't that hungry yet.

But what are you going to do about the aching loneliness?

I had other friends besides Amelia. Mates from my MI5 days. I could call loads of people up for a quick drink, but they would all require some level of effort, and I was not in the mood for effort. But no way in hell would I tell East that I wanted to stay. He wanted me gone, and I wasn't going to shove into where I wasn't wanted.

"No, stay. I can't eat all of this by myself, and of course, your stomach is grumbling, because I guarantee you forgot to eat."

"I did not," I lied easily.

"You're not even lying well. Sit. Eat."

He stood and marched into the kitchen, bringing out plates and serving spoons. When he unwrapped what we had, it was beef and broccoli, honey glazed shrimp, and a mountain of dumplings. My stomach full-on roared.

East chuckled. Actually chuckled. And for a split second, I could remember what it was like a week ago when he still cared about me.

Suck it up, because it's never happening again. Remember what it was like when he cut you off.

Yes. I remembered that. And that was the memory to hold on to.

We dug into our food, laptops open, scanning and searching. "Are you looking in the archives of the school?" I asked.

"Yeah, I'm looking. And there is a Henry Warlow, but there are no photos, no nothing. It's like he was a ghost."

"If you can get me a class roster from one of his classes, I can run through it and ask around to see if anyone has any recollection of him."

East raised an eyebrow. "What are you going to say about why you're questioning them?"

I chuckled. "I'm going to tell them I'm an Interpol agent."

He laughed. "You're going to lie?"

I nodded. "Yep."

"Wow. I see you have fully lost your relationship with the truth."

"Yeah, you know, once you start to sin, all your morals go out the window. That's survival."

His gaze stayed on mine for a long stretch. It made my skin hot and tight, making me pulse and ache in places I would rather not think about. When he spoke, his voice was gravel laced with silk. "You haven't been sleeping well. I can tell."

Yeah well, whose fault is that?

"I sleep just fine. Let's get back to work."

His gaze narrowed and he continued to study me as if waiting for something. But suddenly he sat back, blinking as if a spell had been broken. And just like that, the sliver of warmth between us vanished. "Right. Yeah, back to work."

I hated shutting him down, but it was too tempting. Too easy to let him in. And after what he'd done, the way he'd shut me out without talking to me, I couldn't do that again. It was better to be on my own, alone, than to have people I couldn't count on.

"All right, I found a class he was in with a list of attendees."

"Okay, I'm on it."

"It's late in Milan."

"It may be late, but I do still have a friend at Interpol, and she can at least get me updated phone numbers for all of these people."

I stood to make my call, meandering over to the table every now and again to come back and take a bite. And with every bite of the savory food, I moaned. And with every moan, East's gaze flickered to me quickly and then backed away again.

I wasn't doing it on purpose, but God, I was hungry. I made a mental note to eat more.

East screamed, "Eureka!"

I whipped around. "What? What do you have?"

He clapped then stood up and did this butt-wiggling dance, showcasing his spectacular arse. "I found a fucking picture."

"Stop lying."

He shook his head. "Come look for yourself." I crowded around his laptop, and he laughed before grabbing a small remote and clicking two buttons, and then a projector came down. A photo appeared on the projector screen showing Henry Warlow's class photo. "Unfortunately, it doesn't identify them by name. But I could probably run some facial recognition software. People look different though, and we would have to age them thirty years."

"You can do that?"

"Doesn't Interpol have fancy facial recognition programs that you can do that with?"

"Well, I guess. But why do *you*, a civilian, have such things?"

He arched a brow, the move accompanied by the dark stubble on his jaw, making his beautifully handsome face into something more rakish with a dirty-bad-boy vibe. "Are you really going to ask me that kind of question?"

I handbagd my lips. "Never trust a hacker."

He nodded. "Never trust a hacker."

He was quick. Watching his long skilled fingers as they flew at the keyboard, I was more and more aware of my body, the throbbing ache between my thighs, how much I missed his fingertips over my skin. His voice in my ear telling me that everything was going to be okay. We'd only been together for a couple of weeks, but in those couple of weeks, I had been myself. Entirely, wholly myself, and I missed that. Because I had no idea who I was now. Without my job. Without him. And I didn't even want to think about the fight with Amelia.

He sat back. "Well, facial recognition is running, but it's going to take a while. Do you have anything?"

"Well, I spoke to my contact at Interpol. She's going to give me updated phone numbers of classmates, so I can call them in the morning."

He nodded slowly, and I couldn't meet his gaze. I had to look away. And the only thing to look at was the photo on the projector, since everything in the penthouse reminded me of the last time I'd been there and all the places he'd had me. And then I frowned, stepping closer. "East?"

I was shocked to hear his voice directly behind me. Low, and mellow, and fuck, so sexy. "Yeah, Nyla?"

He might have said yes, and my name, but it sounded like he was saying, 'Bend over, so I can fuck you.' Which, of course, he wasn't saying. I pointed at the projector. "Who does that look like to you?"

He squinted. "It's a faded photo. I don't know. Maybe he looks familiar?"

"Yeah, that looks like Garreth Jameson."

He frowned, leaned forward, squinted, then stepped back a little. "I mean, a little. Around the eyes, maybe the forehead. But Jameson is my age. He's thirty. He couldn't be in that photo."

"No, but it could definitely be his relative."

"Maybe. Maybe his father."

"Is there a list of names with that photo?"

He shook his head. "It only names a few of the students, but it doesn't identify what name goes with which face. One thing of note. One of the blokes in the photo is Marcus Van Linsted. That's all I've got."

"I'm telling you, that's the elder Jameson. If he knew Warlow, he could lead us to him. Obviously Van Linsted won't help us."

"Well, we'll do some more digging, and then we'll see if you're right."

I crossed my arms, because I knew I was right. I *knew* it. That man in the photo was the elder Jameson. Which meant that Jameson knew Warlow. And maybe all we needed to do to get answers was to ask.

CHAPTER 11

East

I'D LIED TO MYSELF.

I knew I didn't want to work with her, but I'd told myself that I could. That it wouldn't cut deep.

That was a lie.

The night after Nyla and I began the search for Warlow, she joined us at Bridge's house for a Theroux meeting.

Every move she made, every breath, I could sense her. I could fucking smell her. And now she was shifting on the couch, rubbing her thighs together as if she was trying to get comfortable. But of course, I kept thinking about why she was pressing her thighs together. Did she miss me? Was she thinking about me?

No, you knob.

Drew was the first to stick his nose where it didn't belong. "Got to say, it's good to have you back. Someone's trying to hide his true feelings, even if he still looks angry."

I scowled at him. "She's not permanent. Don't get used to her."

Nyla's brows furrowed, but she didn't say anything. She merely crossed her arms and narrowed her gaze. A part of me wished she would fight back, give me some of that fire I'd seen the night I'd watched her in her flat, or some of the fire from the lift.

All the blood in my body started to rush south with that thought, and I willed that shit off. All I had to do was think about walking into that secret flat of hers and seeing the photos of me and my mates everywhere. I did not want that viper anywhere near us, but at the moment, we had no choice. I had to work with her. Which meant, my team had to work with her as well. But it was only temporary.

If you say so.

I tried to ignore her. If I could just pretend she wasn't there, maybe it would make that feeling go away. That constant hum that was present whenever she was around. That restless energy buzzing through my body, demanding that I touch her, or hold her, or talk to her. When the fuck had that happened? I had never had that problem before. The complete inability to focus on anything else. Bridge and I were the logical ones. Think it through. Don't get emotionally involved. It was easy.

Until Nyla.

She leaned forward. "Well, Drew, thank you for having me here, and I thank the rest of you for not trying to shoot me when I walked in, East notwithstanding. Um, the good news is we have some information on Henry Warlow. The bad news is Francois Theroux is demanding it in person, and I don't like it. It's dangerous. He's letting us decide the terms of where to meet though."

Livy piped up. "Obviously, it should be somewhere public. No chance in hell you two should walk into anywhere that's closed off and secluded. That's a recipe for disaster."

I watched as she joined Nyla on the couch. What, the two of them were friends now?

Nyla nodded. "No, that's not an ideal situation. Fortunately, we don't have all the information on Henry Warlow. We just have a photograph, and we need Theroux to verify it's the right guy. He has no reason to hurt us, especially since it's only a small part of what he asked us to do in finding him, but since there's just two of us, he could hold one of us until the other completes the job, so I don't like that either. I agree, public is best."

So what, she and my friends were pals now? Everyone else could just forget that any of this had ever happened? Well, I couldn't. I needed this over. The sooner we picked the location and came up with our plan, the sooner she would be out of my hair. "Okay, let's focus. What about Grimwald Square?"

"You mean right next to the train station?" Nyla asked. "I mean, it could work. It has a big open square. Multiple points of entry and exit. It's entirely possible."

Bridge leaned forward. "Safety is what we're looking for here. And we need to be armed and ready as well, but carrying is a problem. Even though the square is massive, and yes, it's always busy, there are lots of alleyways and exit points."

Nyla gave him a direct look when he said that. "Excuse me, Mr. Edgerton, I don't see how that would work. I've been suspended, so I'd get in as much trouble as anyone else if I were caught carrying a gun. Besides, I need Theroux. If we spook him and he's in the wind, I'll have nothing. So I won't be the faulty wheel here."

Bridge held up his hands. "Well, I'm saying you're an unknown quantity. Not that I don't trust you."

"No, I get it. East doesn't trust me, so you don't trust me. Fair enough."

It was Telly who waived away the notion. "No, you already

proved your trustworthiness. We're better as a team. Working together. If we go in small, anything could go wrong. If one of you gets captured, then you can't make the meet."

Ben was sprawled back in Bridge's club chair, looking every bit a king on his throne. "Telly has a point. There is no purpose to keeping this small. Yeah, poor Bridge and Drew could freeze their balls off, but mine are already in Livy's handbag, so I'll be fine."

Livy coughed a laugh. "So I made you pick wedding colors the other day. Jesus. Are you still mad?"

"I'm mad that I now know the difference between mauve and wine. No self- respecting man needs to know that."

"Well, you didn't have to help."

I sighed. Things were deteriorating fast. "Please focus. I'd like to get this over with."

Surprisingly, it was Nyla who helped me. She leaned forward. "All right, if the meet happens, then Grimwald Square is the best option for us. We have these possible exits." She used the Skittles that she and Livy had been sharing to mock us. "If this is us, Theroux would likely put his men here." She put all the purple Skittles on the rooftops in sniper positions. Despite myself, I leaned forward. She was right; those were the best positions.

"You think he'll have snipers?"

Nyla shrugged. "I have no idea. He knows we have no choice but to agree to meet him, but if he gets wind of this game, or he gets spooked, he might start shooting."

I didn't want to respect her or her intelligence, but she was smart. Which was what made her dangerous. And she was right. If Theroux was indeed watching us, we had to be very careful. "Nyla and I are going in together."

Her eyes went wide. "I don't think so."

I lifted a brow. "What, now you don't want to work together?"

"No. We have a common goal, but it just doesn't make sense for us to go together."

"Are you afraid?"

She pressed her lips together in a tight line, and there was an urge that made me think about kissing it off her face. "No, I'm suspended, they've taken away my firearms at the moment, so I just have my bare hands."

Livy leaned forward and clasped her hand. "Something tells me that, even with only your bare hands, you're pretty dangerous."

Nyla smiled. "I'm decent. I can take care of myself. I'd still feel better with a weapon."

I don't know what made me say it, or why I volunteered, but the moment the words were out of my mouth, I regretted them and wanted to cut out my own tongue. "You won't need a weapon. You'll have me."

―――――

Nyla

IT'S NOT REAL. *It is not real. Goddammit, it is not real.*

I didn't know how many times I tried to mentally tell myself that East, with his arm around me, holding me close, nuzzling my hair, wasn't real. My body apparently didn't believe that massive lie.

As I curled into him, I placed a hand over his heart and wrapped an arm around his waist as we walked together to Grimwald Square, seemingly lovey-dovey, and my body believed it. She believed that after this, East and I were going home together, that East and I were going to tear off the sheets and make up for the last week of being cold and apart, make up for lost time, make up for it all. My body was a moron.

That was the only explanation. My body had a death wish. Because clearly, my heart couldn't take whatever the hell he was doing right now. And I needed to remember that. But oh no, I wanted what he was selling. His cologne hit me like a whiplash of sandalwood, and God, he smelled so unbelievably good. I just wanted to lean in and sniff. But that was dumb. I knew better. The last thing on earth I needed to do was to lean in and sniff the man as if I wasn't being punished enough already. This wasn't real. And I needed to remember that, otherwise I was going to groan.

"It's not real," I murmured softly, but it didn't escape East's ears.

"What's not real?"

East's voice was husky, and the heat of his breath sneaked up my neck as I answered out loud, "Nothing."

"More secrets you're keeping?"

"For the love of God, East, if you don't—" I cut myself off. "It doesn't matter. But I do have to give you credit. The way you did it was spectacular."

He frowned down at me. Everything about his body language said, we were a couple in love on a romantic stroll on an autumn evening. But it was a lie. Just like everything else.

"Oh, you're giving me beef for the way I handled every-thing? It was best for both of us. Clean. But it seems like you found a way to stick around anyway. Ugh, we're not doing this now."

He was right. Now was the world's shittiest time to discuss it. But as he'd been avoiding me and we hadn't really had time to be alone, I took the chance to at least ask something. "Do you want to at least tell me what you were doing in my flat while I was gone?"

His step faltered. "I was picking up something I'd left behind."

"You could have just called me for it, and I could have left it with your doorman."

I felt rather than saw his hard swallow. "It was something I didn't want to be seen by anyone else."

"Are you going to tell me what it was?"

"Nope."

We were almost at the clock tower, and his grip on me tightened.

"So we're just going to pretend that nothing happened and that I didn't exist to you?"

He still didn't answer me. Instead, his feet faltered just a little and he held me even tighter. "Something isn't right."

"Yeah, it's not right. You can't just freeze me out, East. Not without a grownup conversation, at least."

It took me a moment to realize that he wasn't talking about us. He meant that something wasn't right about the meet. The air. It was too still.

I halted alongside him and breathed deep. "We're being watched."

He nodded and dipped his head down. His lips were a whisper from mine, and I froze. Oh, hell no, he was not going to kiss me. Not fucking now.

But he clearly wasn't. Instead, he used the opportunity to whisper to me, "Not only are we being watched, but we've also got a tail. West exit. Obviously, I can't see behind me, but I'd bet the south exit too."

I did my own assessment, and he was right.

"Yep, I see him. In sweatpants and camo. Looks like he's stretching."

In our earpieces, Livy sighed. She was the closest to that exit. "Yeah, let me see if I can waylay him."

Ben's voice was loud and clear. "You will do no such—"

From what I could see, Livy was already on the move. Never mind what Ben had to say about it. I'd always liked her. Ben's curses rang loud and clear.

Bridge, from his position at the southeast exit where he was doing some light window shopping for some Prada bags, said, "What are we going to do? Do we abort? Do you think they're Theroux's?"

I snuggled into East even more, my heart hammering. It was a comfort to feel the rapid *ta-pa-ta-pa-ta-pa* of his heartbeat. "That's not where Theroux would place his men. Honestly, if I were him, I'd be very well hidden. You wouldn't even see my men."

From wherever the hell he was, Ben just muttered. "They're not Theroux's. Too sloppy."

I watched the one to my left who appeared to be running through the park at a nice and easy slow pace. I frowned because he stopped at a bench to presumably tie his shoe. A shoe that hadn't been unlaced.

And then I saw him press his fingers to his ear. I kept my voice low, but it was clear and harsh. "Abort. Abort."

East's grip tightened on me again. "What? What do you see?"

"To the east, by the bench. He's a cop. I don't know what branch yet, but he's police for sure."

There was cursing ringing on the line, and Bridge grumbled. "East, what's your call?"

East leaned down, his gaze searching mine. His eyes held mine for a long moment before he muttered, "Abort. Meet back at the Long River's point."

The Long River's point was Bridge's house. There were many ways in and out of Belgravia Square, and everyone on the team all had different exits.

It was then that East leaned low. I knew he was following our protocol for our exit strategy, the one we'd come up with last night, but it was probably apparent that I wasn't thinking clearly, because he wrapped his arms around me and let out a low rich laugh.

He's playing the part. He is playing the part. Do not buy it.

And then he picked me up and twirled me around easily. The swing and the rush of the air made me dizzy, intoxicating me. When he put me down, I knew what was going to happen next. If he nuzzled me on the left, I was to go around and go with Livy. And so we would kiss, turn back around, head for the cafe, and then we would make some show of having forgotten something. He would then go and retrieve it, presumably from the car. And that would leave me to go ahead to the cafe where I'd meet Livy and leave together. If he kissed me on the right, I was to join Bridge at his post. If he kissed me on the lips, I was stuck with him.

As his lips drew near, I didn't know what I was in for. I didn't know what was going to happen. All I knew was that his lips were coming near me, and I needed to control my response. When his lips brushed over mine, my heart froze. Instant recognition flared in my heart. I knew what it was like to be with him. I knew it as I remembered it, like my own instinct.

Jesus Christ. I was rewarded with the *tap-tap-tapping* of his heart under where my hand laid on his chest. Well, at least I wasn't the only one being tortured. When he pulled back with a smile, he took my hand and we headed north to our back up. That meant someone had been watching us a little too intently. Jesus Christ. How had this gotten so fucked up?

With my hand in his, we moved with the lazy confidence of people who knew exactly where they were going, knew exactly how long it would take to get there, and how quickly they could move without drawing suspicion.

Two squeezes of his hand told me that we were being followed. Up ahead, there would be a doorway. It would lead to the back of a tavern. We'd follow that, head out the front door, come out on the other side of the square, and then we'd go east.

I couldn't breathe. Jesus Christ. What the hell was going on? What in the world was happening?

When we vanished into the alley, he released his hold on my waist but tugged me through by my hand. "Keep up."

"I can keep up just fine. Let me go."

"Hey, this isn't for my benefit. I'm just trying to keep you alive."

"So sorry to be a goddamn inconvenience."

"Jesus Christ, did I say you were an inconvenience? Is that what I said?"

"Isn't that what you meant?"

"Fuck, woman. Just once, can't you be easy?"

I picked up my pace, running alongside him. "I'm so sorry. I don't live to make your life easy."

"That's not what I fucking meant."

"You know what, just shut up."

We bolted through the back of the tavern, surprising one of the servers. East though, was quick with the lie. "Oh, sorry, my girlfriend wasn't feeling well. We went out to the back to see if she could, you know, exhaust it all up. Didn't though. I left my wallet at our table."

The girl nodded mutely. "Yeah, of course. If you don't find it, check with Travis at the bar. Someone might have turned it in already."

East beamed a smile on her, and she flushed deeply.

Yeah, of course, she did. Because why the fuck not? Inside the tavern, it was packed, crowded, with a lot of boisterous revelers. Someone's birthday maybe. It was difficult to get through. We were jostled and bumped. Then a big redheaded bloke

127

wrapped an arm around me and pulled me close. "Ah, sweetheart, how about a kiss? Where are you heading off to?"

East whirled on him with a fury I hadn't seen since that day with Jameson. "Let her go, mate."

The redhead only laughed. "Easy, mate, we're just having a laugh."

East stepped up to him, his voice low and menacing. "Let her go."

Before the beef turned into something too difficult to outrun, I stepped between them. "Okay. All right, easy does it."

One of the redhead's buddies said, "Chance, the lady decides where she goes, and right now, it's with him."

The Irishman frowned. "Oh, love, you're breaking my heart."

"Sorry to disappoint."

"Well, there's nothing disappointing about you, love."

The look East gave him was pure menace, and he automatically released me. "Just having a laugh. Wow, what's his problem?"

When I was free, I took East's hand again. It was warm and waiting. And it felt like coming home.

Stop it. You're not helping yourself.

I followed quickly behind him, nearly tripping through the clash of bodies. And then the relief of fresh air hit me in the face. I was free. East was tugging me with him. He walked briskly, speaking in a low murmur. "Bridge, have everyone check-in."

Ben swore he'd had a tail, but he'd lost him. Bridge too thought he might have had a tail, but he ditched him easily by hopping in a taxi.

Livy had better luck. She'd met up with Telly, did a girl-friend-hug thing, then ducked into a bar. "Yeah, whoever was tailing me ran right by the bar we were sitting in."

Ben breathed a sigh of relief. "All right, you two stay there."
"Drew. Drew, check in."

It took a long moment for Drew to answer. And when he did, he was out front. "Christ. I was still roaming about through the park. These assholes had me jogging for real. It's not even Tuesday."

Every Tuesday, the four of them tried to get together for a run. East had told me Drew was always finding some excuse to beg off. And just as we were about to duck onto a pathway that would have taken us to the next exit from the park, I saw him. Denning. And he was coming directly toward us. I didn't think he'd noticed us yet because he was busy cursing in his earpiece.

I grabbed East then and kissed him deep. He froze. And somewhere in my mind, I could tell myself that he kissed me back, but I couldn't be sure because as soon as Denning passed us, I pulled back. East's gaze was lazy at first, and then it sharpened to hyper-focused. "What the—"

"Denning. They're Interpol."

He muttered under his breath. I thought for a brief moment that we were free, and then I heard Denning's voice behind us. "Hey, you two, what are you doing?"

East wasted no time. He took my hand, and we darted down an alley. There were footsteps behind us, rapidly chasing. God, it felt like Monaco all over again.

Despite our pace, East muttered into the coms, "We're exposed. Denning Sinclair might have seen us. We won't make Long River's point. We'll make the secondary rendezvous."

Secondary rendezvous. That was his penthouse. We made a sharp left and then another right.

We were along the river, when out of nowhere, a chip flew from a stone by East's head.

I shuddered as I gaped. "Fuck, was that a gunshot? What the fuck are they shooting at us for? They're not authorized."

"Fuck, authorized or not, you need to move your arse."

We made another sharp left down a darkened alley. It was another pathway that allowed people to get from pub to pub on that side of town.

"Jesus Christ."

"Come on, Nyla."

We were both moving as quickly as we could, neither of us willing to slow the other down, but we were still holding on for dear life to each other.

Into the coms, East muttered, "Liv, you and Telly should get out of there as quickly as you can. Get in a cab. Get to the secondary rendezvous. They're shooting."

Ben's curse was loud and clear. "Fucking hell. Who the hell is shooting at you?"

East's breath came out in heavy pants. "I don't know. Go for the secondary rendezvous."

As we ran, we ducked. Then East pulled me to slow down. "Quick change."

He let go of my hand and we both shed our jackets and turned them inside out. My interior was red. His was a lighter blue. We both zipped up, no longer holding hands. I turned my hat inside out to match my jacket. So now, I had a bright red beanie over me. "I'm going," I muttered as I made a move to go my own way, but East stopped me.

"Don't."

"The plan is to go separately and meet at point two, right?"

"I don't like it. We should go together."

I knew what he was saying was only for the purposes of keeping Interpol off our asses. I knew that. But I still couldn't hide the warm rush of emotion it gave me. He didn't want me on my own. I nodded. "Okay."

There was a cluster of people up ahead. A street performer did a beautiful rendition of a song, and a crowd of onlookers settled around. East put an arm around my shoulder, nuzzling me. We moved into the back of the crowd to see if we could scoot around them, but they were too packed in. To my left, my gaze caught Bryant. He was an Interpol agent. We had been through training together.

"Up ahead, on your two o'clock."

East muttered. "Yeah, I see him."

Bryant searched out into the crowd, pushing people aside. There was another sharp crack on the stone above my head, and we ducked toward the crowd around us, So did the Interpol agent as he looked around in panicked surprise, wide eyed.

"I don't think it's Interpol that's shooting at us."

East dragged me into a doorway that had a vestibule just big enough to hide our bodies, and he covered mine with his. "Let's stay here for a minute."

The sounds of police cars in the distance sent the crowd dispersing. Everyone was running. Panicked. East looked down at me. "Breathe. We're going to get out of this."

Then Ben's voice was on the coms. "East exit?"

East muttered. "Yeah, east exit."

With his body, he acted as my shield, gave my hand a squeeze, took a deep breath, and then silently mouthed the words, *one, two,* and *three.* On the final number, I ran with him, joining the rest of the crowd. As we hit the east exit, there was a black Range Rover SUV waiting at the curb with Ben behind the wheel. The doors swung open, and East shoved me inside and followed right on my heels. Ben was already moving before the door slammed shut. If Interpol wasn't the one shooting at us, then what the hell was going on?

CHAPTER 12

East

"Would you hold bloody still?"

Nyla squirmed on the edge of the loo sink. "It's okay, I'm fine."

I glowered at her. "You're not fine. We were just shot at. You've got some bumps and scrapes. I'm just trying to make sure you're okay."

"I'm fine, East."

I didn't even realize she was bleeding until we were in the car. She hadn't had a direct hit, but must have caught some debris because she have cuts on har arms and on her neck. I hadn't had time to fuss over her then because I had to make sure that Ben's SUV was wiped from all the CCTV cameras. It wasn't until we reached my flat that I realized she'd likely been hit by one of the shards of stone caused by a bullet ricocheting off the wall. "Just sit fucking still and let me deal with this."

"Don't order me around. You are not my father."

"No, I'm not. How is the arsehole anyway?"

"I'd rather not talk about it." Then she winced. "Ow."

"An ow from the one who claimed she's just fine?"

"Shut up."

"Gladly if you'll just stop bleeding all over my loo."

"I didn't ask you to patch me up."

"What, I was just going to toss some gauze and antiseptic at you so you could take care of yourself? Fuck, Nyla."

"Well, can't say you probably didn't think about it."

Okay, fine, there was a part of me that had thought that, but only in terms of self-preservation. That would have kept me from having to touch her and be close enough to inhale her honeysuckle scent. As it was, I was barely standing after being so near her the whole damn night. I was practically crawling out of my skin. God, why did she affect me like this? Why the fuck was I such a goddamn pussy? I couldn't just put her out of my mind.

When she was all cleaned up, I stepped back, threw everything in the trash, and then washed my hands. I avoided her gaze on me. But before I could leave the confines of the loo, she whispered, "Thank you."

I shrugged. "Next time, don't get shot at."

"The last I checked, you were right there with me."

"Do you want to tell me what the fuck Interpol was doing there?"

She blinked at me. "Are you serious right now? I have no fucking clue."

I turned around slowly. "You expect me to believe that you didn't sell us out?"

"Are you insane? I need Theroux. What happened today probably spooked him, and now I have nothing to show for all this bullshit."

"What is he giving you anyway?"

She stared at me. "He said I can be the one to bring him in. He's my ticket out of cold storage."

"And you want me to fucking believe that you wouldn't sell me out to get your ticket out of cold storage?"

"Sorry, but you and your mates are not big enough fish compared to Theroux. Besides, this isn't just about getting back into Interpol for me. With a properly placed apology, I could have that tomorrow. This is about bringing in Theroux. Respect. The kind I've never had before. This has nothing to do with you. I didn't sell you out." She winced as she hopped down. "Have you heard from him yet?"

I shook my head as I grabbed my phone and checked. "He won't be happy."

"The question is, what the fuck was Interpol doing there and who was shooting at us?"

"I don't know, but I have to find out."

Out in my great room, the gang was all there. Drew had gotten a minor graze on his shoulder. "It looks worse than it is. I caught one when I was trying to cover you and Nyla as you left. One of those idiots saw me. I ran from Interpol and then caught the fucking slug. It's fine."

I frowned at him. "Let's call the doc."

He shrugged it off. "I've taken worse."

Ben glanced around the room. "Anyone else injured?"

Liv and Telly were fine. In fact, Telly seemed to think she was having some grand adventure. Bridge was fine, but he kept staring at Nyla. And I didn't blame him.

Nyla didn't appreciate it though. "Do you have something to say, Mr. Edgerton?"

"No, not much. Except, what was Interpol doing there?"

Nyla sighed and pinched the bridge of her nose. "Jesus Christ, like I told East, I have no idea. And since nothing is ever kept secret between you lot anyway, just so you know, what I'm getting from Theroux is that he agreed that I could be the one to take him in. I had nothing to do with this tonight because I needed it to work as badly as you did."

Livy frowned. "No one's suggesting that you did."

Bridge raised his hands. "Well, actually, I am kind of suggesting exactly that."

Livy scowled at him. "Oh my God, what is with you? It took you a while to come around to me too. She clearly wasn't shooting at herself. That had to be Theroux and his men."

I shook my head then. "But that doesn't make any sense. Theroux needs us. If he's been watching us, and I suggest he has, there have been a dozen times where he could have taken me out easily."

Nyla nodded. "Me too. It doesn't feel like him, and Interpol had no reason to shoot at us. Those were sniper shots. They were high-caliber weapons, and they were silenced. Something else is going on here."

I had to agree with her. "Yeah. As much as I hate to admit it, it doesn't feel like Interpol. This isn't their playbook."

Drew ran a hand through his hair. "Then whose playbook is it? Because I, for one, am tired of being behind the eight ball all the time."

Ben scrubbed his hands over his face. "Okay. Let's just all take it easy. Let's regroup tomorrow at a neutral location. Maybe the restaurant? Call up Lucas and Bryna. We need to get everything we can get on Warlow and Theroux. East, as soon as you hear from Theroux, let us all know."

I nodded. "Yeah, I'm on it."

Nyla inclined her head toward the hall, and I followed her. "So I'm going to go."

"You should crash here tonight. I don't want you going back to your flat by yourself. Especially not with Denning and his penchant for breaking in."

She laughed. "Oh no. No can do."

"You want to be by yourself? We were just shot at."

"Yeah, and again, I have a license for a concealed firearm. I didn't give it back. I can protect myself. It's fine. You don't need to worry about me."

"I'm not worried about you."

"Oh, that's right. You don't care about me at all. I remember. You made it perfectly clear."

"That's not what I meant, damn it."

"Um, you know what? I'm too tired for this conversation. I really am. So, let's just forget what happened. I need to soak in a hot bath and catch up on about three days of sleep. The adrenaline coursing through me was more than I had planned on tonight."

"Nyla..."

"No, I get it, East. Persona non grata. Honestly, I even understand why it has to be like this. I just... I'm tired. God, I am so fucking tired. I want to know who was shooting at me. I want to know why. I want to know what I've done to deserve this. I want to know why Interpol is after me, or Theroux, or whoever the hell it was. I want to know it all. But I'm not going to get answers tonight, so I'm going to go and have a bath then get to bed."

"At least let me get you a car home."

For a moment I thought she was going to argue. But then her shoulders sagged, and she nodded. "Yeah, that would be great."

She looked tired. Worn out. The instinct to hold her hit me hard and strong, and the words tumbled out before I could stop them. "Look, why don't you head to the guest loo to take a bath. My tub is bigger than yours and has jets. You really look like you could use it."

As soon as the words were out of my mouth, I wanted to call them back. What the hell was I thinking? I was inviting her to strip down naked, in my penthouse. The words my brain couldn't ignore were *naked* and *wet*.

How the hell was I supposed to concentrate knowing she was just down the hall wearing nothing?

Walk away mate.

As dumb as I was, as shattered as my mind was, there was no way in the world I expected her to say yes.

"I'm... You know what? I'll actually take you up on that. Have a good cry in private."

My brows furrowed and my gaze pinned to hers. "Nyla..."

"Oh relax. I'm only taking the piss. I'm going to have a soak then go home and not wake up for two days."

What I should have done was walk her to the first guestroom down the hall and show her where everything was. What I did instead was incline my head in the general direction of the loo. "You know the way."

Her sigh was soft and exhausted. The full weight of the day was evident on her sloped shoulders. "Cheers."

I swallowed hard, my mind offering up all sorts of images of Nyla naked and wet, with her thighs spread, her fingers under the water on her sweet pussy, taking away some of the tension of the day.

I swayed toward her and had to lock my jaw before I said something truly daft. She smelled so damn good. Her honey-suckle scent made me weak. With a sharp snap of my head, I lurched back. "Brilliant."

Real loquacious. But still I forced my body around her. One step in front of the other. I could do this. I was walking away. I was choosing sanity. Another step. Wasn't I a grown up? So impressive.

Except on the third step, when my brain gave the command, I couldn't follow. With a deep breath I tried to concentrate again.

You're pussy whipped. You might as well do what you want.

But it wasn't about what I wanted; it was about what I *needed.* There was no staying away from her. With a feral growl, I turned around.

———

East

It was automatic, this need to take care of her, this need to make sure that she was safe and happy and cared for.

Because you are a glutton for punishment.

Son of a bitch.

I had extra towels and a robe for her. When I knocked lightly on the door, Nyla called out, "Yes?"

"I've got a robe for you. Extra towels, too."

"Just a sec." When she opened the door, she already had a towel wrapped around her, and I could smell her skin. With the bath already running and the steam filling the loo, the scent of honeysuckle was strong. Oh God. I could do this. I could hand her this robe and walk away. That part would be easy.

Lies.

I quickly averted my eyes because that was what you were supposed to do. But what I wanted to do was pin my gaze directly to her tits. To the soft swell of skin pushing up over the towel. I knew all it would take was one small shift and I'd be seeing nipple. And if I saw nipple, it was going in my mouth. So there was that.

"Oh, uh, thanks."

Like an idiot, the sound of her wary voice had me automatically shifting my gaze to her.

Rookie mistake.

Her eyes were wide, dragging me into their hazel depths.

And Christ, all I wanted to do was lick her. Kiss her. Make her mine. All I wanted to do was sink into her and never come back out.

"Nyla."

She swallowed hard. "East. I'm—"

And that was it. The soft whispering of my name on her tongue, and I didn't know what to do with myself. I couldn't function. I couldn't focus. And so I kissed her.

The moment my lips met hers, she gave me a low, rolling moan.

My cock kicked against the fly of my jeans, and I shoved her back into the loo, shutting the door behind us and locking it. Then I dove for her, my mouth on hers, my tongue sliding in, demanding entry because after the raw pain of the last ten days, clearly, I hadn't had enough punishment. I wanted more. I wanted her to own me. I wanted her to rip me to shreds and then burn me down to ash. Because I was an idiot.

As I kissed her, her nails dug into my shoulders, the little pinpricks of pain sending flares to me that said yes, this was what I had been missing. Needing. Christ. I was going to explode.

I turned her around, looking for a flat surface. But all we had was the tub, the sink. Oh, the vanity.

When I picked her up and seated her on the vanity, her towel fell open, and I could feel her soft curves pressing into me. All the while, she moaned.

I dragged my lips from hers, kissing up her jawline and on her neck. "Fuck, why do you feel so good?"

"Stop talking. Just stop talking."

"Roger that."

I put my lips and tongue to use in other ways. Sucking at the column of her neck, my hands skimming up over her hips, her waist, palming a breast and testing the weight. As if somehow, I would have forgotten. I ran my thumb over the tip of her nipple, and she groaned. "Oh my God."

And so that she would know the full depth of my depravity, the full depth of how desperate I was, I pinched it until she hissed. And when her breath came out in short needy pants, I released her, rubbing and soothing the tip again. "Yeah, that's it."

Her hips undulated against me. I palmed her arse with my other hand, scooting her closer so she could ride my dick. I wanted her close. I wanted her to feel the full length of it.

Before I knew what was happening, she was pulling at my shirt. Tugging, and I was inclined to help her. As I reached back behind to the back of my neck and started to pull off my shirt, she worked the buckle of my belt.

My dick was attempting to punch its way out. Nobody told him that he couldn't do that. He figured he was hard enough. He could make it work.

Once my shirt was off, I returned to kissing Nyla's lips. Tasting her, trying to absorb every ounce of her before I had to give her up, before I had to walk away, before, before, before... Holy fuck.

She reached in to palm me. Her slender fingers encased my cock, and I threw my head back with a shuddering gasp. "Oh, oh fuck. Fuck me."

She said nothing but worked my dick just how I liked it. A nice strong stroke to the tip, making use of her palm. All the while, Nyla said nothing, just made these little soft cooing sounds at the back of her throat like she was appreciating this. Fuck, why did I always feel like this with her? Why was she the one? Why couldn't it be someone else that I felt like this with, just not her.

It didn't take long before I could feel the tingle in my balls. "Nyla," I groaned, practically growling the implicit command for her to stop. If I was going to come, I wanted to be inside her.

Yes, this was very ill advised. Yes, I still hated her. Yes, she had broken any trust I could possibly have for her, but that didn't mean that I wasn't an idiot and wasn't still desperate for her. Desperate to be inside her, to touch her. Just fucking desperate because, fucking hell, she was *mine*. And the fact that I wasn't allowed to play with my toys was not sitting well with me.

With her other hand, she started tugging my jeans off, shoving them down past my hips. Freeing my cock. Then as she glanced down at me and licked her lips, a bead of precum leaked out. She rubbed her thumb over the head of my cock, and my knees wobbled. "Fuck, Nyla."

And then she did something I hadn't expected. She eased her hips forward, angling me just so, and positioned me at her slick entrance. I'd have sworn I saw stars. The heat of her, the impending tightness, as the head of my dick notched at her sweet, sweet core.

I wrenched my eyes open to meet her gaze. "Ny?"

But she wasn't looking at me. She was looking at *us* where we were almost joined.

But she didn't place me all the way inside.

Instead, her slim hand wrapped around the base of me as she coated the head of my dick with her juices. Easing it all around her slit, drenching me, making me desperate. Making me want her. Making me ready to give her anything just to have her one more time.

It will never just be one more time.

I knew the truth of that statement. If she let me have her again now, like after the lift, I would come sniffing back, angry about it but begging and desperate. Then the tip of my dick hit her clit, and she threw her head back. "Oh my God, East."

I wasn't sure which view was better, her face or where my dick was.

So my gaze ping-ponged between my two favorite places.

And then she was working me over her clit again. Using me to wank herself off.

I licked my lips because I wanted to taste her as she came. But I didn't dare suggest it. So I watched. I watched as she teased us both. I watched as she drove me wild. I watched as she got herself off.

Up and down over her slit she teased me, from above her clit all the way down until my dick hit her tight pucker and we both froze. Oh God, I'd never had her arse before. But the way her mouth fell open and she wiggled as if surprised, but pleasantly so, made me curious. I notched my hips forward just a little, and her eyes snapped open as she stared at me. I bit my bottom lip and watched her, but she didn't stop me. Her eyes just stayed on me as the tip of my cock sat at her forbidden hole, begging and praying one day for entrance. Willing to slay dragons, willing to murder assholes. Willing to do her bidding, just for a taste.

Then the teasing was over as she worked me back up to the top. This time I notched up inches into her cunt, and my eyes fluttered closed as a groan escaped me. Thanks to my hips, eager to do what I could not do, and her hips, eager for me, I notched further inside.

I gripped the edge of the counter, because I knew if I gripped her hips, I was going to impale her. And fuck the consequences of no condoms and the fact that we hated each other. We'd already taken a risk once in the lift, but I knew it was dumb to take a risk again.

The lift... That wasn't a risk; that was punishment.

Yeah, but that kind of punishment could end in a baby. And a baby with a woman I did not trust would be its own special brand of torturous hell.

I could feel her silken walls contract around me as her

breath came in those short, throaty pants. "Oh my God. Oh my God, oh my God."

I leaned forward and kissed her. I put my hand around the back of her neck, sliding into her hair, kissing her deep. I was trying to convey all kind of messages in that kiss. 'Please, God. God, please, God, let me. But also, don't let me. Please, please, please, don't let me do this.'

And also, 'If you keep that up, I'm going to come hard, right in your cunt. Do you want that?'

If I could convey all that with a kiss, that's what I was doing. But maybe all she heard was, 'God, fuck, that feels so good.' I licked inside her mouth deep, stroking like how I wanted my dick to slide home.

She notched her hips back just a little and squeezed tight. I wrenched my lips away and dropped my forehead to hers. "Fuck that. I don't know if I can."

"I don't know if I want you to."

"Okay. Okay. We can stop this."

But then she notched her hips forward again, and I said, "I thought you didn't know if you wanted to."

"I don't."

But my entire crown was inside her, her heat surrounding me, pulsing around me. And I could feel the lightning starting to spark at the base of my spine. "Jesus Christ, I could come just like this. Just like this."

I was shaking, and apparently, I was also at the begging stage of this whole ill-advised adventure. "Fuck, Nyla, please, let me. I just... I need it."

"I need it, too. But I don't think I can."

"Please, just let me. Just say yes. I'll do all the work and none of it will be your fault." I notched my hips forward just a little bit until she moaned. "I want it. I want you."

I palmed her breast, pumping it. Squeezing it just a little too hard.

She gasped. "East."

"Tell me yes. Tell me fucking yes. I'm not giving it to you until you tell me yes."

As if I had any bargaining chips. As if she didn't have me literally by the balls.

"Yes."

That one word. That one word sent me home. I withdrew to slide back. It tortured us both. And there was a banging on the door. "Oi, mate, come on. We have to finish this."

My gaze snapped open. "Fuck off."

Drew's voice was a low chuckle. "I hear you, but there's work to be done, so hurry up in there."

I glanced down between us. My dick was notched at her core. I knew what I wanted to do.

I wanted to lean down and lick her tits. Sink home, fuck her, and fuck her, and fuck her, and then put her in the tub and fuck her there. Roll onto my back, have her ride me, fuck me. Jesus, I needed that.

But your mates are in the house. You've all just been shot at. You need to get to work.

With a muttered curse, I forced myself back. My dick was straining for her, begging as if he could detach and go where he knew was home.

I squeezed my eyes shut, panting. But when I opened them and glanced up at her, she had her head back against the mirror, eyes closed, thighs parted. And fuck me.

I couldn't help it. I went back but this time with my mouth. I planted my lips over her clit, and sucked hard.

Her fingers immediately latched into my hair. "East. Oh my God."

I wasted no time. I slid one finger in her tight pussy and

another one in her ass, and then she convulsed against me as I licked and sucked at her clit. Her orgasm was quick and violent. And then I fucked her with my fingers and loved her with my tongue. She shattered around me, drenching my chin in her juices, and my dick wanted to explode. I could feel the vibration and tingling all over my goddamn body. But instead of driving home, taking my pleasure where I needed it, I stopped and pulled back, but even as I stood, I gently rubbed my thumb over her clit. And then I pulled up my fucking boxers. My cock was not willing to listen to any of this nonsense. He pulsed, threatening angrily. *I will leave you, you know. I will fucking detach from you and leave.*

He had a right to be angry. Fuck, I was angry.

And still I pulled up my jeans.

Nyla stared at me. "What the fuck?"

I stared at the robe and the towel that had fallen on the floor. I didn't dare pick them up.

"You should have your bath."

She stared at me as I pulled my shirt from the floor and then yanked it on angrily. My belt. Jesus Christ, this fucking belt. There was no way I was going to be able to buckle it, but I needed to.

It took some rearranging of my dick, but finally I was dressed, just as presentable as before.

"Have a bath. We'll talk when you get out."

And then I left her.

Each step away from her was like being stabbed. What had I almost done? I'd begged. I'd fucking begged. I had begged and begged and begged, and I would have kept begging. Because she was what I needed. She was my destroyer.

CHAPTER 13

Nyla

I STAYED in the bath longer than was really necessary. My skin had started to pucker and prune. The water stayed toasty though, as the thermometer on the side of the tub sent a digital signal that triggered more warm water out of the faucet.

I might have to forgive him just for the tub.

No. There is no forgiving.

The problem was that my brain and my libido were of two minds about what had happened earlier. I craved him on a cellular level. The moment he touched me I lost all rational train of thought. My body wanted what it wanted and if I dared deny it, it threatened to combust on its own.

What the fuck had happened earlier? He'd knocked on the door and presented me with a robe, his gaze raking over me head to toe like he wanted to swallow me whole. Then his mouth was on mine, his hands on my arse, grabbing so tight I knew I'd have fingerprints on my skin.

Then came the groaning and desperation, and I'd wrapped my hand around his cock through his jeans and rubbed just the way he liked. I'd been chasing that high from the lift again. Like a fool.

Luckily, Drew had interrupted. I should have been grateful to him instead of resentful that he'd stopped me from doing something stupid.

East backed up so quickly it was like he thought I was a Venus flytrap.

My head had come online then, and the colossal mistake I'd made had been apparent.

It was only after he'd left the room that I let myself cry. Like properly sob. Letting it all hang out. It was time to let him go.

When I got dressed and stepped out into the hallway, the penthouse was empty. Everyone had left, leaving just me and East. "I'm fine now. I'm going to go."

He looked up from his laptop when I walked into the sitting room. He'd changed into a T-shirt and removed his contacts and put on glasses. Stubble dusted his jaw. The effect was so hot I froze, pinned into position, my body trying to overrule my brain.

His voice was all gravel. "Feel better?"

God, what a loaded question. *When in doubt, lie.* "Good as new. Barely a scratch."

He frowned. "You could have been badly hurt, Nyla."

And we were back to this. "You think I don't know that?"

His eyes were fierce on mine. "If there's something you're not telling me..."

"Fuck you, East. I got shot at, same as you."

He closed the laptop, setting it aside and pushing to his feet. It was the oddest thing to notice, but he was barefoot, and I realized it was the most relaxed I'd ever seen him.

"East, we've already had this goddamn conversation."

"Well, I take it fucking personally when my people are shot at."

"You know that's funny. A few days ago, I would have counted as one of 'your people,' but not so much anymore."

His jaw ticked, but he said nothing.

"You know what, I don't know why I'm bothering. I undoubtedly tripped over some East Hale rule somewhere, but you don't even have the balls to tell me what it is."

"Are you fucking kidding me? You endangered my friends, the people I care about more than anything in the world, and you want to pretend that you don't know why I separated from you?"

"No, I have no fucking clue."

"You're a goddamn liar."

My eyes went wide. "You know full well I don't lie. That is some bullshit. I've never lied to you."

"Yes, you have," he spat.

"I don't even know what you're talking about. I've done nothing to endanger you. All I know is that one day we were on the same page, and the next day you literally shut me out of your life. You went so far as to un-invite me from your place of business, knowing full well I didn't have a badge to get back in and force you into a conversation. Oh no. You went full arsehole. I'll give you one thing. You sure know how to ghost a girl."

His voice went icy cold even as it rose. "Ghost a girl. Are you fucking kidding me? I can't believe you've seriously painted me as the bad guy."

"What the fuck is that supposed to mean?"

I was so tired. I just wanted to crawl into my bed and sleep.

"You know what? Never mind. I'm done. I don't have to do this. I don't need this in my life."

He laughed derisively. "Oh right, run. Instead of having a really hard conversation, you either bury it or you run."

"Me, running? *You're* the one who walked away from *me*. Locked me out. Didn't speak to me. Do you recall that?"

"I call it fucking self-preservation because you're goddamn dangerous. You had me believing in you. You had me believing that I could trust you, and then you lied to me, right to my face. You exposed me and my mates. How am I supposed to fucking forgive that?"

"Well, if you're so sure that I fucked you over, why wouldn't you talk to me about it? Lay it all out? And you're telling me that *I'm* running? You're the greatest coward there is."

"Fuck you, Nyla."

"You don't talk to me like that."

"Ah look, finally, a backbone. Where was that when you were with Denning?"

I whirled on him. "You shut up. You know nothing about my life. You're just another in a long line of people who've walked away from me my whole goddamn life. You're not the first, and you won't be the last. But I promise you, you will not fucking break me."

"You want to know exactly why I walked away from you? I love how you can't even see your own lies, the things that you do that put you in these positions. It makes me wonder what exactly happened with Denning."

"You don't know anything about me. And that's okay. You're not worth the effort."

Inside, I was screaming. My lungs were burning. I wanted to cry. I wanted to thrash. I wanted to hit him with something, because even though I knew where this was going, even though he'd already shown me the depths of his cruelty, I still wanted him. I could feel it now. Even with the tension in our words, my body was coiled, ready for something to happen.

"Fucking tell me. What did I do to you that was so horrible?"

"It was the hit list in your flat."

I frowned. "What are you talking about?"

He couldn't know about that, could he? How?

"Okay, you want to play dumb? I watched you last Sunday. Instead of going to your office like you said, I watched you double back and take the tube."

My stomach pitched. "You followed me?"

"Of course, I followed you. Did you think I wouldn't? I have a team to protect, and you were lying to me."

My knees almost buckled. He had seen it. Fuck me. No wonder he didn't believe me. No wonder he had reacted the way that he had. He had told me before how trust was so important to him. How his family had broken that trust. His own father. And now I'd done the same thing. "East, if you'd bothered to talk to me, you would know that it wasn't like that. Amelia was the one piecing it together. I had nothing to do with it."

"Oh, of course you'd say that now."

"You're such an arsehole. I came to the hotel that day to talk to you. Ask your concierge, Thomas. I left a note very explicitly telling you that you needed to be careful. But either he didn't give it to you, or you just chose to ignore it. I warned you. You didn't listen. Meanwhile, Amelia has got me running to the prison to interview Bram Van Linsted. I saw Jameson visiting him. I was the one who warned Livy they were coming for you because *you* wouldn't talk to me. You know what? I don't even care what drama you're involved in anymore. I don't want any part of it. I played in your sandbox, and all I got was sand in my hair and dirt in my eye. I have zero interest in repeating the experience."

"You expect me to believe that you had nothing to do with that methodically plotted board full of so-called evidence and connections? That the oh-so-tenacious Agent Nyla Kincade wouldn't be after us, wouldn't be coming for me and my mates?"

"What I told you was true. I believed you. I believed that there was something going on, something I didn't know. But then you told me about the Elite and that you guys were trying to avenge your friend's death. I already *had* all the information, so why would I need to keep investigating if you'd already told me? It doesn't make any sense, East. But oh no, you had a major reaction. You believed the absolute worst about me, which, you know, sounds par for the course. I get it. You are loyal to your mates. They're your friends. You *should* be loyal to them. Obviously, you've been through a lot together, and this is a team that I'm not cool enough to be on. I get that. I wonder what it's like to have a family like that. I had started to care about you. I opened up. I trusted you. The funny thing is, we're standing here talking about trust and belief in one another, and *you're* the one who betrayed *my* trust. When you care about people, you talk to them. You engage with them. Ask questions. Instead, you assumed you knew everything. You assumed that I had betrayed you. And God, if that's what you think about me, why did we ever start this? I trusted you when you needed me to. You told me about the Elite. I believed what you were saying about Jameson. I believed you were telling me the truth. But when it came down to it, you couldn't afford me the same courtesy. You were so quick to turn your back on me. So much for that famed East Hale loyalty, right?" And with those parting words, I turned to go. "I don't need you to show me out. I know the way."

My legs were still shaking as I left him standing in his living room, the lights of London twinkling through his windows. I was stunned that he had assumed that I could hurt him like that. That instead of just asking me about what he saw, he assumed that I could betray him, when in reality, he was the one breaking my heart.

———

East

151

ABOUT FIFTEEN MINUTES after Nyla finished verbally handing me my ass, there was a knock at the door, and a rush of hope flooded my veins so quickly that I almost choked on it. I yanked it open, expecting to see Nyla, but instead it was Ben. "Mate, what are you doing here?"

"Liv's with Telly in my old flat downstairs."

"Is that wise? She was attacked in there last year. I wouldn't think she'd be comfortable waiting there."

"I know. But she's the one who actually said that she'd wait for me there instead of the office or downstairs in the lobby."

"Why, what's up?"

Ben rubbed his jaw. "Listen, mate, I couldn't go home without saying something."

I braced myself, because for Ben to leave Livy, it was something serious. "Yeah?"

"I know it's none of my business, but the Nyla thing... I know you don't trust her, but she took gunfire, not only for herself, for *us*. I know you don't trust anymore, and I know that you're likely to turn all your attention toward her and the seventy-five ways she could betray us again. And while I appreciate that, I don't think this has anything to do with her. If it does, her own men shot at her. Which is useless and a quick way to get an agent dead."

I held my breath. "Yeah, I know. I hear you. You came back up just to tell me that?"

"It's bothering me. We're not seeing the picture properly. First of all, what the hell was Interpol doing there? Secondly, who was shooting at us? Because Nyla was right; it wasn't Interpol. It's someone secondary. But it leaves me to believe that we've had a leak somewhere. It's making me nervous."

I nodded because I was thinking the same thing. I'd assumed our leak was Nyla, but again, it didn't make sense that her own people were shooting at her. "Theroux?"

"Maybe the shooters, yeah, but it doesn't make sense that he'd call Interpol on himself."

"Well, he did tell Nyla he'd turn himself in."

"Maybe, but he would control that situation better, and you and I both know he's not really going to turn himself in."

"Yeah, tell that to Nyla though."

Ben winked. "I'll leave that to you. So now we're stuck."

"I know. I'm on it. We'll figure it out. We always do."

"Yeah, we always do." As he turned to leave, he gave me a brisk nod. "Just think about what I said about Nyla. You think you're the one outside looking in and that what she did was fucked up. I know that. But maybe you should ask her about it and talk to her. Because otherwise, it's going to eat you up."

The only thought that ran through my head was that I hated it when he was right.

CHAPTER 14

Nyla

NEVER SAY NEVER, because chances were, at some point, you'd have to eat your words.

A big heaping serving of them. But there was no way around it. We kept running into roadblocks with the search for Warlow. Amelia wasn't speaking to me, so I couldn't ask her for help, and I knew it would come back to haunt us somehow anyway. I was working my contacts, but there was a limit to the information I could give or get. I was between a rock and a hard place, and there was only one thing I could do to soften that hard place.

When my father suspended me, I'd told myself I was never going back. I was never going to put myself in the position again where I would have to beg for attention, or scraps, or anything else from him. But there I was, waiting in the Interpol visitor's conference room like I didn't belong there, like I hadn't spent countless hours searching for kernels of information, cataloging financial crimes. I'd spent years of my life in this place or other rooms just like it.

Instead, I was the one being offered coffee like I was some kind of tourist. When my father walked in, he hesitated when he saw me, and I quietly said, "I was told to come on in. Sorry, if I should have made an appointment."

"We don't have anything else to say to each other, unless you have an apology ready. And even then, there's not much you can say."

I had to force myself to swallow the retort that he wasn't the damn one who should ask for an apology. I had to force myself to bite my tongue, to not scream and let the rage out. I wanted to yell, *You were supposed to be my protector. Stand in my corner.* Instead, I bit my tongue.

"Actually, I *do* have an apology. It's probably been a long time coming. In hindsight, Denning and I working together was probably an error in judgment. While Agent Sinclair is a fine agent, there were so many reasons why we didn't mesh, and it caused a clash in our working situation."

As apologies went, it probably lacked the flair that would satisfy Denning, but it was the best I could do. Like hell were they going to get me to say I'd been at fault. "Dad, I know that you're disappointed in me." That was accurate. He *was* disappointed in me. "But I would like you to know that it was never my intention. I've worked hard and have done my best to be a good agent. I'm tenacious, and smart. I work my butt off."

"Nyla, no one is concerned about your work ethic. If anything, your inability to let things go is the problem."

Bile tried to claw its way up my throat, but I managed to keep it down. "I do need to learn to let things go and walk away. The thing is, in the last several days that I have taken and used the opportunity to reflect on my life and my career, I've discovered there isn't anything else I'm suited for. I was meant to be an agent. The people in this building are my family. And you actually *are* my family. Denning too. As much as we... uh... disagree,

I'm part of a team here. I need this team, and I'm ready to be a team player."

My father watched me warily. I liked being part of a team. I did. I just wasn't very good at waiting for the rest of my team to get on board with things. When I was right, and I knew I was right, getting me to slow down and include everyone was difficult.

Queasiness unsettled my stomach as I recalled Amelia's words. Jesus. Was that how she saw me?

"You expect me to believe that you've changed your perspective?"

"Yes. I don't know what it's going to take to prove it to you. My point is that I'm willing to try. You were right; Denning and I were a powder keg, and I was harboring resentment. I put that and my feelings toward him before work, and I shouldn't have. It was a lapse in judgment, and it won't happen again."

He frowned, watching me closely. "I have to tell you, Nyla, I'm surprised that you're even here. I never expected you to say any of these things."

"Well, I have had some time to reflect, and it has changed my perspective."

"Yes, I'll bet it has." He nodded steadily as he leaned back against the conference table. "And your relationship with East Hale?"

I blinked rapidly to suppress any lingering feelings. "It's over. A passing dalliance. I know what's important now. I should have regarded Agent Sinclair's concerns with more seriousness. I'd ask a few things upon my return though. One, that I'd be allowed back on my team and on my old cases, even if it's a provisional status. I'd like to be given an opportunity to show what I can do without being under the auspices of Agent Sinclair. Maybe if there was a buffer between us, or if there is another team available, perhaps financial crime?" I would rather die than move to financial crime, but I was there to humble myself and get my fucking job back, because who was I if not an agent? And also, it was what I needed to do to move things forward with Theroux and the London Lords.

Are you going to do everything Theroux tells you to do?

That was a very, very good question. And the answer worried me. But I wasn't about to do anything illegal. Before I met East Hale, the idea of even having a gray area made my blood run cold. But I was learning to walk in the gray now, because sometimes, one needed to be in those kinds of situations in order to get to the good side of things. "Nyla, this might not be a good idea. Maybe now is the time for you to explore another career."

"I don't want another career, Dad. I want *this* one. I've worked hard for this. It's the one I made happen with blood, sweat, and tears. I don't want anything else."

"Just because you want it, doesn't mean it's the best thing for you."

"I know, I know. And I have a lot to make up for. If you want, put me on probation. I will prove to you I can do this."

And in a matter of time, I'll bring in Theroux, and you will have no choice but to see me.

He frowned. "You want your job back? You want to be off the desk? In the field?"

"Yes." I wasn't sure what he was trying to get at.

"Fine, then you will have to exhibit that you're up to the challenge and show me that you really mean this. You only need to do two things."

"Okay." I would do whatever it took because I was going to make this happen.

"One, you report to Amelia. She'll be your supervising agent."

My heart squeezed. But it was Amelia. There was a time

when she'd been my best friend. I didn't give a shit who I reported to. She was good at her job. Things might be awkward for a bit, but we'd figure it out. "Okay. And the other thing?"

"Amelia now reports directly to Denning. She will manage your daily ins and outs and interactions, but you are still on Denning's team, which means that you need to apologize directly to him."

I blinked. "What?"

"You heard me. You will need to apologize *to Denning*."

"I—" I swallowed.

"I know I didn't stutter."

"Of course, you didn't stutter. No... You're actually right. I just need to figure out a way to do that."

"It's really simple. You let him know that you have no plans to cause problems again, and that you're here to work. None of your outside life becomes a distraction."

I didn't really have any choice. After all, I was backed in a corner. "Fine, I'll do it."

My father's gaze on mine was steady. "Do it now."

There was no arguing with him. After all, I'd come to get my job back, and I needed to do this. If he wanted me to apologize to Denning, I'd fucking apologize to Denning. I could play nice, do what I was supposed to do. "Fine, where is he?"

It was as if Dad was waiting for me to balk, to refuse at the last moment. But I kept my cool. "I believe he's in his office. So, what do you say? If you can do this, you can have your job back."

Goddamn it, I *could* do this. I *had* to do this. "All right, lead the way."

Again, the halls felt familiar. They felt like home, and at the same time, they weren't. It was like an alien had completely taken over my space. It should bring me comfort, but it didn't. We found Denning in his office as my father had said. We knocked, and my father went in first. Denning looked happy to see him. He looked significantly less happy when he saw that I was trailing behind my father. "What the hell is she doing here?"

Dad, ever the politician, smiled at him. "Well, Denning, my daughter would like to say something to you."

What, now? With him watching? Ugh, God. I immediately hated Francois Theroux. I hated him with the fire of a thousand suns for subjecting me to this moment.

Nothing lasts forever.

That was true. Besides, who gave a shit? Denning Sinclair wanted me to crawl and lick his boot. But soon enough, I would have the collar of a lifetime. And what would he have?

I took a deep breath. "Hello, Denning."

Denning just glowered at me. "Again, with all due respect sir, what the fuck is she doing here?"

That raised my hackles. I had more right to be there than he did. But I had to keep it tight. "Look, I know you're not particularly happy to see me, and I understand that. I recognize that my actions..." God, what was I going to say? I needed something that was feasible enough. I tried again. "I know that my actions have been a cause for consternation for a prolonged period of time, and I just want you to know that I apologize. From now on, I will be the team member you need. No arguments, no circumventing the system. Whatever you need, I'm here. I'm just here to do the job, and it's a privilege that I get to do it."

He smirked at me with a cruel smile. I knew that punishment was coming. And unlike with East, it wouldn't be at all pleasurable. "Okay, fine. But what about the little problem of who you're dating?"

No, I was not consenting to that, but what choice did I have?

"Well, I'm no longer dating East Hale, but whoever else I date is not your concern, or anyone else's. That's a breach of privacy and shouldn't be a public record."

Something in Denning's eyes told me that he wasn't happy with that, but there wasn't much he could do because I had a solid point. He didn't really have a right to ask about my private life or to butt in whenever he liked. "So just like that, she apologizes and she's back?"

My father sighed. "You know, Denning, while I did want Nyla to show some humility, I think you need to as well. Let's not forget, you were the one in her flat, unannounced, uninvited, and for no good reason. I haven't actually forgotten that."

Denning sputtered. "I was merely protecting her because she was not—"

My father shook his head. "I never thought I'd have to say this, but Denning, you need to get yourself together. Nyla walked in here and did what she needed to do for the good of the job. You need to keep your emotions in check, Agent Sinclair."

My heart soared. My father had never done that for me. And I mean *never*. I still couldn't believe it. I could not believe that he'd backed me for once. Denning clearly couldn't believe it either. "Sir, of course not. I'm just speaking as her supervisor."

My father continued with his truth bombs. "About that... Nyla is coming back, but she will be working under Amelia as her direct supervisor. Not you."

Denning tried to hide the disapproval on his face, but it showed anyway. I tried to wipe any gloating expression off my face, because, after all, I was a picture of contriteness. "But sir, East Hale is—"

"Enough, Denning. I don't want you turning up in her flat. You two are no longer dating, so why you even thought it would be a good idea to breach her trust by showing up at her flat unannounced is beyond me. You're lucky she didn't kill you. And that's all I need to hear ever again about that. Do you both understand?"

I was quick to nod.

Denning followed through. "Yes, sir."

My father nodded. "Good. Now that that's out of the way, Denning, as I said earlier, she'll be working directly with Amelia, so make sure she gets settled. She's still under your team, but I want the two of you working one-on-one together as little as possible because I like my peace and sanity."

I ground my teeth, but at least he was on my side.

I was back in the fold, just like I'd wanted. Now all I had to do was make sure I didn't squander that chance.

CHAPTER 15

East

ALL NIGHT I'd tossed and turned, waiting for a call from Theroux... waiting for the other shoe to drop.

Bullshit. You're thinking about what Nyla said.

I didn't want to think about what she'd said. That I was acting obsessive. That I had no right to her body, her mind, her emotions. I was not hot and cold. There was no decision to be made. I didn't want her.

But you can't stay away, can you?

Fucking hell. I'd seen it. Her *hit list*. I had nothing to apologize for. I'd protected my family.

But my brain kept trying to go back to the day in that flat. Back to the moment of seeing our names on the board. All the questions, the red lines of yarn, trying to piece together... what?

There was something I was overlooking. A thread was missing, and I couldn't quite lock onto it.

It didn't matter. I had bigger fish to fry.

Drew had been off his game, and it was time I figured out why. I hadn't been surveilling him, but when we were together, he was always withdrawn, quiet. Out of it. If we were going to survive this, we needed *all* of us functioning on all cylinders. So if something was up with him, we needed to know. And we needed to know now.

I'd taken half the afternoon off and driven into Chiswick despite the wild traffic. I could have called my driver. Hell, I could have done anything other than driving myself, but I needed the time to think. It was bloody Thursday, and Drew worked from home on Thursdays so he would be there to take his daughter Annabelle to riding class. It was their thing, and I always admired that about him. He fulfilled his commitments.

But what if he's not sticking to the other commitments he made?

I rang the doorbell, and a member of the staff in full livery opened the door. I couldn't believe that they had their staff wear formal uniforms. My staff did, but that was because they were employees of the hotel, not a personal residence. "I'm here to see Mr. Wilcox."

"Yes, he's in the study, sir. Shall I direct you?"

"Nope, I know the way." The butler was a kid, not much older than we'd been when we joined the Elite. But he was freshly starched and ever so formal.

I went up the stairs at a jog. Annabelle wouldn't have riding class until later this afternoon, so hopefully, I'd caught Drew at a good time. I knocked on his office door and opened it before he could even say, 'Come in.'

I found him at his massive oak desk with his head thrown back, euphoria on his face. "Jesus Christ, mate, are you wanking off?"

His head snapped up and his body jerked as someone under the table groaned.

I turned around quickly and sent my eyes skyward. "Mate, your kids are in the fucking house."

"My kids know how to fucking knock before they walk in."

"Is this what's up with you?" I expected Drew to send out whatever maid, or assistant, or personal blowjob-giver he had under the table. Instead, several seconds later, it was Drew, not the person under the table, who strode toward me, leading me out of the office.

"Let's go downstairs to the terrace."

"Who's under that desk, Drew?"

He sighed as he shoved me out of the door and closed it behind us. "East, fucking leave it alone."

I held up my hands. "Jesus, sorry to embarrass your maid, or assistant, or fuck, is that the nanny? Not that I don't want plausible deniability. That way, when Angela comes for your arse, I can deny everything if I didn't see her. Jesus Christ, Drew."

He shoved me toward the stairs. "Shut the fuck up. Think about all the things you have been up to over the years, and I've said nothing."

I glanced over my shoulder at him. His face was beet red, and a muscle in his jaw was ticking. "Fine. Next time lock the fucking door."

He grunted, still shoving me until I started to trip down the stairs. "Okay, okay, I got it."

When we got downstairs, I made a right toward the living room. He followed me and gave a quick snap to his servants to bring us tea.

"Drew, you dirty dog. God, I'm not sure I'll ever erase the look on your face out of my head. It's seared right in there."

"Fuck you. What do you want? And why didn't you call first?"

His gaze was wide-eyed. Alert. Was that fear? "Mate, you do what you want. But I need to warn you, this is dangerous territory. You know who Angela's father is."

His skin was still blotchy, and he was still sweating as he ran his hands through his hair. "I know. I just... You were right. I was... careless."

Angela Blankenship-Wilcox was the daughter of Lord Frederick Blankenship. He was one of the Senior Elite council members and carried a lot of weight. "Okay, look, I was just taking the piss. Who you shag on the side is none of my business. But we are mates. You could have told me. I would have told you to be careful, but still."

He dropped his head and scrubbed both hands over his face. "I know. It's just... I'm not exactly fucking proud of it. Everything is fucked." Then I watched him pull that affable Drew mask back into place. "Sorry. I'm fine. What are you doing here?"

"Believe it or not, I'm checking on you."

Drew swallowed. "Cheers, mate." He rubbed at the back of his neck. "I'm fine."

I lifted a brow. "You sure about that? Ever since Ben was named Director Prime, you've clearly been off your game. Now I find out you're getting some strange from God knows who, in the house you share with Angela where she could have easily discovered you. I'd say... You're not *fine*."

"It's just that a lot has been going on."

I sighed. "Well, I wanted to know what the fuck is up with you. I could have found out the easy way. I could have been poking where I didn't belong. But we had a deal, you lads and I. I don't go poking where I might not be wanted. In fact, there's this shit called friendship. It's where I ask you questions, and you tell me what's going on with you."

Drew ran his hands through his hair. "Nothing is going on."

I watched him warily. "Look, I checked. You were off coms for a full minute last night. You've been cagey for weeks. Testy. What is up with you? It's like you don't want to put this shit behind us."

"Trust me, I want to put all of this behind us. Some days I wish we had never even started down this path."

I studied him closely. "What does that even mean? You don't want justice for Toby?"

"Mate, of course I do. It's fucking *Toby*. But it's just a lot. I have my family to think about, but you lot are my family too. This is just too fucking hard right now."

"I know. There have been a lot of mistakes, but we can fix them. We will get to the bottom of this. We will keep it away from you. Are Angela and the girls okay?"

He sighed then ran a hand down his face, pinching the bridge of his nose and surreptitiously wiping at his eyes.

"Drew, what the fuck? What is going on with you?"

"Nothing. It's just been stressful, mate. You know how married life is."

I frowned at him. He was giving me some kind of bullshit lie, and I didn't know why. "What I saw upstairs, is it a fucking problem?"

He swallowed. "No, it's not."

He was lying. I could tell by the flush in his cheeks and the way he fidgeted before shoving his hands in his pockets. "Are you fucking in love or some shit?"

He swallowed hard. "I—I don't know what I am."

I whistled low. "Mate? Are you fucking serious right now? How do you think this is going to go? Blankenship is going to lose his shit if you hurt Angela."

"I know, I know. And it wasn't supposed to get this far." He ran his hands through his hair, looking like a man on edge.

"What are you going to do?"

"Fuck if I know."

"Mate." I glared at him. "This should be a no-brainer."

"It's not that simple."

"Make it simple. You can't do that shit in your own house." I jabbed my finger toward the stairs. "This isn't just about you."

"I know. You're right. I'll figure it out."

"Don't you fucking get it? You're not alone. It's not for you to figure out on your own. Just don't take risks, and we'll get it sorted."

"I'm just in over my head."

I slumped back against the railing. "Been there. There's an answer. And I promise you, it's not fucking with Blankenship."

The last thing we needed was that kind of trouble.

East

LATER THAT NIGHT at Ben's we were going through our Theroux options. I kept an eye on Drew, who was sucking back scotch like it was his lifeline. I prayed to God he held it together.

Nyla sat back and crossed her arms. "Fuck me if I ever join a secret society. It's just too much. Is it always like this? Blackmail, thieves coming after you. Why would you even want this?"

Ben shook his head. "None of us did. But we have a job to do. Take down those involved in Toby's death or covering it up. We have to get rid of Garreth Jameson. Francis Middleton is next. After that, I couldn't give two fucks about what happens to the Elite. But we need time, so we're going to have to deal with Theroux if he's trying to take us out."

Bridge leaned forward, placing his elbows on his knees. "Still radio silence?"

Nyla and I exchanged glances, and we both shook our heads. "We still don't know what happened."

"I'm going to check in with my Interpol contacts." Nyla said.

"It's a delicate procedure since I just went back and I'm still on probation. I don't think they've picked him up, because when I last checked the website, he's still on the top ten list. I mean, they could have taken him to a black site, although they generally don't operate that way. He's not dangerous. He's just a thief. He doesn't usually *kill* anyone, so there would be no reason to take him to a black site unless he stole something he really wasn't supposed to. Something related to espionage. Who knows?"

Ben nodded. "Yeah, stay on that Nyla. Report back when you have something."

"Yup. Can do."

I frowned at that. The way that the team just reinserted her back into a position she never had. As if nothing had happened.

But what if nothing did happen? What if she's telling you the truth?

I didn't want to think about it. Right now, there were too many irons in the fire, and I didn't have time to focus on Nyla Kincade.

The longer I looked at her, her dark hair over her shoulder in a messy braid, the more something so deep pulled at me. She had been mine. The question was, could I let go and trust her again?

But what if she did nothing wrong? What if she was telling the truth and you were wrong? What if you're too late?

I shifted my attention back to the conversation, and Livy was talking. "'Marry a billionaire,' they said. 'Everything in your life will be on easy street,' they said. So much for that. This isn't an easy street. Is there any way we'll ever return to our normal lives again?"

I winked at her. "I thought you said once that normal was boring."

"Yeah, that was the *past me*. Past me didn't know that people would be coming for us all the time."

Ben put a hand on her knee. "But we're stronger together. All of us, we watch each other's backs." He turned his attention to Nyla. "That means you, too. As soon as you hear anything about Theroux, let us know. We might be able to leverage him in some way."

"All right," I said. "It looks like we're about to be in the fight of our lives." But unfortunately, there was no way I was keeping Nyla out of it.

CHAPTER 16

Nyla

I COULD FEEL him watching me. I was sure he didn't think I knew he was there, but how could I not? My body was so attuned to every part of him, his look, his scent. I could feel him following me.

Leaving Olivia and Ben's place was easy. There was a tube station nearby, so I set out walking toward it. I knew I had a shadow from the moment I left the gate. He'd been talking to Bridge, and then suddenly, his voice went silent. But I just kept walking and didn't turn around once. I was so good. All I had to do was get on the tube and make it home.

Camberwell was my beacon. If I could make it that far, I would be free. I wouldn't have to think about East. I would be well on my way to being cured of my addiction.

The problem with that sort of thinking was that I had no choice in the whole matter, no choice about what my heart wanted or what my body craved. In reality, there was no choosing not to be with him, not to let him touch me. That wasn't a choice that I had, period.

I could choose to *pretend* that I didn't want him, to *pretend* that he didn't occupy every single thought that I had. I could put on blinders and pretend that the hole in my heart wasn't there. And most of the time, that choice felt like bloody heaven. But I knew now it was only a panacea. It wasn't real.

Because all it would take was one look, the sound of that low baritone voice, an accidental brush of one of his knuckles across my arm, and I would be right back to wanting and needing and longing for him.

Being with East Hale was a thing you didn't recover from.

I rode in silence on the tube. I hadn't seen him follow me off the train, or even up the escalator. Maybe I was crazy, and he hadn't been following me at all. Maybe I'd made it all up.

When reached my townhouse, I started to honestly think that my wishful thinking had manifested shadows of him following me. In my relief, or perhaps my disappointment, I said aloud, "You really are losing your shit, aren't you?"

There was a low rumble that was almost a coherent sentence in the hallway behind me. "What the fuck do you think you're doing walking home alone from the tube?"

Panic seized and squeezed my heart, and I whirled around in shock. "Jesus fucking Christ, East. You scared me half to death. I knew I felt you. I couldn't explain it, but I knew you were following me."

"Are we going to go inside?"

My gaze flickered to my door. "I'm not sure that's a good idea."

"Nyla, we need to talk. And you *know* we need to talk."

I slid my key into the lock, then opened my door. Maybe if I rushed to close it, I could close him out of my heart. No such luck. He was right behind me.

Come on in why don't you?

I dropped my keys onto the table in the vestibule and turned to face him. "I have said everything I intend to say to you. I have no words left, East."

"Fine. Then I have some words for you."

I lifted a brow. "You have something to say to me? What could you possibly have to say that can be any worse than what you already said and thought about me? There's a thing called death by a thousand cuts. You have cut me infinite times in the last two weeks. I can't take much more."

His next words were so rushed I wasn't sure I'd heard them correctly. "Nyla, I can't do this anymore."

"What?" I asked as he stepped further out of the shadows, letting the light illuminate his gorgeous face.

"This," he said as he waved his fingers between the two of us, pointing back and forth. "I don't want to do this anymore. But I can't stay away from you."

"Can't or won't?"

He sighed and pinched the bridge of his nose. "Okay, fine. Won't."

"That's not how this works. You think I betrayed you. You think I looked you in the eyes and lied. That's what you think. You have zero faith in me, but I'm supposed to throw caution to the wind and have all kinds of faith in you?"

He shifted on his feet. "Nyla, try to understand. What I saw in that flat... I couldn't let that go."

"We're back to the same thing East. Instead of talking to me, trying to see what the hell had gone wrong, you assumed that I could do such a thing because that's what you think I'm capable of. What kind of person do you think that makes me?"

He ran his hands through his hair. "I don't know what the fuck to think. I wanted you so badly, and to think that I'd been wrong about you, about everything, I just couldn't take it. All I knew was I had to get away from you as fast as humanly possible. I had to cut you out. I had to perform surgery on my heart with no field dressing, just bleeding out everywhere. I had to in order to protect my team."

"Jesus Christ, you still don't get it. You didn't *have* to do that; you *chose* to do that. I let you get closer to me than anyone else in the world. I opened my heart to you. And you trampled on it, because God help you if you had to have an actual conversation with me. No, it was easier if I fit into some mold you imagined. Unfortunately, East, it's not easy for me to forgive that, and you lost that chance when you just deliberately set to cut me out knowing everything you know about me and my family. You broke my heart."

"I didn't know it then, but I was breaking my own heart too. I didn't know at the time that you were in my bones. In my blood. I thought I could protect myself. Protect the team. The only thing I was doing was fighting myself. All I really wanted to do was find you, wrap you in my arms, and shake you until I forced you to tell me what the fuck was going on."

"Then why didn't you do that? Why was your solution to freeze me out?"

"I've never let anyone close before, Nyla. Sure. I've thought I had, but it wasn't anything like *this*. I've never felt this *shattered* about a betrayal. You broke me."

I couldn't help it; I shoved at his chest, but the arsehole didn't move. "I never betrayed you. From the moment I saw what Amelia had planned, what she was looking for, I've been trying to deter her by my damn self. All because you can't see past your own obtuseness to see *me*. To *believe* me."

He stepped closer. "I see you. I've always seen you. Even when I was so busy running away from you, I couldn't fathom you doing this to me, but it still hurt. And it hurts only because I care so fucking much, and I don't want to. But you're here, and you're not leaving. And I can't fucking stay away from you. So stop asking me to."

I threw my hands up. "I never asked you to stay away from me. That was your choice. I only asked you to stop hurting me."

And then he did the thing that I didn't know he could. I watched him forgive me, and let go. There was nothing to forgive of course. But his mind had still been holding on to that piece of Nyla he thought could do something like that to him. He had to reconcile her with reality and the truth. And only when he did that would he be able to see where we were. It happened in front of my eyes as he watched me, as the full acceptance sunk in. The tension of mistrust rolled off of his shoulders only to be replaced by worry and shame.

"I can't imagine how much it took for you to choose to protect my friends. Have I cocked it all up? Are you capable of forgiving me for not seeing the truth?"

I shook my head, trying to back away from him so I could think, so I could breathe. "East, I don't know."

For some reason he looked relieved. "I can work with that. I know I don't deserve a second chance. Not after what I did with my first one, but I swear before God, I will work to earn back your trust. God knows I don't deserve it, but I'm not going anywhere."

"And if I don't ever forgive you?"

"Then I'll pine for you for the rest of my life. But even if you don't take me back, there is no way I'm leaving without you."

"That's going to make it awkward for my next boyfriend."

The feral snarl that rose up from his chest was quick and decisive. "What fucking boyfriend?"

His expression told me he was deadly serious. "You have got to be kidding me."

I watched him as he swallowed hard and tried to compose himself. "Sorry, darling. It's going to take some time. A lot of time. But if you don't want me, I'll have to respect that. Unfortunately, I will still always see you as mine, so I might make his life difficult."

"You know that makes you a stalker, right?"

"I'm okay with that." He closed the gap between us, taking my hands tentatively at first, and then more firmly as he pulled me flush against his body. "Now, I'm going to attempt to kiss my way into your good graces. I know it's not enough. And I have much groveling to do. But let me kiss you. Let me take you to bed and give you enough orgasms that you'll forget the last two weeks. It's a start. That's all I'm asking for, Nyla."

No one had to tell me this could end badly. My brain had already run through all the infinite scenarios where I'd get screwed. And not in the fun, eyes-rolled-to-the-back-of-my-head kind of way.

But I could see the anguish in his eyes, and I *believed* him. Just like he should have believed me. And maybe that was going to take some time to get over, but I wanted him so badly. I didn't want some rushed, dirty, clandestine meeting in the lift or some desperate bumbling behind a barely closed door. I wanted it *all*. I wanted him. And that was my stupid heart willing to risk it all *again*... for him. For this man.

"Take me to bed."

East

THIS WAS the shot I needed. The chance I probably didn't deserve.

Don't fuck it up.

I didn't even know where to start. I was bloody nervous.

Nervous. Imagine that. The relief flooded my veins and told

175

me that everything was going to be okay. I just needed to not fuck this chance up.

I took a step toward her, and the smile she gave me was tremulous. My heart broken in two because I was the reason that she was unsure. It was my fault. I hadn't talked to her. I had assumed the betrayal. I hadn't trusted her at all. So why should she trust me now?

Get your head in the game. Make this up to her.

It was only when I reached for her that I realized I was shaking like a schoolboy about to get his dick wet for the first time.

With my arms wrapped around her waist, she tilted her head up, her gaze open, searching mine. And I knew in that moment that I would do anything, whatever she asked. It didn't matter. She was mine, and I was hers. I leaned forward, and our foreheads touched. Her question to me was soft. "East?"

I inhaled deeply. "I missed your scent."

"I'm right here."

"I know."

I picked her up. Right off her feet. Her shocked gasp came out as a squeak and then a giggle, and then I tossed her over my shoulder.

"Oh my God, East. Put me down."

"Nope."

I carried her over my shoulder to the master bedroom and marched over to the bed. With my back facing the bed and the backs of my knees hitting the mattress, I eased her down my body, her curves pressing into my muscles. And then her hitched gasp took on a different note. A throatier one. One that told me exactly what she wanted from me. "Not very caveman of you."

"I have it on good authority you might like a caveman."

She laughed and shook her head. "All right, caveman, show me what you got."

With my arms still wrapped around her, I took her with me as I fell back on the bed.

I wrapped one hand around the back of her neck and drew her down to me. Molding our lips together, reveling in her taste as her tongue tentatively met mine.

With a little pressure, I angled her head so that I could deepen the kiss, and then I went from gentle and exploring to desperate and needy.

I pulled her with me as I scooted even further back. I didn't stop until my head hit the pillow. I kicked my shoes off and then adjusted us until she straddled my hips. "God, you're so fucking beautiful. I really, really, really don't deserve you."

"Yeah, tell me some shit I don't know."

With both of us quite aroused, I levered myself up to reach her and kiss her again. She tasted so damn sweet. The flavor of fine wine that I couldn't describe but knew the taste of intimately. Like she was a vintage made just for me. With my hands in her hair, the silken tresses falling over my fingers, I kept kissing her. If nothing else happened, just the ability to freely kiss her without feeling that tightness in my chest was a gift. One I probably didn't deserve. She rocked against me, the heat beneath her leggings hitting me exactly where I needed her on my dick. She rolled her hips tentatively, and I groaned into her mouth. I didn't have to tell her what I needed. I didn't have to ask her to do anything, she just moved. Rocking over me with our clothes on, making every moment dirty and thrilling and something I craved.

I wasn't sure which one of us was in charge at that point. Me with my hands on her hips gently rocking her back and forth, or her, on top of me, knowing me well enough to know just how to drive me mad.

And then I felt it, that tipping point where it changed from slow and sensual to desperate and dirty.

It was like someone had pressed a nuclear detonator inside the both of us and, then we were tearing each other's clothes off.

When she sat over me in just her bra, she pushed me down hard and then reached behind herself and unclasped the bra in one swift movement of her fingers. When her breasts were free, I stared at them. I needed to worship them.

I sat up propping myself on my elbows again, reaching up to palm one of them, rubbing my thumb over the dusky tan nipple.

Nyla threw her head back, her breath coming in short gasps. "East."

"You're tits are fucking perfect. Did you know that?"

She arched her back even more, inviting me to keep going.

"Do you have any idea how many times a day I wank off to thoughts of you?"

"Do you now?"

She asked this even as she rotated her hips in a circular motion with that fever pitch of the slightly forbidden, just like when we were young. That need to have the other person but not quite knowing what awaited you. But knowing it was going to be beautiful.

Tracing my other hand up her back to give her support, I leaned her more so I could access both of her breasts. Kissing the tip of one, pulling it into my mouth, laving it, trying to inhale her honeysuckle scent, trying to make her permanently part of me.

When I moved over to the next one, she groaned loudly, perching herself slightly upright and digging her hands into my hair, holding me to her breasts. For some reason the right one was a little more sensitive. A fact I happily exploited.

As she held me to her, I sucked, nibbled, bit, licked.

All the while I could feel it coming, that sort of mind-blowing orgasm just on the precipice, sneaking up my spine like a tease. The kind that would surprise you and blow your fucking top off.

Fucking hell.

I should stop this, or we were going to be done before we even began.

When I tried to pull myself away from her, she held me fast.

I had to smile at that.

Fuck. I would rather be inside her, but if this was what she wanted, then this was what I would give. Because she deserved to have everything she wanted.

But then she pulled back. When I released her nipple, I stared at it, and it was red and abraded and puckered and looked well loved. My cock pulsed.

"Nyla, fucking hell. I could do that all goddamn night."

"I almost want you to."

"I have much more fun things planned too."

She shook her head. "No, I have something else in mind."

The way she said it as her eyes twinkled and danced told me that there would in fact be torture in my future.

She started to scoot back out of my arms, and my instinct was to hold her tight. "Where the fuck are you going?"

"Release me."

I groaned but did as I was told.

And then she started to slide back. When she'd scooted back enough and her hips straddled my thighs, I watched her intently. Oh God, if she touched me, I was going to blow.

I would absolutely 100% blow.

My dick thought this was a fantastic idea.

But in my brain and my heart, I knew better.

I had one rule. Ladies first.

Nyla knew my rule, but she said, "There's something I've been dying to do."

A groan tore out of my chest. "Ny, I don't have any control. We can do this later, Just let me—"

But her delicate fingers were already wrapped around my cock and fucking hell, I saw stars.

The spike of pleasure hit me so hard I was pretty sure I started to shake, and I raised my hips to help her a little. Jesus, why did it feel like this? I thought I might die if I wasn't inside her soon.

But still, I wanted to come. Right the fuck now. No waiting, selfish. But I had to calm down because I had plans for her. So many plans...

She slid back even more, and my plans were forgotten the moment her tongue laved the tip of my dick.

I could feel it coming, the rush, the tingle... But then Nyla drew back, her long breath a mere whisper.

When I drove my eyes open and looked down at her she just gave me a beatific smile. "Oh, you didn't think I was going to let you come, did you?"

My mouth fell open, and I laughed as I dropped my head back. "Oh my God, you plan to make me pay."

"Hell, yes."

When her mouth was back on me, I wanted to yell glory to every single saint I'd ever heard about in church. But once again, she wasn't letting me lose control. This was about playing. About making me pay. When my hands went into her hair, she stopped altogether. When I gave her a questioning glance, she said, "Oh no, you don't get to control this. I'm in control now."

I shoved my hands into the duvet and made tight fists. Jesus she was going to kill me.

And she was giving it her best effort.

Her tongue stroked along the underside of my dick, stopping just when it reached the tip, flicking back and forth. She was an expert. This was all before running her hand up and slowly back down and then sucking me in whole.

Oh fuck. I was going to die. I was going to die of pleasure.

I kicked out my legs, gritting my teeth, tried to focus on anything but the heavenly sensations on my cock. Nyla didn't let up. I kept trying to warn her. I kept trying to tell her that this was a train I couldn't stop once it started.

But each time, she knew exactly when to stop, exactly how to torture me, and every time she stopped, all I could do was grip the sheets and moan my frustration, my need. I wasn't above begging. "Baby, please. Love, I know, I was a bad boy. I am sorry. Just please, fucking hell I need to come."

"Oh, do you? You need to come?"

"Yes, love. Fuck, Nyla, please."

"So, these two weeks when I've been all alone, what were you doing?"

"I told you what I was doing." Oh fuck. "I was wanking off to thoughts of you. Watching surveillance of you and wanking off some more. Wanking off to you in the shower. And then there were several times I wanked off to you in my office and then had to take a shower after that. Are you sure you want to hear this?"

She released the tip of my cock with a loud resounding pop. "Yes. I want to hear this. Because I want to know that you were just as tortured as I was."

"Yes. I was. I was horribly tortured. Please. God. Nyla."

But the torture continued. Didn't matter how much I begged.

She had zero interest.

At one point she sat back and smiled at the pre-cum leaking out of my tip. "I want you to know I'm still mad at you."

"Uh-huh, yep. Mad. I hear you."

I didn't care how mad she was. I needed to come. I needed to be inside her when I did.

This isn't about you, asshole.

That little voice of reason was the one I should've listened to. But God, it was so hard to listen because Jesus Christ, the woman could give head.

If there was a head-giving championship, I would volunteer as tribute to be her partner. Forever.

Her hand stroked over me lazily, keeping me just on the edge, and my hips rose involuntarily as she asked, "Oh my love, is there something you need?"

"Yes. I need to be inside you. Goddamn it, Nyla."

"Should I take mercy on you?"

"Yes, fucking mercy. God, I'm begging."

She raised her head, her gaze meeting mine. "You're begging?"

"Yes, I'm begging. Whatever you need, however you need it, please. I will take whatever you give me."

Then she sat back and scooted off the bed. I wanted to scream. I wanted to pull her back. I wanted to demand to know what the hell she was doing and where she thought she was going, but I didn't.

Instead I watched as her fingers went to the back of her leggings, hooked her thumbs in the elastic and tugged them down.

"Oh sweet fucking Jesus."

Once her leggings and knickers were gone, she climbed back on the bed. "You can touch me now."

I didn't need to be told twice. In one move, I pulled her up to me, melding my mouth with hers, my tongue playing over hers. Against her lips, I whispered. "You're a naughty girl."

"I'm pretty sure you liked it."

"Yes. Now, it's my turn to be in control."

Her eyes went wide as I easily rolled her on her back and

was between her thighs in seconds. "I want you to hold onto the headboard. Let's try not to break it, yeah?"

A smile played over her lips, and then I slid home deep. No preamble, no checking to see if she was ready because I already knew. Her hands clutched at my shoulders, and I held perfectly still. Fucking hell. So good. So goddamn good.

Her breath was hot against my ear. "Yes. God, I missed you so much."

And it was those words that I held on to. Those words that told me I had a chance to fix my colossal fuck-up. And I wasn't going to waste it. I wasn't going to ruin it. I pushed back to my knees while using my palms to widen her legs and to pull her to me as I rode her. I was not going to come under penalty of death. Not until she did.

I could feel her though, she was close. Already so close, my beautiful Nyla. My hands slid up her thighs, close to where we were joined. Her eyes went wide, and her hands looked like they wanted to move.

"Do you want to touch me?"

"Yes. I do."

I reached for her, and pulled her up, taking her thighs and bringing them up over mine so that she was seated in my lap. I melded my lips to hers, and we rode out the pleasure. Stroke and slide as I worked my thumb between us and slid over her clit. The trembling started in her legs, and I could feel her shuddering moan on my tongue. I slid one hand to her ass, palming it tight, my fingers gripping, holding her as I pumped. Sweat dripped from my forehead. And as she shook, her lips were still melded to mine until I slid my finger to her tight pucker. Then she tore her lips from mine and screamed, "East, oh my fucking God."

With an evil grin, I laughed and then pushed. Just the tip of my finger inside her arse and she exploded around me. There was no soft flutter and quiver, just a deathly vice grip like she was attempting to cut my cock off with her pussy, and I was here for every bit of that.

I wish I could say that I was able to shag her all night long. I wish I could say that I gave her some epic ride in the first go around. I wish I could say that I lasted for hours. But there was no way. No way I could hold back any longer. And I exploded. The bright white of bliss completely blinding me, as the two of us fell to the side, me still inside her, pulsing. Her around me, pulsing. The two of us intertwined, our foreheads touching, our noses pressed together, our breaths commingling. And then she opened her eyes, "Wow."

I gave her a smile. "Yes. Wow indeed."

CHAPTER 17

East

I KNEW it made me an absolute creeper to watch her while she slept.

But I couldn't help it. She did this thing with her mouth when she slept, like she was sucking on an invisible pacifier. Her plumped-up cheeks looked so adorable.

There was a part of me that worried if I slept, she'd wake up, change her mind, and run.

It's her flat. She's not running.

Goddammit, you know what I mean.

My subconscious didn't care. He was more than eager to point out that I was a complete and total arsehole. I had walked away from her. What the fuck was wrong with me?

You're damaged, that's what's wrong with you. Now don't fuck up this second chance.

"You're cute when your cock is stirring."

I blinked when I realized her eyes had fluttered open and she'd been staring at me too.

"Good morning, love." My voice came out huskier than I planned. But she seemed to like it. She gave me a soft smile.

"Good morning yourself. I didn't know you were staying."

Shit. She was still cagey and on edge. "I didn't have anywhere else to be. I meant what I said last night. Right here is where I plan on being, so if you want rid of me, you're going to have to explicitly kick me out. And even then, I might not get the message the first four or five times, not in a creepy, stalking and dangerous kind of way, but more of a—"

Her lips twitched. "Creepy, stalking, dangerous kind of way."

I frowned. "I'm not dangerous."

Her words were soft. "Yes, you are. To me."

"I was thinking, you should come stay at the penthouse."

Her eyes went wide, and she blinked at me. "What?"

"Just, you know, temporarily." *Not at all temporarily.* "We just got shot at. I want you with me."

"I appreciate that, but I have a place. And I like my place."

"I know. But even you can't discount that the penthouse is safer. And if you like we can stay in separate rooms."

She laughed but then sobered quickly. "You're kidding.."

"No, I'm not. Or I can have some men come and build in a panic room over here, maybe change your windows to tempered glass. My place is bigger though."

"You're serious?"

"When it comes to you and your safety, yes, I am."

Her brow creased ever so slightly as she considered my offer. "Can I think about it?"

"Of course. And while you think, let me show you just how dangerous I am." I lifted the sheet and crawled toward her as she giggled.

———

Nyla

I WAS BEING ABSOLUTELY a hundred percent truthful with myself. East Hale was my kryptonite. Two weeks ago, when I was drowning in the fog of despair, I had sworn to myself I was not doing this again. I was not going to let him walk back into my life and pretend as if nothing had happened.

But then he'd been there last night on my doorstep, insisting that we weren't done. He admitted that he had fucked up, and he wanted another chance. Not that he deserved one, but God, it was so hard to say no. And then he'd said the one thing that tipped the scale. "I know what it took for you to choose to protect my friends."

But it had been easy to choose to protect them. A little too easy. The old me would have never shared information like that with them. But I'd done it because they needed the protection. I was seeing things in all different shades of gray now. My mother died of cancer, and I felt her loss so viscerally every day. But I couldn't imagine the visceral loss of a friend and knowing that people you cared about and trusted had something to do with it. That's why I'd chosen to help them. Also, it might have been possible that, despite my words to my father, I still hated Denning.

East said, "Can I ask you something?"

I nodded, leaning into his fingers as his thumbs stroked my cheeks.

"Why did you go back to Interpol? Your father didn't respect you. Denning treated you like dirt, and if you ask me, he's a creepy stalker. But most importantly, you don't feel good about yourself there. You are so sexy and confident most of the bloody time, but working under them, it's like you're trying to dim your light to match theirs. Why? Why would you go back?"

I bit my bottom lip. It was an excellent question. Why had I gone back?

Well, the truth of it was, I had my eyes on the prize. And I wasn't sure how much of that I was supposed to tell him. But when in doubt, I opted for truth. "It was one of my early bargains with Theroux. He said he needed me inside Interpol."

East cursed under his breath. "What?"

"I know. I don't know what he wants from me, but he demanded that I be an Interpol agent again, so it must mean I can access whatever he wants."

"Why didn't you ever tell me this?"

"Well, it didn't really come up. If you remember, you and I weren't exactly being honest and forthcoming with our feelings when he paired us up to work together."

"Fucking hell. You have got to be kidding me."

"I know. I know. I wish I was. I thought you knew."

He rolled his eyes. "No, I didn't fucking know."

"Well, that's why I did it."

"You should have told me."

"For what? What would be the purpose in telling you?"

"Don't you see? You should be asking what he wants from *you*, Nyla. You and I both know he has zero intention of handing himself over to Interpol."

My stomach knotted. I knew he was right. Hell, I had already anticipated this, so why did it hurt to hear him say it? "Oh, I know. I'm just trying to get close enough to tag him."

He stared at me then. "You plan on tagging Theroux?"

"Yes. If we'd had our meet, I could have accomplished it. They have these tracking devices that are wafer thin. I might have acquisitioned one or two from Amelia."

He blinked at me. "Who are you? The Nyla Kincade I know is dogged, determined and absolutely fierce, but there's no way in hell she'd take that kind of fucking risk."

"Look, I tried not going back into Interpol. I tried to pull off half the things I've been doing *without* Interpol. But I need to be inside. I need it for access, Theroux needs it for whatever he's doing, not to mention that it could be useful to the London Lords as well. So it's done."

He sat up. "Like hell, it's done. If you need something, you tell me, and I'll get it."

I laughed, and his frown only deepened. Perhaps laughing was not the right choice. "Oh, like I'm the little missus? This little missus is very good with guns."

"You're not even supposed to carry a gun."

"I know. And I generally don't. It's because I'm former MI5 that I still get to have mine. It's in my safe."

He frowned at me then. "You weren't a field agent for MI5, were you?"

I frowned. "What do you mean?"

That deep crease in his brow only grew deeper and deeper. "Were you a field agent, or weren't you?"

"Yes, but as it turned out, I was better suited for something like Interpol. Oddly, I'm happier there, even with the stress and pressure of having my father and Denning around."

"You were a field agent?" He was genuinely surprised.

"For the last time, yes. What's the problem?"

"I just... I don't know. I knew you'd been MI5 before. I had assumed just as an analyst."

"No. Field Ops."

"That would certainly explain how you know how to fight."

"Yes, but why are you making such a big deal out of this? It's really not."

East rubbed a hand through his hair, making him look even more sexily disheveled. "I just... I don't know. I knew you were Interpol, and I knew that you were dangerous to me. I just didn't picture you being, you know, *in the line of fire* that often."

Ahhh, he was going all protective. "East, I'm sorry you didn't understand." I sighed. Why did I even need to reassure him? "Okay look, Interpol isn't really even an agency in and of itself. Technically, I'm still an MI5 officer. Hence, I have a gun. Think of Interpol as a giant inter-agency task force. We're all on loan from our respective agencies, and we all work together. So, while my father and Denning are my bosses, I still do monthly reports to MI5 on any urgent cases I'm working on." I tried another tactic. "Okay, what worries you about me and Theroux?"

He frowned. "What worries me is what he has you doing. The risks he asked you to take."

"Those are risks that I stand up for. Even as an Interpol agent, I take risks every day. When I was chasing you lot down, at any moment, I could have been hurt or discovered. And can I just say that Ben and Livy are extremely difficult to track? Just the two of them. I had a team watching everyone at that Gem Gala thing, but we got nothing because the stupid lights went out."

His lips tipped into a smile at the corners.

"Oh, wait... You had something to do with that?"

He shrugged. "Carry on."

"All I'm saying is that I face danger every single day in some form. I went back because I'm good at my job. It's possibly the only thing I'm good at. Obviously, I am shit with relationships."

"Something we are rectifying."

"Oh, *we* are rectifying? Because I swear to God, you're worse at relationships than I am."

His jaw dropped, and he looked mock affronted. "I'm not that bad."

"Yes, you are."

He shrugged. "Okay fine, I am. I just don't trust Theroux."

"Good. I don't trust him either. What I do trust is that no

matter what he's got on you or whatever reason he wants me back at Interpol, even if he thinks he's using me, I have every intention of bringing him in. He can act like he's playing me all he wants, I'm okay with that. If I even get *anything* on him, that's already a huge clue because he's such an enigma. For once, I want to be able to do something big, something important, and prove that I am my own person. I don't want to be Roger Kincade's daughter or Denning Sinclair's jilted girlfriend, though those comparisons are really unfair."

"They are unfair because Denning's lucky you even went out with him in the first place."

"Right? But anyway, my point is that I went back because even if Theroux plans on double-crossing me, I get a real shot at bringing him in. A real shot. Closer than my father has ever been. I get to make my own mark. And to be honest, it's easier to chase things down if I'm inside Interpol. The civilian life sucks. I'm no super hacker."

"But I am a super hacker. And even then, sometimes it's hard to get information."

"Exactly. But anyway, that's why I went back. And I can use that access to help you lot as well."

He cradled my face in his hands then. "Nyla, I don't want you to get hurt. I feel like the farther you go down this path the more likely it is that's going to happen."

"I'm not. And before you ask, I did tell Amelia about Theroux. But no one else in Interpol. Amelia has been so focused on the London Lords it hasn't come up again. I haven't told anyone else at Interpol what's happening. And let's just say she's not speaking to me at the moment, so it's unlikely she's even thinking about Theroux."

East frowned. "Any chance you guys will work it out?"

"I hope so, but it seems unlikely. Although now she's my new boss, so that makes things more awkward."

He pulled me close. "Just be careful. There are too many players. I don't know what's happening, and it worries me. All I want to do is wrap you in a sheet of bubbles so you won't get hurt."

"What about you? What if you get hurt? You know I'll avenge you, right?"

He chuckled. "You will avenge me?"

"Yeah. I am a great avenger."

"You know, I don't think that's the name of the movie."

I frowned. "Oh, someone's funny. I can be just as fierce as you can."

"Oh, I know." He stared down at his chest. "I have claw marks to prove it."

A flush crept up my neck. "I... Uh, sorry about that. I guess I was a bit of a tigress?"

He laughed heartily and then wrapped an arm around me and pulled me underneath him. "This is me acknowledging your fierceness and ferocity. And also me pulling you in for a kiss."

"I am fierce," I muttered, even as I leaned in for my kiss.

"Can you do me a favor? Just so I sleep a little better at night?"

I nodded. "Yeah, what?"

"If Theroux contacts you again when I'm not on the call, at least tell me first what the hell is going on."

"I can do that."

"Thank you."

"My pleasure."

"Okay. Now, since you're up and I can stop creepily watching you sleep, what's your preference?"

He kissed the crest just below my breast. "Breasts?"

He kissed between the valley of my breasts again, this time tracing his fingers where his mouth had just left. "Fingers?"

His fingers rolled down my body. The juncture between my

thighs was already pulsing, thanks to the way that he was kissing me. "Or do you want something stronger?"

I couldn't help the giggle that escaped. "I'll pick something stronger please. Always something stronger."

"I was really hoping you'd say that."

CHAPTER 18

Nyla

I WAS in my office when I got the call that we had a walk-in.

I was just finishing up a document when Amelia popped her head in. "You here? We have a walk-in."

"Yeah, I was just headed downstairs. Do you know for what case?"

Amelia shook her head. "No, but she requested the two of us."

I grab my jumper and followed Amelia down the hall and then down the front stairs. When we checked in with security, they pointed us into one of the small conference rooms. There was a woman inside with dark hair and a slight build. She couldn't be more than in her mid-twenties. She looked so young, which made me think twice again about just how young Hazel looked. And what Denning was doing with her. But that was a whole other question for another day.

With a slight knock, I let myself in. "Hello. Are you Chantal?"

She stood and shook both of our hands, and Amelia introduced us both. "Hi."

We took our seats, and then Amelia took over. "Ms. Anderson, thank you for coming today. We were told that you wanted to speak to us, but you wouldn't say what about."

"I'm sorry, I didn't mean to be vague. But I just know that these men are powerful, and I didn't want to say something I shouldn't."

Amelia nodded, opening her notebook and putting her pen to it. "Okay, why don't you tell us what we can help you with."

Chantal's gaze slid toward me, and I gave her a warm smile. Or at least what I hoped was a warm smile and not one that said *I didn't get a wink of shut-eye last night because my boyfriend, who I got back together with, wanted to spend all that time making up. Enthusiastically no less.*

"I spoke to Britney Jenner a couple of weeks ago. She told me that you were interviewing girls that used to do those parties, you know for the spoiled rich boys at Eton."

I immediately sat forward. "Yes?"

"I, um, I was visiting family. I just got back. I didn't know, or I would have come in here sooner."

Amelia started writing rapidly in her notebook. I just kept eye contact with Chantal. "Chantal, you were at those parties?"

She gave me a nod. "Once. I was fifteen."

My stomach churned. "Jesus Christ. And your mom? She didn't know where you were?"

She shook her head. "My cousin took me to the first one. She'd been invited. She asked if she could bring someone. She didn't want to go by herself."

Amelia and I both nodded as if that seemed perfectly reasonable.

Meanwhile, in my head at least, I was thinking, *you have a young impressionable cousin, you don't take her around skeevy old geezers.*

"Right. You and your cousin spent a lot of time together?"

"Uh, we did for a bit there. But, you know, after the party I went to, I didn't do much of anything. So I, um... My parents sent me to stay with another cousin in Australia for a bit. You know, when things weren't seeming to get better here."

In a calm voice, Amelia said, "Okay, why don't you just tell us what happened."

Chantal's hands shook as she wrapped them around the Styrofoam cup of tea she'd been given. "It was a party. At first, I was excited, you know? It was fancy. They provided dresses that were nicer than anything I'd ever owned."

I nodded.

Amelia was writing furiously.

"It was like a camp, you see. They trained us, told us all kinds of things about the boys that we'd be meeting, what they were like, who they knew. I thought it was a bit odd, but the weekend before the party my cousin just said that they were important people, and we were going to earn a little cash. I thought it was just like a hostess gig."

Her gaze flickered back and forth between me and Amelia. "I swear I didn't know."

I reached out my hand, upturned so that she could see I meant no harm. "No one is judging you, love. I'm sure I would have gone to a party my cousin deemed would be fantastic."

"She didn't know either, and we just thought it was a... So anyway, we go to this party. We were told everything about the boys we'd be meeting. Specifically, I was told about this boy, Bram. What he liked to talk about. His school interests. What he studied. We actually had a lot in common. I guess I thought so, anyway."

Amelia kept writing. And then she prompted. "So you went to the party and you met him. What happened?"

"It was different than anything I'd ever seen before. When I was introduced to Bram, he seemed nice. Like he liked me. No, that's the wrong way to say it. He just, I don't know, he looked like he'd hit the jackpot or something. Anyway, at first, he was fine. I was supposed to hang on his every word and laugh at his jokes. He wasn't that funny, but I could fake it. It was nothing I hadn't done on a date before."

I kept watching her, thinking how young she'd been.

"And then at one point, the woman who'd trained came and whispered in my ear that there was more work to be done, and I went with her. I told Bram I'd see him later, and he seemed excited. And then that woman, led me to a room and told me I was supposed to get undressed and—" Her hands started to shake as she took another sip of tea.

My stomach churned. "It's okay, take your time."

She took a deep breath. "I wasn't supposed to do anything. I just had to sit there and wait."

Amelia frowned. "Wait for what?"

"Twenty minutes later, that nice boy Bram came in. And I thought we were just going to, you know, hang out. I didn't"— she shook her head—"I didn't understand."

I hated to make her say it, but we needed to know. "You didn't understand what?"

She sighed. "I didn't understand what was expected. What I was really there for. I was there for Bram, but not to talk to him or keep him entertained for the night. Bram expected sex. And I'd never done that before. It wasn't a hostess job after all."

Amelia cursed under her breath and stopped writing.

I glowered at her, but then I saw that her eyes were shiny.

"At first, the kissing was nice. And I thought maybe it wouldn't be so bad, but I didn't realize what he liked."

I swallowed, trying to force bile back down where it belonged. It was Amelia's choked voice that broke the silence. "You can tell us, Chantal. What happened?"

"He, uh, he liked innocent girls, girls who had no experience, and he liked it when they fought. He liked fear. Seeing them scared."

Amelia cursed under her breath.

Meanwhile I kept my hand on the table, and Chantal finally took it. Her delicate hand coiled in mine. I squeezed it tight, trying to convey to her that it was okay. That she was safe with us. "I'm so sorry, Chantal."

She nodded as her voice shook. "I didn't want to do that with him. He wasn't gentle, and he wasn't kind."

"Did you tell anyone? Did you say anything to your mom, a friend, anyone?"

She shook her head. "I only told my cousin. And I don't know. She wasn't much help. I think maybe she had it worse than I did. Afterward, we didn't really talk anymore. She got into drugs and stuff."

I bit back a curse. "I'm so sorry. Were you able to leave after that?"

She nodded. "That woman, she came back and gathered us all up. She told us we were to report back in two months for the next initiation, and she'd give us a new file. I knew I was never going back. She tried to threaten us. Told us we'd all signed a contract. But I knew she was lying because I was underage and she couldn't make me do anything, contract or not."

My heart was breaking for her, but we had to hear the rest of her story. "What happened then?"

"I don't think mum really knew what was going on with me. Why I changed and became so sullen."

"Okay." I didn't know what to say. I had to keep her talking. I chanced a look at Amelia, and her face was ashen. Her dark brown skin had taken on this gray ash pallor.

"Anyway. I thought it was over and I didn't have to think about him again. I thought I could go back to school and live my life. But he found me. I don't even know how. I hadn't given him my last name, but he still found me and said I had to meet him."

Amelia leaned forward once again. "Did you meet him?"

She shook her head. "No. I refused. And he told me he was going to ruin me. There was a video."

My stomach turned.

"He said he was going to post it everywhere, and my friends and my father would see it. He said that I shouldn't have been such a slag."

I squeeze her hand again. "I promise you, Chantal, none of this was your fault."

"He wouldn't leave me alone. He kept calling. So I ran away to Australia. My aunt and uncle have a farm there, mostly off grid, and they let me stay with them. I changed my name, just desperate to have a new life, I guess."

"Of course. That makes absolute sense."

"Maybe a couple years afterward, Mum said that boy that was looking for me had finally stopped calling. I didn't dare come back though. I was too worried, too scared."

"Of course. When did you come back?"

She licked her lips. "Two years ago, and I've been back and forth between here and Australia since. So I missed it when the news reports about his father came out, but when I found out, I knew I had to say something."

I squeezed her hand. "You are so brave. Thank you for doing this."

Amelia added, "Thank you for your statement. If you think of anything else or you know anyone else who may need to come forward, bring them in or tell them to talk to us."

She nodded as she gathered her things, and she swiped the tears off her face with the meaty part of her thumb. It was inelegant and raw, but it was the truth. "Thank you for listening. I didn't think anyone would. For so long, everyone told me I should just forget about it. Take the money he offered."

Amelia dropped her notepad. "He offered you money?"

"Yeah, apparently that's why he'd been trying to reach me in the first place. To sign paperwork. He tried to make my mum sign one too, some kind of NDA or something."

If there was one word to describe the look on Amelia's face, it was haunted. Like she'd been at the brink, looked over and seen the horror scape below.

When Chantal was gone, I stood at the doorway trying to catch my breath.

Amelia called out to me. "Nyla—"

"I need a minute." I couldn't talk to her now. Not about this. My focus was on putting some space and distance between myself and what I'd heard from that poor woman, Chantal. She was never going to be the same because of a man like Bram Van Linsted. And I felt ill at the idea that I was at all connected to him.

And I wasn't ready to hear it if Amelia was still willing to work with him, even after everything she knew. I just wouldn't be able to deal with it. So I did the only thing I could.

I ran.

———

Nyla

THE FOLLOWING DAY, on my way to meet my new team about the Theroux situation, I opened the door to find Amelia on the threshold. I lifted a brow. "Is this urgent? I have somewhere to be."

She took in my attire in one quick glance. I might have worn a little makeup, and perhaps brushed my hair even. And fine, I had on earrings. Not that this was a date, but East always seemed to see me mildly frazzled. So I'd tried to put in a little effort. Not that I was ever going to admit that to anyone.

"Oh, sorry. You look like you're going out."

"I am. What's wrong? Is it the case?" Thus far, she'd only talked to me when it pertained to the case.

She winced. "Actually, can I come in?"

My stomach flipped. The last thing I wanted to do was get in another shouting match with my best friend. She might not consider me her best friend anymore, because apparently, I was the worst best friend on the planet, but she was still mine.

Stop being melodramatic. She had a couple of good points there.

And maybe I was just always used to following my gut instincts. They were rarely wrong. But maybe I didn't give her enough credit. Maybe all the years working under me had made her resentful, and maybe she was entitled to be so. She hadn't had the same opportunities I had. She'd come from Scotland Yard. All her colleagues and professors loved her, so why was I the one who had moved up, and she the one who had stalled? I'd never thought of it before, But maybe I should have. But I still, under no circumstances, ever wished her harm. We eyed each other as I stepped back into the flat. "Um, yeah, what's up?"

She indicated my earrings. "I always loved that pair. You would never wear them."

The threaders I'd stuck in my lobes were stunning. Silver, with the bottom portion encrusted with diamonds. They were thin and delicate though. And you would only notice the glam factor when I was in the light. "Thanks. I never really have much cause to wear them."

She nodded slowly. It was like we were strangers instead of having spent the last three years working cases together.

She rocked back on her heels and ran her hands through her braids. "Look, I'm just going to say it. I'm sorry about our argument."

I nodded as I watched her warily. "The thing is, Amelia, I'm not entirely sure you need to apologize, but maybe I do. Maybe I'm not directly at fault for the way that you've been feeling, or maybe I am. Maybe I've always sort of automatically taken the lead and didn't give you enough opportunity. Trust me, your words sit with me every day. So just know that I'm thinking about what you said."

She nodded and shifted her gaze down to her feet. "Yeah, thanks for at least acknowledging that."

"I never said you weren't capable, Amelia, I just want you to know that I always wanted you to have everything you deserve. Even if things were unfair, I will always be rooting for you."

She nodded and shoved her hands into her pockets.

"Okay, what gives? You're acting weird. What's going on?"

"I would very much love to eek an apology out of you, but unfortunately, this time, I'm the one who needs to give it."

"Why?"

"Bram Van Linsted."

I groaned. "Oh God, what now?"

Her brow furrowed and she chewed her bottom lip, as if trying to figure out the right words to use. "You were right about him."

I narrowed my gaze. "Okay, but why do you suddenly think I'm right?"

"Well, for starters, that statement we took from Chantal Anderson yesterday. And what you said last time... I couldn't let it go. It was just in my head over and over again. His own corruption, what he gets out of this, etcetera. But then, I spoke to some of his father's victims, and while we can't connect Bram to his father's activities, we most certainly can look at Bram's own victims. There were a number of women besides Chantal who referred to him as the devil incarnate, and not in a good way. He's corrupt, ruthless, and will ruin people at the drop of a hat, and I should have listened to you."

"Um, okay, apology accepted, I guess." Something she was saying didn't ring correctly though. "But you knew this before even speaking to him, so why now?"

Amelia sighed. "Well, not that this affects you at all, because I doubt that you were in Grimwald Square, and I seriously doubt that you and your boyfriend were there to meet, oh, I don't know, a notorious thief, because that's not something you would do."

I could feel the bottom drop out of my stomach. "What are you talking about?"

"Right. I have a good resource that would swear men working for Bram Van Linsted took shots at who he *thought* was East Hale and my agents in Grimwald Square four nights ago."

I held my breath. "Shit."

"Shit is right."

"He's in prison. How did you get this information?" I sputtered.

She sighed. "Okay, let's just cut the shit. I had a guard in holding with him. He found a piece of paper that showed the layout of Grimwald Square. And on it was written the names of the London Lords and one other name, Valter Kinnick. A little research turned up the fact that Kinnick is an assassin and former German KSK. Dishonorably discharged. He's a sniper for hire now."

My mouth fell open. "Oh my God, he wants to kill them."

Amelia rocked back on her heels. "It would appear that way. So I went to Grimwald Square with Denning and the team."

I tried desperately to keep my face impassive. Showed no emotion, gave nothing away. But she knew me better than anyone. She had to know I was withholding something. "Okay, so you went there to work the assassination tip?"

"Something like that. But while we were there, apparently Denning got a hot tip that Francois Theroux was on his way to maybe meet someone. So Denning has it in his head that Theroux was there to meet the London Lords, so he's coming for them."

I nodded slowly. "All right. That's interesting news, I guess."

I was desperate to get out of there, to reach out to East and the lads and let them know what I'd heard. If it was even useful information. But Amelia was still talking.

"Fuck. I'm sorry, okay? I fucked up. I wanted my shot so bad I was willing to ignore the fact that I had an unreliable witness. And something tells me you're in the crossfire of something dangerous, and I just want to help. I know things are weird with us right now, and I'm sorry. You've never been anything but amazing to me. All the other shit really has to do more with Interpol and my career than anything else."

I studied her closely. "You don't have to apologize for all the other shit because there's truth to it. When I'm on a case, I can't even hear anything else, so there might have been times you were trying to talk to me, let me know how you felt that I wasn't listening. That makes me a shitty friend."

"You're not shitty."

"Well, sometimes I am."

"Well, if you wanted to maybe notify a certain Englishman, let him know who was behind taking shots at him the other night, not that I'm saying he was the one who he took shots at, but just in case, because you know, reasons."

I could barely hold back my smile. "Right. Reasons. Ah, thank you for the heads-up, I guess."

"Yeah, of course. I'll just, um, get out of your hair."

She turned to leave, but I couldn't let her walk away like that. "Wait, Amelia, wait."

She halted and turned. "Yeah?"

"Stop being so sad. Do you want to come with me? I'll fill you in on what I'm working on."

She frowned. "Shouldn't I already be in on what you're working on?"

"Yes, you should. But this is important Amelia. And we haven't been exactly chummy these past few days, so..."

"Because I refused to listen, was absent, damn near got you killed probably... not that you were there."

My lips twitched again. "Not that I was there."

"What's happening? What are you up to?"

"There's a lot going on that I really haven't exactly shared with you. I just want to make sure first that you trust me. And if you do, we can go. But be warned, your whole world might turn upside down."

Her gaze met mine and searched it, waiting for me to reveal that I was lying or joking, or that something else was going on, but all she saw was the truth. "What's going on, Ny?"

"We're getting closer to closing the Theroux thing. Do you want in?"

Her eyes went wide. "Are you shitting me?"

"No, I'm not. Come with me, I'll tell you on the way."

CHAPTER 19

Nyla

SINCE WE HAD a problem with trust, I opted to text East before I headed over to Bridge's house. No doubt he would lose his shit when he saw Amelia. But if she'd come to warn me, they needed to know that.

The car service dropped us off in Belgravia Square in front of Bridge's house, and Amelia gawked. "Wow, you've come up in the world."

"Nope. It's not my house."

She nodded with a laugh. "Okay, good point. But still, nice friends."

"Yeah, well, the jury is still out on whether or not they're my *friends*. I think East and I are back on track, but Ben and Bridge will probably take more time to convince. Actually, just Bridge. Ben will go the way of Livy, and she likes me."

"Even after we pretty much turned her life upside down?"

I winced as I rang the security gate. "Do you have to say it out loud though?"

"Well, we sort of have."

"I know. And she's been nothing but gracious. Which is almost worse. She's so nice."

"Well, maybe if we catch the arsehole who's trying to kill us all, they won't be mad at us."

I turned and gave her a wide smile. "I like the sound of 'we.'"

"Yeah, me too. And can I just say, it felt weird not having you and me being a team effort. Don't quit again, okay?"

"Is that what they told you? I didn't quit exactly. I would never quit. What, and give Denning the satisfaction?"

"That's a good point. I should have known something was up when you told us that you would no longer be on the team, per your choice. I guess I interpreted that as you quit, but now I think your choice was to tell him he was an arsehole to his face."

I grinned. "Well, I still have my mouth."

"And what a mouth it is."

We were buzzed in the gate and marched right up to the front door.

She fidgeted nervously, shuffling from foot to foot. "Are you sure this is okay?"

"Well, East knows you're coming, so I'm sure he's warned the others. If Bridge brings out the pitchforks, I'll protect you."

"At least I can count on you for that."

"I know, right?"

When the door opened, Bridge's gaze went straight to Amelia. "Great, more coppers. None of the mates I grew up with would ever believe any of this shit. But since you're here and are apparently saving our lives, come on in."

I had to give Amelia credit. She didn't falter in the least at Bridge's stern gaze or at his dark words. She gave him a wide smile and stuck out her hand like we were strolling into a business meeting.

Reluctantly, her complete indifference forced him to be polite. He shook it as she said, "Agent Amelia Jansen."

"Welcome to my humble abode."

She coughed at the word humble, but nonetheless she followed him, and I trailed behind.

When we walked into the study, everyone had a drink. Livy and Telly gave me warm smiles and Amelia curious glances. Ben, well, he scowled. But more at Amelia and less at me. Completely untrusting this crowd.

But don't they have a good reason?

I sought out East, who came over from the bar and held out a drink for me. "Vodka tonic. For the nerves."

I took it and then handed it to Amelia. "Something tells me, I'll need all my senses tonight."

"Yeah, by the time Bridge is done with you, probably."

Amelia sighed. "If me being here is a problem, I'll go. But at least let me tell you what I know first, and then I'll be out of your hair. And for the record, I'm the one with the murder wall. Not Nyla."

He nodded slowly. "Right. I suppose you were just doing your job."

She shrugged. "Yeah, but getting in bed with the devil is never a good idea."

East seemed to ease up a little as he grinned at her. "Well, it depends. How good is the devil in bed?"

Amelia studied him for a long time, and then her lips quirked into a smile. "I can see why she likes you."

"Well, I am pretty brilliant."

I could only shake my head. "Yes, and so modest."

When everyone was seated, I saw that Prince Lucas and Bryna had joined us. Ben gave Amelia the floor. "Everyone, obviously, we have a special treat. We have a real live Interpol agent with us."

I frowned. "Hey, I'm an Interpol agent too."

Ben rolled his eyes. "Sort of. If you get suspended, then

people start to squint at you when you say you're an agent."

I muttered under my breath. "I got suspended *one* time."

Ben ignored what I said and nodded at Amelia. "This is my family. I understand that you're Nyla's family?"

I gave him a firm nod, and winked at Amelia.

She sighed. "Yeah, I am. Look, whatever you dragged her into, I don't love it. But I also trust her and her gut, and she wouldn't believe you so passionately if she wasn't on to something. And I'm inclined to believe you now because of what was found in Bram Van Linsted's cell."

Everyone leaned forward. She pulled out her phone and passed it around. "Obviously, I couldn't get the original, but that's a note from his cell. Someone, we suspect Garreth Jameson, passed it to him from the visitor's lounge somehow. There was no touching allowed, so we'll have to watch the tapes to see how it happened. But it's a confirmation of an attempt on your lives at Grimwald Square."

Everyone was dead silent and so still they could have easily been mistaken for statues. But it was East who spoke first. Ever watchful, ever vigilant, the most concerned about safety. "Theroux? But why double cross us?"

I frowned at that. "I don't think so. He had to run just like us. If anything, he would have tried to take us out himself. And he would have gotten the job done, and we would never have even seen him."

Bridge leaned back in his seat, clinking the ice cubes in his glass together. "She has a point. Theroux can get to any of us. We're not hiding. We're easy to find. If he wanted to take us out, he could have. Besides, he's made it clear that he needs us for something."

Ben rubbed his jaw. "So who is Van Linsted working with?" Livy patted his knee, trying to get him to calm down.

She chewed her bottom lip before adding, "It makes absolutely a hundred percent sense why Van Linsted would have a vendetta against you guys. Because of you, he's not where he thinks he belongs. Because of you, his father is in jail, and your hatred of each other is well documented. I mean it stands to reason Jameson is involved."

Bridge continued to clink his ice cubes. "The question is, who was the original mastermind of this plan to take us out? Jameson or Van Linsted?"

Drew stood quietly, impassive. "They plan to pick us off."

Bridge stood and approached him. "We're surprisingly hard to kill. Especially pretty boy."

Drew pushed away from the fireplace. "You think this is funny, do you?"

East stood to separate the two of them. "Jesus Christ, this doesn't help. We're on the same team."

Amelia's eyes went wide. "Wow, that's some family dynamic shit."

I shook my head. "It's a long, complicated story. But yeah, fun times."

Amelia leaned forward. "I feel like I'm missing backstory here."

I sighed. "Yeah, I guess we have to catch you up. Um, the Elite is real, and Ben's the head of it, and Bram Van Linsted wants to be the head of it, but he can't be." I glanced over to East. "Did I get it right?"

He shrugged. "In a nutshell."

"Okay, while you guys are arguing, I'm going to use the loo. Bridge, where is it?"

He guided me to a door at the back of the study. "Down the hall, first door on the right."

"Yeah, thanks."

I didn't want to leave Amelia in the den of wolves, but East would make sure no one ate her

After I used the facilities, I stepped out and accidentally made a right instead of a left back to the study. Hushed voices had me rooted to the floor.

Bridge whispered in a harsh tone, "You need to leave."

"What? That's absurd. I'm part of this. Ben invited me. Are you going to tell him that you're kicking me out?"

"If I have to."

The woman's more feminine voice said, "You can't kick me out. Everything that happened affects me too. Besides, what's your deal anyway? What does it matter to you if I want justice for my brother? What does it matter to you if I'm willing to do whatever it takes to get it?"

"Because you think you're playing, but this isn't a game. The other night, someone took shots at us. Actual real bullets. It's not one of your fancy dress parties where you get to play spy. This is real life. People are going to die if we're not careful."

"Who the hell appointed you my brother?"

There was a pregnant pause.

"God, what is your problem with me? You've always hated me."

Bridge's voice was tense and low. "I haven't ever hated you, Emma."

I racked my brain. Emma, Emma, who was Emma?

Oh yeah, I remembered East mentioning Emma. Toby's sister.

I hadn't seen anything in the records I'd pulled about her and Bridge having a relationship though. But the kind of fight that they were having, that was some we-fucked-once kind of energy.

"Goddamn it, what is your problem, Emma?"

"The problem is you. You can't control me. Since Toby died, I've wanted only one thing, and that's for the people who were responsible to pay. And if that's you, so be it."

"Don't you understand? I'm trying to keep you safe."

"Yeah, you're just forgetting one simple fact. I never asked you to keep me safe. And I don't want your help. If I have to do this myself, I will."

"The hell you will—"

A door opened somewhere, and there was another feminine voice. "Okay, clearly I've interrupted something."

I knew I shouldn't be standing there listening. I knew it. But I couldn't help it. It was like I was in the middle of this drama and couldn't turn away.

"Is this your *girlfriend?*"

Bridge's voice went tight. "Mina, let it go."

"Let what go? If you're inviting your whores over, the least you can do is tell me."

"Mina, stop."

Emma just laughed. "His whore? From what I hear, you already occupy that role."

And then there was a crack. I didn't know what happened, but it sounded like a smack. Then there was deadly silence and the second woman said, "I'm tired of this. I want them all out of my house."

Bridge laughed low. "First, you will never put your hands on her again. I don't care how pissed off you are. Ever."

There was a long beat of silence, and I inched closer.

"Second, this isn't *your* house. Until we get married, which you keep putting off, this is *my* house."

Another long pregnant pause and then a sniffle. "God, I knew you were cruel, but this, this takes the cake."

There was thumping and stomping, a muttered curse from Bridge, and then more shuffling. I eased backward. I shouldn't have been listening. It didn't matter how curious I was or what the hell was going on, it wasn't my business.

But damn, it sounded like Bridge had problems.

CHAPTER 20

East

WHEN NYLA RETURNED from the loo, she was giving me a *Can we keep her?* face. When I'd gotten her text earlier, I had been willing to hear Amelia out, but that bridge didn't quite extend to bringing her fully in.

Isn't she fully in already? Look at Nyla.

Nyla, Telly, and Amelia had their heads buried together talking about something. Livy came over. "You care about her a lot."

My chest ached. "Yeah, I do."

"I know this is hard for you."

"It's not hard caring about her. Well, not now."

She laughed. "It just took you a while to realize you were being an idiot, right?"

"I'm so lucky that I have you lot to tell me when I'm being an idiot."

He laughter was a soft trill. "Well, you can always count on us for that. So, new member, huh?"

I glowered at her. "Amelia is *not* a new member, we're not keeping her."

"Have you told that to Nyla?"

"I don't think Nyla is making decisions here."

"Well, she's with *you*, so she's in the group. And she walked her friend in here with her, so it's highly likely Amelia will be with us permanently now too. After all, Telly and I were a package deal."

I scowled at Amelia. What was I supposed to do with this information? I had to get to work. We had the Elite coming for us, had Interpol inadvertently on our assess, and a master thief demanding our attention, all because I'd been careless.

Ben joined us, and he wrapped an arm around Livy. "So, are you telling him that Amelia is in or not?"

Livy laughed. "Well, he seems to think that we shouldn't cave."

There was no fucking way. It was difficult enough having Nyla in this, and now we had this new wannabe member. We didn't know her or what she wanted from us, so why should we take the risk? I was getting deeper into my own thoughts, and I didn't realize that the room had grown silent.

I looked up at Nyla, and she raised a brow. Amelia, to her credit, just stared me in the eye. Telly decided to be as unhelpful as ever. "Oh, don't mind him. He's just territorial."

"I am *not* territorial. I'm just trying to keep everybody alive."

Amelia put up her hands. "Look, I know. Two weeks ago, I was coming after you. I get it. If I were you, I wouldn't trust me either. But Nyla trusts me."

Nyla nodded. "Yeah, I do. When things look bleak, Amelia is the one I turn to. She can help us. And at least she's not persona non grata at Interpol. The higher ups will listen to her."

"Right now, I have no clue what your intentions are, Amelia. Zero. So if you want to take part in this mess, do it on your own.

No disrespect, but you can't stay. I can't be sure you're not going to get us all killed."

Nyla was unimpressed with my speech. I could tell by the set of her jaw. "And I'm telling you, we *need* her. Imagine what we can do with two Interpol agents, instead of just one. Just think about it. She's an asset. And you're being ridiculous if you think shutting her out is a good idea."

"Nyla, be reasonable. It's my job to make sure we stay protected and covered. Adding Interpol to the mix is not the best way to do that."

Nyla glowered at me. "Like I said, you're being ridiculous."

"I'm just being cautious. You might not like it, but it has kept us alive so far."

"Look, I hear you, but this isn't just your call. You guys are a team, right? And you have a leader. Who is the team lead?"

Ben grinned. "She got you there mate. But I'm sorry, Agent Kincade, when it comes to matters of security, we defer to East. But... If I do get a vote, I think it's not the worst thing in the world to have Interpol on our side. It certainly can't hurt adding one more agent."

"Can't you all see how this could benefit us? Denning Sinclair is after you."

Amelia came forward. "Look, I get it. I came for you, and I wasn't nice about it. I tried to put you in jail that one time, and I owe you for that. But you've forgiven Nyla, so I'm hopeful you'd do the same for me. Keep in mind, the real bad guys are out there, and that's who we're trying to deal with. I came to you without any inhibitions or any ultimate goal. I just want to help. But I get it. You have to do it your way. I'm not going to fight. I'm not going to beg."

Jesus. "So, what? I'm the hold out now?"

Ben shrugged.

At that moment, Bridge walked in with Emma in tow. "Jesus

Christ, Emma too?" I blurted out, though a part of me knew that Emma had more right to be here than any of us.

"Ah, this looks tense. What are you voting on?" Emma said.

Bridge scowled at her. "You don't get a vote."

"Oh yes, I do. Ben invited me, so I get a vote. What were you voting on? Come on, tell me," she pleaded before joining me with a broad grin. "Hey, handsome."

"Hey, little Tobes." I hugged Emma, and Nyla eyed her up and down.

"Hi, I'm Nyla, East's girlfriend."

They exchanged glowers. I grinned then, seeing Nyla's jealous move for what it was. "Yes, she's my girlfriend."

Emma laughed. "*You* have a girlfriend? Be still my heart."

"Hey, even the best of us fall sometimes."

She laughed and extended her hand. "Hi. Emma Varma. Toby was my brother."

Nyla nodded and shook. "I'm really sorry. I didn't know him, but from what East tells me, he was the best."

Emma nodded. "He was. So, why the grim faces? I know Bridge doesn't want me here, but Ben asked me to come, so I assumed you need all hands on deck."

Bridge scowled. "We can't let Emma in on this. And the same goes for Amelia. No offense, but we barely even know her. You all know full well what's at stake here."

Drew laughed. "I say they're both in just because it means getting to watch you two bicker and lose your shit."

Nyla laughed. "Amelia can actually keep government secrets, so she's not a security risk. Besides if she goes, I go."

My head snapped around, and I could hear my low, feral growl. "You're going nowhere." She merely lifted her brow.

Ben rolled his eyes, and Livy snapped her fingers loudly. "Enough. They both stay, because we've been trying to do this ourselves and so far, we don't have any answers. So, welcome to the team, you two." Then she turned to Bridge and I and leveled a direct gaze at each of us. "Both of you, deal with it. Figure it out or whatever you have to do. I don't care. But get over yourselves."

Nyla turned and grinned at me, and I knew I was going to regret this.

———

Nyla

AFTER DROPPING Amelia off at home, I headed back to my townhouse. East would be by after he finished some work, and I had just the thing to surprise him. My breasts grew heavy just thinking about it.

You really think this is going to last, don't you?

A frisson of dread snaked up my spine, but I refused to let it take root.

I waved at the doorman before jogging up the stairs to the hallway, where I saw my neighbor, Mrs. Briggs. She gave me a wide smile that wrinkled up her face like tissue paper. "Hi, love."

"Hi, Mrs. Briggs. How are the new flowers?"

"Oh, my hydrangea? I keep trying, but I have the worst black thumb."

I laughed. "Well, maybe we should get you another hobby."

She chuckled and waved her hand in the way of old grand mums. "No, I just love them. And sometimes, I get lucky."

I grinned at her. "Well, I wish you all the luck then."

She passed me in the hall, and then she paused. "Oh, I think your visitor went inside. It wasn't the usual young man I've been seeing you with, but anyway, he's in your flat."

I kept a smile plastered on my face. I didn't want her to worry and then get nosy enough to come looking for me.

"Thanks for letting me know. You have a good night now."

"You too, love. Do you want me to pick you up some biscuits from the shops?"

"Oh, you're the best, but no. I'm back at work now, so I must stay focused and eat less biscuits."

"No fun, is it?"

I laughed. "No, not much fun at all."

I forced myself to keep my voice light and airy. Just as she rounded the corner that led to the lobby, I reached into my crossbody bag and palmed my Mace. Keys in my right hand, I was able to unlock the door deftly enough while still gripping the puffer. I stepped in, noting the lights were low, not unlike how I normally left them. "I already know you're in here. Time to come out."

I didn't know who I was going to find. I assumed it would be Denning. If he thought I wouldn't Mace him, he had another think coming. It wouldn't be my father, or Mrs. Briggs would have recognized him. But even he would have called first.

"Your neighbor is lovely, I must say."

I whipped around toward the hallway, and out of the shadows strolled none other than *Francois Theroux*.

His face was so familiar. He'd been at my father's office glaring back at me from a case file for years. "What the fuck are you doing in my flat?"

He put up his hands. "Easy does it. How about you put the Mace away before one of us gets hurt?"

"You realize I'm MI5, Interpol, and know how to use a gun. I think I'm capable of not fucking up with Mace."

"I do not doubt your skill level, but maybe you should pay attention to the man I brought along." The closet door eased open, and I nearly jumped, but I didn't take my eyes off of Theroux. Instead, I reached in my handbag, grasped the hilt of the knife I always carried, and pulled it out.

Theroux chuckled softly. "Well, it seems that you stay handily armed."

"Yeah well, I've had to. What are you doing in my flat?"

He waved off his goon, who leaned back against the closet and crossed his arms.

I just rolled my eyes. "If that's meant to calm me down so I'd put this away, you don't know me very well."

"Well," he said as he approached slowly, "I know you better than you think I do. I must say I was disappointed we couldn't meet last week. I was excited to see you and Mr. Hale in action."

I knew that Bram Van Linsted had sent a hit squad, but he didn't know any of that, so I pushed him a little. "Were those your goons shooting at us?"

"'That was unfortunate, and certainly not classy. Shooting in public? I'm a gentleman thief. What do you take me for, some kind of hoodlum? No. I prefer the subtleties in life."

"Ah, yes, you just prefer to try and kill me in my flat. Did you think no one would notice?"

His smile was easy. "I noticed you said, *try* to kill me."

"You think I'm going to make it easy? No, I won't. So, can we get on with your agenda or not?"

"Congratulations on no longer being suspended. Excellent work. I wish you'd chosen that route first though. It would have saved you time."

He sauntered past me, even though I kept my weapons trained on him, and he didn't even seem to notice or care. "Henry Warlow, where are we on finding him?"

So, he was going to just pretend he hadn't broken into my flat and wasn't standing in my living room uninvited? "We're tracking down leads. I don't know how fast you thought this was going to go, but the guy vanished. He's a ghost. So it's taking time, but we'll find him," I said with determination.

"My, my, you are a little thing, but so much strength, so much zeal. The kind of daughter a father could be proud of."

"Yeah, well, you should probably tell my father he should be proud, because he doesn't seem to know."

"Oh, I guarantee you he knows. He's just too much of a twat to tell you."

I coughed, fighting to hold back my laugh. "Considering you're his number-one enemy, I think you have a very specific opinion of my father."

Theroux shrugged. "Let's just say I've been evading his capture for a long time. Running from someone tells you a lot about them. How they think, how they pursue, and whether or not you want to get caught."

"Why do you want to get caught? Why do you want to let *me* take you in?"

The look that he gave me was merry assessment. "Because I find you delightful, and I know that it will irk him greatly that he's not the one to get the glory. Let's just say that I'm guaranteed to stay alive while you process me, and he won't get the credit. That's pleasure enough for me." He placed a hand over his chest as he walked, and I followed him into my living room, careful to keep my back to a wall and my weapons handy.

"Why are you willing to do this? Why are you even allowing yourself to be brought in? Clearly, you know how to evade arrest. Clearly, you don't need to walk in there, put your hands up, and surrender."

"Oh, but what fun would that be?"

"What is it with you and him? I'm sick of this. I'm sick of the game. Either you have something to tell me or you don't. Either you have something that I need to know pertaining to Henry Warlow or what I'm working on, or you don't. If not, stop wasting my time. I don't want to play games. I want to get you what you want and bring you in. And then—"

He nodded at me, brows lifted, as if encouraging me to keep talking. "And then what?"

I frowned at that. "What do you mean, then what?"

"So you'll take me in, and then what happens?"

"I get the respect I've earned."

"But you don't *need* respect; you already have it. Your colleagues, whether they like you or not, they respect you. Well, except Denning. But that has to do more with his fragile ego than anything else."

"How do you know Denning?"

"Like I told you, Agent Kincade, there's very little about you that I don't know."

"Are you stalking me?"

"No, my dear. I am far too old for those kinds of pursuits. That's really where your boyfriend, or partner, prevails. Which is it now? Have you two reconciled or not? Quite frankly, I was saddened when you split the first time."

My jaw unhinged. "What?"

I knew he'd been watching us, but that closely? Holy hell.

"Stay out of my business."

"Well, my dear, I wish I could. But since you're doing me a favor, technically working for me, *your* business is *my* business."

"I'm really over the patriarchal shite."

"It's not about controlling you. It's about getting what I need. Where are we on Warlow?"

"We're working on it. You sent us in to find a needle in a haystack."

"Is that an excuse from you, Agent Kincaid?"

I clenched my jaw tight. "No. I know what's at stake. I'll find him."

"See that you do, Agent Kincaid. See that you do."

East

Theroux's impromptu visit at Nyla's had us pressing to research Henry Warlow. Our inability to find anything on him returned us to the one place we had a lead. We needed a better look at that image in Lord Jameson's office.

Nyla was due back at Ben and Livy's as soon as she was done with work. And I couldn't deny I was pretty antsy to see her. Since Theroux had shown up at her flat the night before, I was nervous when she was out of my sight.

Bridge stared at the map of the Jameson estate. "So we're really doing this bit of crazy?"

Ben nodded. "Yeah, we really are." He leaned closer, dropping his voice like he had to keep a secret. "Yeah mate, speaking of crazy, what the hell is going on with you and Mina?"

Bridge rolled his shoulders. "There's nothing going on. Everything is fine."

Ben laughed. "Okay, if you say so. Except I don't believe you."

Bridge rolled his eyes like Ben was nothing more than a

gossiping schoolgirl, which to be honest he really did resemble. "Emma and Mina had a disagreement at the house last night during the team meeting."

"What, did Mina catch you and Emma in another disagreement and tell you to play nice?"

He shook his head. "She found Emma and I talking, made her own conclusions, got in an argument with Emma, and it didn't end well for Mina."

"What do you mean by 'didn't end well'?"

He sent his gaze heavenward. "She called Ems a whore. Ems said that she was the one who was the whore. Mina slapped her." My jaw unhinged. "Then Mina tried to kick you lot out and I might have reminded her that until we get married she's not lady of the house."

I winced. "Holy shite. Why didn't you call us to come in and watch? That sounds epic."

He sent me a glare. "Come on, as if you would want to watch that. This is not about your sex life, East."

"I regret telling any of you that I like to watch. Remind me to never tell you lot anything again."

Drew just chuckled. "Wait, Mina actually slapped her?"

"Yeah. Legitimately. No questions asked. It was a full on I'm-not-fucking-with-you slap."

Drew's laugh was low. "Mate, what did you do after? Knowing Mina, she must be well ticked off?"

"Later, I told her that she was never to lay hands on Emma again if she knew what was good for her."

We all just stared at him as Ben said, "Jesus Christ, mate, have you no sense of self-preservation?"

He shrugged. "Well, she *did* deserve it. She had no right to call Emma a whore, for Christ's sake."

I winced. "True. What the hell is wrong with her?"

It was Ben who cleared his throat and asked the question,

"Did she have a reason to think Emma was behaving like a whore?"

Bridge scowled at Ben. "Fuck no. She's Toby's fucking sister."

Ben just held up his hands. "Easy mate. I'm just asking a question. Questions are important. I was just curious if you and Emma had ever gone there, because sometimes it seems like you have."

"I never would have done that to Toby. She's his little sister, mate."

Bridge had always had this thing about Toby's little sister. It was as if Emma couldn't look after herself, couldn't have destroyed any man who looked at her cross-eyed. Emma Varma was a force, and the only one who couldn't see it was Bridge.

"Mate, do you have a thing for her? Because that changes everything."

He scowled. "I do *not* have a thing for Emma. I'm engaged, remember?"

I shrugged. "Okay, if you say so."

Ben just chuckled. "I remember when I told you I didn't have a thing for Livy."

"Ah, the good old days," I muttered to myself.

Bridge wasn't having it. "I don't. I just... Long before he died, Toby asked me to look out for her if anything ever happened to him. You know, some basic shit we all say. But I took it seriously. Obviously, I didn't know what was going to happen, but now it's like I can't let it go. He said look out for my sister, so I do the best I can. At least as much as Emma allows anyone to look after her, which isn't much, because she's stubborn, and mule-headed, and a pain in the arse."

Ben, Drew, and I exchanged glances. We were all desperately trying to hold back our laughs.

How could he not see that, for all his protests, Emma had wound her way under his skin?

"So, just to make sure I have this right, Toby asked you to look after Emma."

Bridge nodded. "He did."

"And you thought what, that was for perpetuity?"

Bridge rolled his eyes. "All I know is my mate asked me to look after his sister, so I have. I should have looked out for her brother better."

That was a tough one to swallow because, yeah, we *all* should have looked out for Toby better. And as much as we tried to rectify that, it was always going to be a sore spot. We had failed him. And Bridge felt like he was failing Emma.

"Mate, I know Toby was our friend, but just in case you did have a thing for Emma, which you don't, obviously, but if you did, I'm pretty sure there's no one he'd want to be with her more."

"Are you daft? Are you forgetting I'm already *engaged*?"

We all knew that was the magical word that meant *shut the fuck up.*

Bridge had a blind spot when it came to Mina. There was a part of me that thought she could be good for him. And in the beginning, he'd been obsessed with her. He'd thrown himself headfirst into the relationship, and something about her had calmed him down.

He'd been less angry, less closed off since he'd met her. And so we'd celebrated her sudden appearance in his life, his sudden establishment of her as the woman he wanted to be with. We accepted all of it, but it had never felt like something that *should* be happening. It had never seemed like something that was on point.

And then we'd discovered the one thing that would be guaranteed to split them up. But he was happy, so I'd fought Ben on telling Bridge the truth. But in hindsight, that was the wrong way to go.

"Right, Mina. Of course."

Bridge scowled at us. "You lot have got to let this Mina thing go."

Ben put up his hands. "We've let it go. We didn't say anything about Mina, okay?"

Bridge changed the subject. "Can we get back to the task at hand? Jameson?"

I guess that was that. "I'm on it. I'm trying to find a way in. Maybe a remote camera if we can get a workman to smuggle it in. I'll ask Telly for help."

Drew clutched his hands to his chest. "God is real. If you're going to ask Telly for help, what has this world come to?"

I rolled my eyes. "Ha-ha, very funny."

Still chuckling, he shook his head. "I could do this all day."

I looked to Ben. "If you can't shut him up, I will."

He laughed. "I hate to say this but maybe Lucas is the one to go in."

Bridge laughed. "You know full well it won't be simple and that he won't be contained. He'll rob Jameson blind."

I laughed. "Yeah. But, it would be brilliant to watch."

Bridge nodded. "Yes, but it would bring a slew of complications. But hey, who wants to do anything easy?"

Drew raised a hand. "Me, I like it easy."

We all chuckled.

"Jameson will be a problem," I muttered.

Ben's voice was low, "Yes, but this is the in we need. Besides, Jameson elder and younger were always in the crosshairs. Any connection to Warlow just speeds it up."

East

An hour later, the team was all together, and we were reviewing the map of the grounds on Ben and Livy's massive coffee table.

And the woman I loved suggested she draw the short straw to get us the image from inside Jameson's office. "I don't like it." I stared at the plan. "I have no idea about their security. This is bad. This is a bad plan."

Bridge clapped me on the shoulder. "Oh yes, East, forever our worry wart. Relax, Thanks to Telly finding out the security company and working her contact there, we know all camera placements. We know the pitfalls."

I scowled at my mate. "I'm sorry, are you the security expert? No, right?"

Bridge just laughed. "No need to be so testy."

"I just need more information. No offense, Tel, the information is good. It's just not complete. It's a bloody closed system. I can't hack it unless I'm inside. We sneak on the property and we'll be blind. Like how many, in what locations, and what are they pointing at?"

"I knew he'd be like this." Drew muttered to himself.

"Like what? Trying to keep everybody alive? Pardon me if that's the whole purpose of what I'm doing."

Nyla watched our exchange back and forth. "This is a delight. I love to see other people giving him shit, not just me."

I grumbled under my breath, "This is not funny."

"No, of course, it's not funny. I'm the one who's breaking into a state-of-the-art secured compound. None of this is funny. Matter of fact, this is all downright dangerous. But you will help keep me protected."

"Yes, but the point is, this is so much harder than it needs to be."

She shrugged. "Well, it is what it is. We need access to that photo if we hope to ever have a good lead on Henry Warlow."

The shitty part was, I'd seen that image the last time I'd broken into Jameson's office. But Warlow hadn't been on my radar then, and I couldn't remember any of the other names.

Telly stepped forward with her laptop open. "Okay, East, what is it that worries you the most? Is it the fact that we'll have to actually search the office physically, the security protocols that we don't know about, or the fact that we have to also be super close to the buildings so that we can hack in?"

"All of the above. It just seems reckless."

Ben nodded. "So noted. Now, if we had nothing to lose, how would we do this?"

Nyla sat up. "Okay, we need access to the photo. East you've seen the photo?"

"Yes, but it's in the heart of the compound in Lord Jameson's office."

"Bryna, you and I will monitor from here." She pointed the egress route that we'd taken that night we'd gotten hit by sprinklers.

Don't you mean the night she rubbed herself all over your cock and you had blue balls for a week?

Yeah, good times.

"Okay, so it would seem that the room you were in is here." Telly pointed out Lord Jameson's office on our schematic.

"Yup."

"And this is what, the front door?"

"Yep, that's the one."

"Obviously, this has to be done when no one is looking."

"Yeah, which is just about never."

Nyla frowned, chewing the corner of her bottom lip. She always did that when she was thinking something through. "Amelia? Any ideas?"

"No. I was counting on your gut to tell you something."

"I wish my gut was operating like that right now, but it's not."

Emma spoke up. "How important is this?"

Amelia and Nyla exchanged glances. "Well, it's everything."

"There's no way you're going to make it in there without anyone noticing you are in there. So the *best* we can hope is that nobody notices. Disguise yourself. Dressing up as a maid is a good one. If we need to physically be on-site for this, you would want to be as inconspicuous as possible."

I tried not to bite her head off. I did. No way were serving Nyla up to Jameson dressed like a French maid.

"Okay, why don't we walk right through the front door?" Nyla asked.

A long exhale escaped out of my lungs as she continued. "Maybe Amelia and I can distract him while, East, you break in and get the photo we need. Hell, this might even be a one-person job. Which I can do. Get into the office. Get a photo you say is there, walk out."

I vetoed that play right away. "The hell you will."

She threw her arms up as if to say, *be reasonable.* "We have badges, and we will walk right in that front door. Hell, we only need one agent to go in. Better if it's me. I'm the one known for going off half-cocked. I can go under the pretense of being concerned about missing pieces of artwork he lost during the Monaco museum forgeries. Amelia that could work, right?"

My bestie nodded as she chewed her bottom lip. "It's simple, and I can cover you better from the outside. In case you get caught or something. I can make calls."

Nyla rolled her eyes. "I'm Interpol. It would stand to reason I'm following a lead."

"Are you insane?"

"No. I'll flash them my badge, and they'll have no choice but to let me in. East, how long will you need to get in and out of the office?"

"Ten minutes if I want to avoid the cameras inside."

"It's doable. And honestly, we just need to see the photo. Trust me, this will work. You'll see."

I had a feeling that every time Nyla said *trust me* it was going to take several years off my life.

CHAPTER 22

Nyla

"WHAT'S WITH THE FACE?"

East had been quiet since we'd left Ben's. East wanted me to move in with him, even if it was temporarily, which... I still wasn't sure what to do with that.

"Nothing. Nothing is wrong."

"Something is obviously wrong. You're never this quiet."

"I can be quiet," he grumbled

"You're cheesed off with me."

A moment of silence ticked by, and I watched his hands grip tighter on the steering wheel of the sports car. I'd never seen another model like it, and with its low carriage and modern spaceship-like interior, it was almost akin to riding inside a hoverboard. The crisp apple scent of the leather screamed of its newness. Or maybe he just didn't drive it often. It didn't smell like him. As I made all my observations, I waited, not so patiently, for him to speak. If he was angry, we needed to talk it out. I'd seen what happened when he didn't talk to me.

"Well, I'm not really thrilled about you and Emma being involved in any of this."

I tried to think of the best diplomatic response, but opted for directness in the end. "We're grown women, East. We make these choices for ourselves."

"Yes, I know. Obviously, women's empowerment and all that, but I care about you, so I'm worried."

"All right, then tell me you're worried. Don't try to control me, or tell me what to do, or tell me this isn't my fight. Because if it's your fight, it's my fight, right? That's how caring about people works in case you didn't know."

He scowled at me. "You know, if you weren't so bloody gorgeous, I might have something to say about your attitude."

I laughed. "*My* attitude. You're the one who's been stomping around all night. Grumpy. Uncommunicative. Remember, we were going to start talking to each other?"

"Yes, I remember. But this is hard. Usually, it's just me. I never have to think about anyone else when I make decisions."

"I get it. You have been living a very lovely and convenient life. It must be nice. Welcome to how the other half lives."

He scowled more. "You know what, I'm not talking to you."

"Oh yeah, real mature."

"Just understand where I'm coming from. I want to keep you safe."

"And just understand where I'm coming from. I'm the one with the gun."

His lips pressed into a firm line. "Must you always remind me of that? It's just, what I couldn't do for AJ, is definitely something I need to do for you. I need to protect what's mine. Call it some kind of primal instinct."

"I hear you. And I'm appreciative. I am. Trust me. I don't want anything to happen to me either. I'm amazing. Or haven't you heard?"

His lips twitched, and I could see some of the tension rolling out of his shoulders. Perfect. Now he might be more reasonable. "I get it. Everything that happened with AJ makes you more aware. More alert. But I'm not someone who needs to be protected. I am a protector myself. So, you should trust that I won't make dumb decisions. When I need help, I'll ask for it. And I trust you. I know that seems weird to you, but I do. I believe that you will protect me in your own way. But also understand I'll protect you. It's a two-way street."

He rolled his eyes hard. "It's not the same, Nyla." Once he parked, he climbed out then came around to my side to open the door.

In the lift up to the penthouse, he turned to me, still scowling, and I couldn't help but poke the bear a little. "I'm just saying, who has the badge?"

He coughed out a laugh. "You can't end every argument like that. I want to keep you out of this."

"I'm sorry, but you can't." Once upstairs and in the penthouse, I tossed my keys onto the tiny porcelain dish he had by the door. I hadn't given him an answer about a more permanent relocation, but I was staying the night.

"It's like you're telling me not to do my job. I'm not going to tell you that you don't have to do this. You and the others have a huge stake in avenging your friend. I understand that. I wouldn't dream of telling you not to pursue the people responsible. It doesn't make any sense. But I also want you to be careful. You know that, right?"

"Yeah, I know. I know."

"*Do* you know? Do you understand that you are very much someone I need in my life? You get it, right?"

"So what you're telling me is that you like me?"

I gave him my most beleaguered, frustrated sigh. "Barely. If you didn't have a big dick, we wouldn't be talking."

He tugged me close. "Big dick, you say."

I giggled and scooted away from him. "I'm serious. I can't kowtow to someone just so he'll give me sex."

"I'm not sure why not."

I shook my head. "Come on, let's order some carryout."

He leaned in, nuzzling my neck, "You'd rather eat than fuck?"

"Well, when you put it so delicately."

"Don't want to talk about the new safety parameters I have installed here at the penthouse?"

I frowned. "Safety parameters?"

He nodded enthusiastically. "Oh yes. I have added your thumbprint and biometrics. Your eyeball scan too. And now, you can voice activate the panic room."

I blinked at him. "The panic room?"

He nodded as if that was the most normal thing in the world. "Yeah. I'll show you." He took my hand, led me down the hall into the bedroom and to the anti-chamber inside the closet. "See? Just say, 'East has a big cock.'"

I frowned at him. "You really think I could say that under duress?"

"Well, we can find out."

He started kissing my neck. "East Hale. Pay attention."

"What? Okay fine. You can change it to whatever you want. You press these buttons here." He showed me a sequence of buttons to press. "And you can change it to whatever you want. It's voice activated. You can also use your thumb or your retina, but in the event that you are injured in some way, your voice will work too."

"Wow, you really thought of everything."

"Well, I wanted you to be safe."

That was the crux of our fight. His pathological need to see me safe. Like he couldn't do for his sister. "I am safe. Is there any reason that I wouldn't be?"

"You don't know the Elite."

I sighed. "Listen, I get it. I don't know what they're capable of, these people, these men in the shadows. I understand that you have legitimate concerns, and I'm with you. I don't want to negate that at all. I just like my life. I like my independence."

His brow furrowed. "I get it, but maybe just for the time being, until we can get all of this under control, you'll consider staying here?"

I sighed. "It's not that I don't want to be with you. I might get used to this penthouse life. I mean, I think it was meant for me, don't you?"

He laughed. "Of course."

"I just... I don't want to move too fast. I don't want to take any of this for granted, you know?"

He palmed my cheeks gently, and his green eyes penetrated mine. "I know. And I'm not trying to push you or force you. It's just for safety. If you want to still, I don't know, *date*, I'm here for doing whatever you want. We can date as long as you like. I have five guest rooms."

I blinked, then blinked again. "Five?"

He nodded as if that wasn't a big deal at all. "Yeah, if you prefer your own guest suite, of course we could do that, but this bedroom is the one with the panic room."

"You're willing to let me sleep alone?"

He shook his head, and his brow furrowed. "Of course not. Where you go, me and my dick go. But if you want to pretend that this isn't the real deal and we're just dating, we can sleep in a bed in the penthouse that isn't *my* bed."

"I—" I had no words. Telling him he was ridiculous would be a futile effort. "No, I want to be with you. And I don't want any other room. I just don't want us jumping the gun."

His voice was quiet when he said, "I'm not Denning. I'm not

going to fuck you over. Just fuck you. Well and pleasurably until you are so exhausted that all you can remember is my name."

"That sounds like a fantastic idea. But this is all temporary, okay? Sooner or later, I'll go back to my life. You will too. And then we'll take this slowly."

He nodded. "Yep. If that's what you want."

"Why do I get the impression that you will take every opportunity to convince me that this is where I belong?"

"Because it is."

"It is what?"

"It is where you belong. Right here. Next to me."

And I knew then that I was in trouble. East Hale had a way of getting to my heart that no one else had ever managed before. And there was no way, after being with him, I could ever want anyone else.

He was dangerous. And it terrified me.

CHAPTER 23

Nyla

"REMEMBER, just stay calm. Direct. Don't stray and don't let on. Just stick to the script. And let me know if you see anything."

I scowled before even ringing the doorbell. "You know that this is actually my job, right? I interview suspects. People pay me to do this."

His long-suffering sigh was barely audible on the com line. "But this is different. He's dangerous."

"Believe me, I know. Let me do my job."

A maid dressed in uniform opened the door. "Can I help you?"

I took out my badge and flashed it, grateful that I had sucked it up and gone back to Interpol. I didn't like it. It felt terrible, but it let me do this, so... "Hi, I'm Agent Nyla Kincade with Interpol. I need to speak with Lord Jameson please." I used my professional I'm-a-grownup voice.

She had me wait for a second, and then she stepped back and allowed me inside the vestibule. Once inside, my gaze nearly went to two sculptures that hadn't been in the foyer the last time I'd been there for the party. Maybe they'd been moved to accommodate the guests, but they were there now in the foyer. Metallic and stone intertwined, and they looked like two giant interwoven penises.

I covered a laugh with a cough, and East was immediately on the coms. "Are you okay?"

I muttered a quick, "Mm-hmm," as I walked and tried to control my head. As an Interpol agent, interviewing suspects was part of the job. You pushed and pushed and wheedled and controlled, but that wasn't the difficult part. And I'd had many people watch my interviews. It was one of those things you got over being sensitive about. That's just what it was. Along the way, people were going to be standing over your shoulder watching you.

It was unnerving, of course. But this, this was a whole other thing. I knew Amelia was there too, so that made me feel marginally better. But I didn't like someone else actually in my head. If there'd been a way to turn off the damn earpiece, I would have. But East had mic'd to me himself. He didn't want to leave anything to chance.

Don't give chance a window.

What the hell did he think was going to happen to me? I'd walk in, ask Jameson a few questions, tag him if I could, and see how to get a response out of him about Henry Warlow.

Bonus if he took me into his office so I could see the photo for myself. How hard was that?

But if he didn't take me into the office, I was going to go and use the loo and then sneak in. Which was risky, of course, but I could do it. I could make this happen.

Luckily, I didn't have to employ plan B. The maid led me right through the massive house, past the great room, the kitchen, the dining room, and the glass doors to the outside patio where we turned left toward the back of the house. I recognized it as the slightly narrow hallway where I'd been the last time. More closed doors. Cameras. Every-damn where. I almost felt the need to salute them as I passed.

She knocked gently on the door, and a booming voice said, "Come on, in."

When I opened the door, I found Lord Jameson behind his desk. The whole room was like an explosion of masculinity with dark oak furniture. So much so that it was hyper. And oh, joy. Was that an elk head on his wall? Oh, he was a hunter. Excellent.

"Lord Jameson, thank you for taking the time to speak with me."

"Oh, nonsense. Anything to help Interpol. Did you know I once thought I wanted to be in the Intelligence services?"

I lifted a brow. "Did you? What stopped you then?"

"Art. I loved it more. Over the years, my family has acquired many pieces. I couldn't leave it behind. I was always a little bit more obsessed with paintings by the masters than I was with actually being James Bond. I think I like the movies better than the discipline."

I forced myself to smile. "Sadly it's not all martinis and baccarat tables. They make it look fun when in reality," I shrugged as I slowly paced around, inspecting the antiques, "it's quite tedious sometimes. Not just field work, but you know, meticulous paperwork. It's shocking how many criminals are caught because of paperwork rather than their primary crimes."

He nodded. "Agent Kincade, say it isn't so."

"Sadly."

"Well, I can still pretend. Please, have a seat."

To avoid sitting, I pointed to one of the carvings on his bookshelf. "Ah, this is stunning. Who is it by?"

His face lit up into a grin. "Yes, I picked that up on a trip to

China a few years ago. It's priceless, you know. Twelfth century."

My eyes went wide as I gently eased my hand back as if I might have touched it. "Maybe you should put that behind glass. To warn people off from touching it."

He shook his head. "No, no. I believe art is to be enjoyed. I didn't know you had an interest. You must come to the house next week then. I'm having a birthday celebration. I'm bringing all the pieces out of my vault."

My eyes went wide. "Oh that's incredibly generous. But you don't have to—"

He cut me off. "Nonsense. You clearly are curious. Come and see. Have some champagne."

I would not be coming for a party, but he didn't need to know that. "Well then, thank you."

"I'll make sure you get all the details. You clearly enjoy art."

"Sure, but you wouldn't want somebody accidentally touching something so priceless. It looks delicate, like I could have broken it."

"No dear, not at all. Have a seat."

But I still didn't, instead choosing to roam around the room, this time keeping my hands in my pockets for safety. When he noticed that I wasn't sitting, he came around his desk, shadowing me. Piece by piece, I asked him about the ones that looked mildly fascinating, like he might be able to speak about them for a moment. And then finally I settled on the photograph that I'd truly come to see. "Where was this taken?"

"Ah," he smiled. "The Aviator Sail in Milan, Italy, in my youth. That was a long, long time ago."

"You all certainly look like you were having fun."

"Yes, boys will be boys. And thankfully, we have all grown up since then."

"Right, you have." This time I let him lead me to a seat as he perched on his desk. "Now, Agent Kincade, what can I help you with?"

"Right. So, as you know, we've been investigating a string of art forgeries. Primarily jewels, but as it turns out, paintings as well. Now, having spoken to a few people, I understand that your family was affected by the art forgeries as well. Is that correct?"

His affable smile fell a little. "Ah, well..." I watched him in a split second make all those calculations about whether or not to admit the truth. "Yes, we were. But we prefer to keep it on the hush, honestly. Scandal. It's the bane of the aristocracy."

"I understand that, but at the very least, you could have talked to Interpol about it at the time. It would have helped us get a full picture of the crimes."

"There was no harm no foul. We have recovered our paintings."

"Yes, but I spoke to AJ Hale. My understanding from what she said was that some pieces of her collection were expertly forged. If they hadn't known to look, it could have been generations before they were discovered. But you say your pieces were recovered?"

He crossed his arms and watched me warily. "That's what I said."

"Right. I'm just curious. Did the thieves make the same mistake? Did they intend to replace your pieces and just run out of time? I'm just trying to establish a timeline."

His brow furrowed, and his general geniality started to crumble the more I probed into the events surrounding the forgeries.

Finally, he blurted, "Must we discuss this? It was such a long time ago."

"Well, it's only been three years, and we would very much like to catch the remaining forgers who are still at large. Miss

Hale told me there had been a discussion amongst those involved. She heard from word of mouth that perhaps one of your paintings wasn't authentic and that's what prompted her to look at her own collection."

He sniffed. "Miss Kincade, if you—"

"Agent, actually."

He frowned. "Excuse me?"

"Agent Kincade. You called me Miss."

That brought down a full frown. "Agent Kincade, you can speak to my lawyer about all of this. We have recovered the painting and prefer to just let bygones be bygones."

"Well, all the same, I would just like to complete the picture. Do you mind if I see the authentication chain and the verification on the piece? I want to be able to cross out any open loopholes. Dot every I, cross every T. I want to see if there were any similarities, any patterns."

He crossed his arms then. "I thought they'd caught the forgers."

"Yes, that's what I thought too. But we only caught three of them, and they were involved in the jewel side of the operation. According to one of the forgers, he was hardly the mastermind behind this, and he won't give up his accomplices. But he did say there were at least two others. Anything you can give us could help."

He frowned. "On your way out, Gemma, the maid, she'll get you the paperwork you need."

Ah, so I was being dismissed. He didn't want to talk about it. But why?

As I turned around slowly, I added the one question I'd been waiting to ask since I arrived. "Um, excuse me sir, one more question, which one of those young men is Henry Warlow?"

His sharp gaze narrowed. "Excuse me?"

"Well, you see his name has come up in our investigations. More relating to an older missing painting some thirty years ago, and I couldn't help but notice the same name was on your photograph. Perhaps it's just a coincidence; who knows how popular the name Henry Warlow is? But since he is in the photo with you, because that is you right there on the left, isn't it? Do you know which one he is?"

"That photo was only taken because we were at some regatta. I didn't know half the blokes in it."

"Right sir, but if you could try to remember, it could be very helpful. If we could connect that thirty-year-old case to the one three years ago in any way... It's a long shot, but it would be a great lead."

His voice pitched low as he pushed to his full height. "I told you, I didn't even know half their names. It was a wild summer. Lots of drinking. And it's been well over thirty years."

I nodded slowly and then slipped my card out and handed it to him. "Fair enough. If you can think of anything else, Lord Jameson, I would very much appreciate it." And then I let myself out.

Lord Jameson's response to the name Henry Warlow sent chills down my spine. The goosebumps on my arms hadn't gone down, and my heart still jackhammered in my chest. I knew East was listening. I knew they were just outside grounds. I was safe. But the fear still skittered over my nerves.

"You must be lost, little girl."

I whipped around to find Garreth Jameson lounging across from one of the doors I was trying to open. "Sorry, I was looking for the loo before I head out."

Garreth eyed me warily. "I know you from somewhere."

"Perhaps we met at your father's party several weeks ago."

"No, I don't think so. Have I fucked you before?"

Bile rose up in my throat. "No, you certainly haven't."

"Are you sure, because—" His eyes went wide as realization dawned. "You, you were at the bar with East Hale."

"Ah, so you do have two brains cells to rub together." His gaze narrowed, and I knew I shouldn't have said it, but I couldn't help myself. "Is there a problem?"

"You're sniffing around my house."

"I had an appointment with your father, and I was looking for the loo."

"Here's the thing. I don't believe you. Why are you in my house?"

He was standing close now. Too close. My heart hammered in my chest and I wondered just what kind of horror I'd gotten myself into.

———

East

AMELIA WAS out of the back of the van almost as quickly as I was. "I'll deal with it. You go back."

She scoffed. "You're kidding right? She's my partner."

"She's my girlfriend."

"What, like that gives you some kind of claim on her?"

"You're just going to get yourself hurt, Amelia."

I chased her across the lawn, around the side of the mansion where Nyla's beacon said that she was.

"Again, you seem to forget that we're not the little women who need saving."

"I didn't forget that, goddammit, since you're both reminding me every two seconds."

"Garreth Jameson is the literal devil, so I've got to get her out of there before anything happens to her."

"Or you could just fucking listen. Do you have a plan, Amelia? Or are you just going to run in half-cocked?"

She glowered at me as she tossed her braids over her shoulder. "I suppose it should be you running in half-cocked."

"Do you even know where you're going?"

She stopped and frowned. "That's beside the point."

I rolled my eyes and shook my head as I led the way to the side window of the small library Garreth had dragged her into.

"It's time to leave this to the professionals," she hissed.

"What, like you? You're hardly a professional. You realize you nearly got yourself and Nyla killed once, right?"

Her eyes went wide. "Me?"

"You and your little trip to see Bram Van Linsted, remember that?"

Amelia winced. "Okay, so I fucked up there. But come on, getting in bed with a thief?"

"If you could just stop for a moment, I can get in there to help her."

All of a sudden Nyla's com went silent. My heart squeezed and started a full gallop. "Fuck."

Amelia's voice was quiet and tense. "What do you need me to do?"

"How about you help me remove this sill? I put this alarm blocker in the last time I was here in case we needed it as an egress. I didn't realize we'd be back."

She helped me remove it. We unscrewed the sills frantically, and I was moving as quickly as I could even while my hands were shaking. The nip in the air didn't help. Good old England, forever rainy and not so much heat.

We worked silently together, moving as quickly as we could to avoid being seen because there would be no explanation for what the hell I was doing there. Amelia could maybe pull off that she was there as Nyla's partner, but she had a point. What exactly was I going to give as an excuse if they saw me in there? But still, I couldn't leave her in there.

Not with him. Not like that. Just as I deactivated the alarm, a voice rang out behind us.

"What in the world do you think you're doing?"

I whirled around at the sound of Nyla's voice. Amelia tackled her with a hug. "Jesus Christ, are you okay?"

"Yeah, I'm fine. Garreth Jameson is a handsy arsehole, but I'm fine. I repeat. What in the world are you two doing?"

I stepped forward and bracketed her face in my palms. Gently, I searched for any sign that he'd hurt her. "Are you okay?"

"You know me, I'm really good at evading." Her voice was choked and gravelly as I pulled her in. Just hearing her in distress, I'd stopped thinking. I'd stopped breathing. I was never fucking going to feel anything like that ever again.

"Yeah. Jameson is a pain in the arse. Like I said, handsy as fuck, but I handled him and let myself out through the terrace. What are you two doing?"

Amelia and I looked at each other. I was the one who said, "Rescuing you?"

Amelia laughed. "I told him you didn't need rescuing."

My jaw dropped. "Horseshit. You were out of the van faster than I was."

She waved her hand dismissively. "Hush, no one believes that."

Nyla laughed. "Oh my God, are you two friends now? This is awkward if you are."

I shook my head. "No, we're not friends. We just share a mutual concern for your safety."

Nyla laughed. "I'm so glad you're getting along now. My bestie and... what are you again?"

"The love of your life. Anyone else want to get out of here before we get caught?"

Nyla nodded. "Yeah, and fucking hell do we have a lot to talk about."

———

Nyla

THERE WAS something off about East. Since returning to the penthouse, he hadn't let me out of his sight. Even as he made love to me, there'd been something desperate, as if he'd been attempting to permanently mark me or was looking for affirmation of some kind.

And afterward, as he held me, it was in the way he wound himself around me like he meant to guard my whole body with his, and he wouldn't hold my gaze, as if he was guarding his emotions. At that point I'd been too tired, too sated and sleepy to dwell on it. I figured we'd talk in the morning.

While I drifted off into a dreamland of chasing bad guys and uncovering secrets, I was confused when my dreams took a turn into me chasing a thief, determined to bring him to justice. And when the thief dropped his mask, God, he was beautiful. He had dark hair, green eyes, and a jaw to make Henry Cavill jealous.

And in my dreams, East was very, very sexy. Instead of running like he should when I told him to freeze, he sauntered toward me, with the devil's own grin and sin in his eyes. And then right before me, he kneeled, lifting my skirt, his eyes challenging me the whole time as if daring me to make him stop. Or daring him to continue.

I did neither. And inch by inch, up slid my dress. Then he backed me up to a desk. We were in some kind of office building? Who knew, it was a dream, and I held onto it tightly. Because God, this was getting good.

He exposed my garters, and then he nipped at the inside of my thigh. I tried to close my thighs, but he wedged his shoulder between them and then commanded, "Wider."

A shiver ran up my spine, and before I knew it I was sitting on the edge of a desk, thighs spread, skirt up, and this thief, this bad guy, was kneeling between my thighs, staring between the junction of my legs like I was his favorite snack and he had skipped every meal for the last three weeks. And then he pulled my knickers aside, and with a long stroke from my pucker to my clit, he licked, moaning and then taking a deep inhale.

I shuddered and said, "Oh, my God."

Then he wound a hand in my knickers, drew back, and stared up at me, eyes once again challenging. I furrowed my brow and tried to meet his gaze at the same time that I tried to close my legs, but I was unsuccessful at both. And then with a grin, he tore my panties clean off.

Wow. Dream East was strong.

He dove back into his feast, licking, sucking, stroking. He slipped first one finger inside me, then another, his mouth closing around my clit and sucking.

My legs started to shake, and I choked out his name. "East. Oh, my God, East."

Dream East pulled back and grinned. "Ah, so you're awake."

I frowned. "What?"

Dream East continued to laugh. "Hmm, maybe you're not awake. Maybe this is all a dream."

My eyes drifted open, and I realized it wasn't a dream after all. East was between my legs. Happy as a clam, mouth over my clit, licking. Fingers inside me, stroking my G-spot. I threw my head back. "Oh, my God. I thought I was dreaming."

He chuckled low as he went back to work. "Oh, no. This is real. All real."

"Oh my God."

"Yes, you can call me God, Jesus, mostly I prefer my name though, East."

I choked out a laugh. "You are impossible. Honestly, does anyone have an ego bigger than yours?"

"And by ego, you mean..."

I giggled.

"Oh, someone's in a giggling mood. That's brilliant." He dove back in, giving me no quarter. There was no rest for the wicked. East Hale had plans for me, and he intended to make me scream.

A lot. And God, I couldn't help it. I slid my hand into his hair and tugged, trying to angle him just how I liked.

Then he did something unexpected. His tongue slid down my slick entrance, penetrating me gently. I lifted my hips, wanting more of him.

And then his tongue kept going.

His big hands held onto my arse, and he tucked in, his fingers bruising my skin.

I gasped. "East."

"Yeah, Nyla."

And he went right back to work. His thumb stroked over my clit, back and forth, back and forth, and my legs started to shake. "East, oh my God."

He laughed. "You can relax, Ny. I'm just trying to make you feel good."

"Oh my God. I—"

Usually, I was proud of my eloquence. I could find words for any situation. But in this one, where East Hale was determined to do every dirty, naughty thing to me, I had no words for that, all I had were my gasps and groans and *Oh, my God and please yes and more there.* That's all I had.

He was unrelenting, as if there was a lesson for me to learn in this particular form of exquisite punishment.

"East, please, I... Oh, my God."

He chuckled. "Now that I have you right where I want you, I need you to make me a promise."

My head thrashed on the pillow. "Anything. Whatever you want. You can have it."

"Wow, aren't you amenable."

"Yes, I am. What do you want?"

He laughed. "I would very much like you to not scare me anymore."

I frowned. "Why would I scare you?"

"You vanished on the Jameson estate tonight."

My brow furrowed. "I didn't vanish."

"Your coms went down, and we couldn't find you. I was scared. I didn't like it. I need you to not do it again." He went back to his feast.

"I-I'll try."

He stopped stroking my clit. "Promise me now."

"Oh, my God. You're the worst. This is torture."

"Yes, I seem to recall that you've done this to me before."

"That was different. I was mad at you."

"And I'm not mad at you?"

I lifted my head and met his gaze. No, that wasn't anger, that was... worry?

"No, you're not mad. You're worried."

"Amelia too."

"Yeah, I know that. Also, I told you two that I can manage it. You have to trust me."

"I do. But I was scared. So promise. No foolish risks, you hear me?"

I nodded. At that moment, I would've promised just about anything. "No risks. No foolish risks."

He sighed then. Putting his thumb back where I needed it.

"Is that a promise?"

I nodded wildly. "Yes, fine. No foolish risks. Now, would you just let me come?"

He dove back in, and my head spun.

He was an artist with his tongue. Idiot knew it too.

He kept bringing me to the edge, and then pulling back, and then back to the brink and pulling back again.

And when I started to let go, to bring nirvana to me, he stopped.

I lifted my head to complain, but then he sharply pulled me down to him, both hands on either side of my hips, and turned me over easily.

When I squeaked, he gave me a quick swat on my arse.

The sting burned. "Hey."

He gave me another one. A harder tap.

"East," I gasped.

"Promise me, never again."

"Fine. Yes, I promise. I promise."

One more tap that stung even more.

But before I could complain, his hands were on my hips, drawing me up to my knees and scooting me back.

And then his mouth was back on me again. "Oh, sweet Jesus."

I wasn't sure if I saw bliss, or nirvana, or whatever it was called, but I was in heaven.

When he slowed, I whimpered. "No, no, no, no. I'm so close."

"Are you now? I'm pretty sure you'll like this."

Then he moved behind me, teasing at my entrance with his

cock. His hand played up my back, applying gentle force and pushing my face further into the pillow.

I glanced over my shoulder at him, and a slow smile spread over his face.

And then he slid home.

His pace was unrelenting, and I could barely hold on.

When my hand started to sneak up my thigh to my hip, that earned me another swat on the arse. "Not until I say, love."

"You want to watch, don't you?"

"I do. But you scared me, and I'm still trying to remind myself that you're real and you're here and you're not hurt. So not until I say so."

As he made love to me, he leaned over, nipping my neck and shoulders, all the while keeping me hovering just on the precipice of bliss.

As his warm body encompassed mine, his hips pumping and thrusting and sliding home, I gasped. He was so deep inside me.

"East, oh my God, please, I just... Please, please, please let me."

He spread his hands down my back as he lifted himself to his knees, both hands gripping my hips tightly as he brought me back hard onto him. "Let you what?"

"Please, please, please let me come, please."

I would do anything. Say anything. Promise anything. And then something, a finger? His thumb? Teasing my back entrance, slowly circling, stroking, teasing.

He continued his onslaught. "What would you give me?"

"Anything. Oh, my God. Anything, please, East. I'm sorry I scared you. God, just let me come."

"Oh, we're getting there. But I was scared, and I couldn't tell you I was scared, and I didn't like it."

Thrust, thrust, stroke. His thumb and his dick were working in tandem, making it difficult for me to think at all.

"This is cruel and unusual, East."

"Well, I'll try anything to make my point."

When he slammed home again, I gasped, and I knew I was lost. I could feel it coming. The orgasm that was going to knock me the fuck out.

He could feel it too, and he delivered another smack to my arse. "Did I say you could go somewhere?"

"I can't help it."

He picked up his pace then, and all I could do was hold onto the sheets for the ride. And I could feel him withdraw from each stroke, as if he got bigger. Harder, more like steel as his thumb penetrated me. I gasped, lifting my head and throwing my hair back.

He wrapped a hand in my hair and tugged. "Fuck, I—" a Low growl tore out of his chest. "You, are in my soul, Nyla. Don't scare me anymore, okay?"

"Okay. I promise. I promise. I promise. Please." And finally, I flew apart with East's name on my lips. I flew apart and knew I was never going to be the same again.

With two more deep thrusts, he fell over me, and we lay there for several seconds, panting and shaking. Every muscle in my body felt little shocks like tiny zaps of electricity. Good God, he was going to kill me. That was it. That was how I died. From being dicked to death.

I laughed, thinking about what my new friends would say.

They would have such a howl. Nyla Kinkade, dicked to death.

As I drifted off to sleep and East rolled us to our sides so he wouldn't crush me, he nuzzled into my neck, and I thought it had a nice ring to it.

CHAPTER 24

Nyla

"Hello, this is Nyla."

"Hello, I'm looking to speak to Agent Nyla Kincade."

The voice sounded vaguely familiar.

I was in the midst of scouring files, Denning had me investigating the Grimwald Square incident, which meant he obviously didn't know I was investigating myself. But, while he was essentially looking for me, I was looking for a way to tie Jameson to a shooter, even if it was a professional.

"Agent Kincade, I see you don't remember me."

I frowned. "Who is this?"

"Ryder Stone."

The name... Why was it familiar? "I'm sorry. Have we met?"

"You have tea with a woman once, and she immediately forgets everything about you."

"Ryder Stone!" He was the fence East had introduced me to a few weeks earlier. I leaned back in my chair. "All right then, can you tell me what one of London's most notorious fences wants from me?"

"I don't want anything from you. Let's just say I've had a change of heart. I'm about to do you a favor."

I laugh. "Once a grass, always a grass, yeah?"

"Do you want the help or not?"

"Oh, I want the help. But I want to know what you expect in return."

"Let's just call it a favor." "

"I don't like owing favors."

"All right then, let's just call it restitution."

I laughed. "You believe in restitution? I thought you swore up and down when I met you a few weeks ago that you were on the straight and narrow."

"And I was. But things have changed."

"Ryder, if you are involved with your old crew again, now would be the time to come clean."

"I'm not. But you should know that if you keep pressing this issue about the art forgers, you're going to get hurt."

I sat forward, dropping my voice. "Did someone already try to hurt me, Ryder?"

There was a beat of silence. "Look, I'm not saying that. But there's a warehouse near the Flint Estate. It's supposed to be a car park. That's what it's zoned for. Proper permits and everything. It's got monthly payments coming from renters to make it look like someone's parking there."

"Okay, what's the address?" He rattled it off to me. "What am I going to find when I go there? Is this some sort of trap?"

"No, it's not a trap. I just don't like having my arm twisted."

The hairs on my arms stood at attention. "Is someone trying to hurt you? We can protect you." I was putting in my earpiece as I grabbed my jumper.

"No, I'm okay. But you'll find what you're looking for there."

"Ryder, why don't you come on down to the station, and we'll get a proper statement, okay?"

"Nah, mate. I'm not coming in."

"Ryder, do yourself a favor. Your partners... If they find out you're giving us the location, that's trouble for you. I can protect you. I can keep you safe."

"You just get down there. Find what you find and leave me out of it."

I had no idea what the hell I was going to find at the address, but I wasn't dumb enough to go by myself.

Yes, you are. Except if you go by yourself and find something, Denning's going to ream you a new asshole.

Besides, Amelia was my boss. So if there was something to be found, I'd rather she be the one to get the credit. Not Denning.

I marched swiftly down to her office. She looked up from her computer the moment I banged on her doorjamb. "What bee's flown into your knickers?"

"Ryder Stone. He's a fence I met when East was helping me on the forgery case. He just called me."

Amelia cocked her head. "A fence? Jesus."

"Well, an ex-fence. Except I'm not sure how ex he is. Anyway, the point is he just called me and gave me an address. Told me that I'd find something very fascinating there. Want to take a ride?"

She lifted her brow. "Nyla? There are procedures and policy."

"We don't know anything. Right now, we're following a lead. A fishing expedition. Any problems, we'll call for backup. But please, please, please, dear God, please, don't make me give this to Denning just yet."

Amelia sighed. "I don't want to be in the middle."

"Um, I'm sorry, but I got you in the divorce."

She shook her head. "Yeah, but he's got custody."

I sighed. "Look, this is on the up and up, okay? I just knew better than to go by myself."

Amelia sighed. "I suppose that's progress."

"Well, not exactly. I knew I'd be in a shitload of trouble if I went on my own. And you're my supervisor now, so I don't want to make you look bad."

She shook her head. "Jesus, Nyla."

"What? I'm getting better, I swear."

We were there within twenty minutes.

And sure enough, the sign outside said it was a car park. But as we went around the back, there were no cars, no attendants, not even a rolling door where people would drive their cars in.

There were no cars being stored there.

Amelia frowned. "Without a warrant, there's not much we can do."

"I know. Maybe we can just look inside a window."

"Ny?"

"What? We're here. Just give me a boost, would you?"

She stood there, hand on her hip, muttering curses at me. But sure enough, she followed me to the window and clasped two hands together, interlocking them and giving me a landing for my boot. I stepped up, praying all the while as she boosted me. And at the top, my prayers were answered.

Mostly I saw crates. Crates upon crates upon crates. But in the corner, there were several that were unboxed. Art. Paintings to be specific, and one or two of them looked familiar. That corner of the room had a long table, white linens placed on top. It was cleaner than the other parts of the warehouse. There were gloves on the table as well.

For handling precious items?

And what was that painting that was under glass? Holy shit.

Amelia lowered me down. "What do you see?"

Instead of answering her, I just locked my hands and hoisted her so she could see for herself. When she whistled quietly, I lowered her down, panting as I smiled. "Well, what's our next move boss?"

She grinned. "Now we call for back up. It looks like there is millions of dollars' worth of stolen art stored in there."

CHAPTER 25

Nyla

EAST DROPPED me off at work. He'd insisted on driving that ridiculously flashy sports car. "You recognize this is unnecessary right?"

"So you're saying I can't drop my girlfriend off at work?"

I flushed and shifted on my feet. "I wouldn't dare say such a thing."

He leaned against the door and pulled me into his arms, wrapping them around me. "And now, you're going to kiss me in front of everyone."

I laughed. "You don't have to do this you know."

"Oh, but I think I do. How else is everyone supposed to know that you're taken if I don't piss all over you."

I choked out a laugh. "That's disgusting. Please don't piss all over me."

He laughed. "Hey, don't knock my kink."

I couldn't help it. I snorted. "If that is your real kink, you know, I'm trying to be good, giving and game and all that. But I couldn't have you actually pissing on me. Not my kink. But maybe, warm tea would suffice?"

It was his turn to snort. "I saw that episode of *Sex and the City* too. We'll need to do a full re-watch together. You recognize if you tell anyone I watched that, I will deny it."

Before I knew what was happening, he pulled me in for a deep, lingering kiss. The kind of kiss that made my toes curl as his tongue licked into my mouth, as his fingertips pressed into the top of my arse, bringing me more firmly against his cock. The same cock that had woken me up twice in the middle of the night and first thing that morning.

East drove his hand into my hair, tousling the loose curls and kissing me like he owned me in front of the world.

When he released me, I was so dazed I couldn't even drag my eyes open. When I was finally able to force myself to blink, I stared at him. "What was that for?"

"You said you didn't like pissing. So that was the best I could do under the circumstances."

"Right. That was much better than pissing."

"I aim to please. Now, get your little sexy arse inside and Interpol things."

"You recognize that's not a verb, right?"

He smirked. "Sure it is."

"No, love, it's not," I said with a laugh.

"I could have sworn you said it was."

He was teasing me. East Hale was teasing me. And I loved every second of it.

Because you are whipped.

From the corner of my eye, I saw the stern, disapproving gaze of my ex at the massive glass doors leading into our section office.

I whirled around. "You did that on purpose."

He merely shrugged. "Yes, I did. I knew he was watching. Like I said, I've licked you. Now he knows you're mine."

I wanted to read him the riot act for being a chauvinist pig. But he *had* licked me, and I was his. So technically he was right. And he fucking knew it. "No more antics."

"I do not agree to that. I will continue to lick you. You're mine. He needs to know that there will be dire consequences if he puts his hands on what's mine."

"We will continue this conversation later."

I ignored Denning as I strolled in. Let him stare. I didn't give a fuck about him. He couldn't ruin my day.

How wrong I was. If I had been more self-centered, I would have thought it had to do with me. But it didn't. The case wasn't going well.

Make that cases.

Our original forgery case was stalling. And then there was the Grimwald Square incident. The team still didn't know it was us, and Denning was leading the hunt. And eventually, his search was going to lead to one place.

I could see the tension lines etched around his mouth. He wasn't giving us any breaks. None. All of us were hopping.

At my desk, I had the forgery files, thanks to a break in the case from Ryder Stone and the bust we made of some of the missing pieces of artwork.

I had another chance to prove myself. Not to my father, or to Denning, but to myself. I'd been so close before I'd been suspended. I just had to figure this out.

There were hundreds of pieces of art that had been recovered. The recovery team was going through each of them meticulously. Identifying who they belonged to through tedious research.

I didn't want Amelia to look bad, as she was now my boss. So I was going through every single piece of evidence twice, as if my life depended on it. Certainly, there was a part of me that couldn't let it go. I knew I could do this. I knew I could make this work, and that if I just stuck to it, I could solve this case.

For nearly three years, I'd been thwarted, trying to figure it out and determine where I'd gone wrong. I was nothing if not tenacious. So I planned to sit there and go through every single piece of the art catalog. Even when everyone else left to grab a bite and eventually, as most were headed home for the night to their loved ones. I'd already texted East to tell him I'd be working late. It still struck me as odd, calling his penthouse home. Not that I wasn't thrilled to be with him. It just felt too soon. Much too soon.

And as a result, I was constantly on edge, waiting for the other shoe to drop.

Which wasn't exactly fair to him. I knew that. And not that I was trying to be unfair, but honestly, the last experience had left me wounded.

It certainly didn't help that Hazel, Denning's fiancée, was quite insistent that we be friends. Every time she came to the section office, she made a point to come see me, suggesting that we get together for a drink or dinner again sometime. But I didn't want to be her friend. Nothing personal against her, I just didn't want to be. Why did she care so much?

She's crazy.

Or she was just honestly being nice. But if she was *so* nice, then why choose Denning? Because of all the nice guys out there in the world, she could have honestly done better.

I looked up at the clock and saw it was 8 p.m. My eyes were tired and felt like someone had blasted sawdust into them. Ugh, maybe it was time to give up for the night. I could finish in the morning. But we were close. I could feel it. I could sense—

I stopped at a photo.

Now wait just a minute, that painting of a woman, the ballerina with her full white tutu flared out. She was on pointe, arching her back. It was a Wilson Collins. I had seen that before. But where? My brain offered no clues, no assistance, no quick memory. I was toast. I kept it out of the pile and put a little Post-it on it with a note. *Where have you seen this?*

It was quite a famous painting. Maybe I had seen it in some gallery. It was certainly valuable. It was a ten-million-dollar painting.

Maybe it was displayed somewhere at the Tate?

Maybe that's where I'd seen it. But still, my brain wouldn't let it go. Wouldn't release that string that I kept tugging on, no matter how hard I pulled. Before I could even grab my coat off of the hook behind me, there was a knock at the door. I glanced around and my stomach knotted up. "Hello, Denning, how can I help you, guv?"

I forced levity into my voice and tried to release the sarcasm. Look at me. Team player.

"How is it going?"

"You know, it's good to be back. Just heading home."

"I noticed that the rest of your team has already gone."

"Well, yes, I think they headed to the pub for a pint some time ago. I declined."

He sighed and crossed his arms. "I don't think we'll be able to work together."

Damn it.

"Are you suspending me again?"

He shook his head. "I'm not sure what to do with you. You should consider a transfer."

"Me? I'm not the one who thinks we can't work together. Working for Amelia has been great, actually."

He sighed. "This is an old branch. You and I, we don't work well."

"That's true. But again, I won't be looking for a transfer. You can choose to transfer me if you like, but given my seniority and the fact that I'm your only representative in this office from MI5, you'll need a replacement."

He narrowed his gaze at me. "Why do you insist on making everything difficult?"

I sighed. "Denning, I'm not trying to make everything difficult. I just want to do my job and do it well. I'm telling you, that's the only reason I'm back. You might not believe me. Hell, you might believe me and just not care. I'm planning to stay out of your way if you can stay out of mine. We're adults. We should be able to make this happen."

He scowled at me. "No one wants you here."

The stab at the center of my chest nearly toppled me, but I stayed on my feet. I didn't waiver, just leveled my gaze at him. "They will have to deal with me. I have no intention of leaving."

He straightened his shoulders. "Are you threatening me?"

"No, Denning, I'm not. And the moment you walked in here, I pressed record on my phone so you can't later say that I did."

His jaw tightened. "You're such a pain in the arse."

"Possibly. Oh, by the way, Hazel seems lovely. She was so nice. Insisted that it might be good for me to work here. Even if you don't necessarily agree."

"Why the fuck would she say that?"

"I don't know. She's not *my* girlfriend. But she seems to want to be my friend."

"You stay away from Hazel." He jabbed a finger in the air toward me.

"Sure. I'm not inclined to be her friend anyway. I feel like she makes poor judgment calls." I was deliberate to not say anything specific, in case I needed to use the recording later.

"Don't you have a lead to chase? I'd rather not see your face."

"Of course, *guv*. Off I go."

He marched out ahead of me. Before I left, I paused in front of the photo one more time. And suddenly, I remembered where I had seen it. In Lord Jameson's house. That was the very same painting in his ballroom. Holy shit. This was the connection I'd been looking for. And I needed to tell East straightaway.

———

East

THAT NIGHT my gaze was trained on Nyla's arse as she bent over my desk, but it wasn't for the reasons I wanted.

Oh no. She was vibrating with excitement about some work thing. "What's this?" I asked.

Since she'd been working late, I'd sat in the office with Ben, talking about one of our Caribbean properties. "Look at it."

Ben leaned over too. "Ah, it's a beautiful painting. It's a Wilson Collins, right?"

She nodded excitedly. She looked like she was about to burst at the seams from her excitement.

"Okay, babe, you have to tell us what's going on. Because I don't think either one of us gets it."

"Okay, It's a Wilson Collins. But that's not the important fact. Nor is it important that it was appraised at a value of ten million dollars before it was stolen."

Ben whistled low. "Well, okay, a ten-million-dollar painting, great. I'm with you so far."

She gave him an exasperated sigh. "Look at it. Don't you recognize it?"

Ben and I glanced down at the painting. It did seem somewhat familiar, but I didn't know why I should know it. It wasn't one of ours from the family collection. It wasn't even the du Mont style. Wilson was too frenetic a painter. His paint was too close to the surface and didn't really fit into our style, so I'd never really tried to pick one up. Still though, it was gorgeous. "Help us out here."

She sighed. "Oh my God, where do you think the last place I saw this painting was?"

Ben shrugged. "Nyla, just tell us."

She pouted. "You're ruining my excitement."

He nodded. "I get that. But just tell us. It would make your life a lot easier."

"I saw this at the Jameson estate."

I sat up straighter just as Ben leaned forward, and we knocked heads. "Ow."

"Son of a bitch," he muttered, rubbing a hand through his hair.

We both rubbed our foreheads and she stood staring at us. "Oh my God, and the fate of the free world is in your hands."

Ben shook his head. "It was his fault."

I merely rolled my eyes at him. "Are you sure this is in the Jameson ballroom?"

"Without a doubt. I remember it from the charity fundraiser."

"Okay, so if it's in Lord Jameson's ballroom, why do you have a file on it?"

"Because when Ryder called and told us about the warehouse where all those stolen paintings were stored, guess what was recovered from it?"

Now I understood. "You're telling me this Wilson Collins was in the recovered art?"

"Yep. And I'm pretty sure, when they authenticate it, either everything in there will prove to be a forgery, or everything in there will prove to be a real thing, which means that Jameson's got a forgery, proudly displaying it. But maybe he thinks it's the real thing. I need those authentication results back."

"Fucking aye."

Ben scrubbed a hand over his face. "But it doesn't make sense for Jameson to be involved in that."

"Unless he *knows* it's a forgery. Maybe the Jamesons are hard up for money, and they're selling off their assets."

"Or," Ben theorized, "they reported it missing or stolen and got the insurance money. Which is a tidy sum, for sure."

"Okay, so, how do we find out?"

She started pacing. I knew this pace. She was excited. She was willing and ready to charge in. I'd seen this Nyla. *This* Nyla also worried me, because if this was true, and she'd seen that painting at Jameson's, then she was in danger and I had to protect her.

She's not yours to protect.

I knew she wouldn't appreciate it. And it wasn't that I didn't believe she was strong. Hell, it was one of the sexiest things about her. But I still wanted to keep her safe. I loved her. I knew what this feeling was. I'd spent weeks trying to avoid them. "Okay, I hear you. But remember, one step at a time. Did you call Amelia?"

She winced. "No, I'll call her now. I mostly got excited, so I came here to tell you first, because I know that you are working on taking Garreth Jameson down."

Ben nodded. "I'm not sure how to use this yet, but thanks for letting us know."

"Why aren't you two more excited? We have him."

"We don't have anything yet. You know this Nyla."

"But come on, he has the same painting, so he is up to something."

Ben chimed in. "The problem is, we don't know what he's up to exactly. And we can't prove anything."

"No, I can't prove anything. Correct me if I'm wrong, but don't you need a lot less burden of proof?"

"You're trying to use this to help us against the Elite? Ny, don't get involved. We have this. We will find something to blackmail him with. We will find what we need. Have faith."

"I have a hundred percent faith in you. But have faith in me too. I can help. This bastard was standing there just smiling at me like I was some kind of nuisance. And all along, he's running around with that forgery in his house. Or, hey, I'm willing to entertain the idea that he doesn't know."

"How could he not? That's literally their whole business."

"And what happens to his business if he has forgeries in his house? It's one of the cornerstones of who they are. Who's going to trust them again? He knows something. You just let me question him again."

East chuckled wryly. "I'm pretty sure Amelia's going to say no to that."

"No, she won't. Why don't you want me to do this?"

"I don't want you to do this because it's dangerous. Garreth Jameson is dangerous, and so is his father. I care about you too much. I know you can do this, but let's take it easy here. Let's wait until the authentication results are in."

She glanced back and forth between me and Ben. "You think I'm crazy? Jesus, you have the exact same look that Denning does."

The fury simmered to life, and I locked my jaw as I turned around. "Stop talking, right the hell now."

She opened her mouth and it looked like she was not going to heed my warning. It looked like she was going to say something else. But then, it was as if she caught herself. "You know that's not what I meant."

"You still said it."

Ben shifted on his feet uncomfortably. "Um, if you lot are going to have a fight, can you tell me now so I won't have to stand here awkwardly experiencing it for myself?"

We both ignored him. "Ny, how could you say that to me?"

"You know that's not what I meant. Come on. You are trying to bench me."

"I'm just telling you to be more cautious. There's got to be another way to do this other than charging right into the lion's den. That's all."

"I'm sure there is, but God, I pulled this great lead, and all you want to do is sit on it."

"I'm not sitting on it; I'm just trying to keep us all safe."

"One of these days, East Hale, you're going to realize that I never asked you to keep me safe."

"You're so bloody impetuous. It's no wonder you were benched. You need to fucking look before you jump." The moment the words were out, I knew they were the wrong ones. I reached for her, and she pulled away. "Ny—"

"No," she said as she packed her files. "I'm leaving."

She might not like it, but I was right. Unfortunately, I'd said the one thing guaranteed to get her hackles up. She was going to make me pay for it later.

CHAPTER 26

East

I KNEW there was no way she'd gone back to the penthouse. She was far too furious. So on the drive between the office and Nyla's townhouse, I tried to figure out what to say to her.

I'd worked myself up a little after she stormed out. I worked myself up even more when she didn't answer her bloody door. But finally, Amelia did. "Give it a rest, mate, she's not here."

"Where is she?" I called past her. "Nyla. Let's talk about this."

She laughed. "She's at my place. Now, I know you know where that is, and you can get there easily and quickly. But note that she sent me here so that maybe I could talk some sense into you before you went charging after her."

I whirled around, more than determined to get to Nyla. Amelia was a poor substitute.

But Amelia was stronger than she looked. She grabbed my arm, and when I went to loosen it, she grabbed me with her other hand and cuffed me to her. "What the fuck?"

She jangled our arms. "I'm keeping you from doing something you'll regret."

"Not my kink, love."

She shook her head. "I have a feeling I don't want to know."

"You have to uncuff me. Nyla is on the road to doing something colossally stupid. When she said she was going to bring in the most wanted thief in the world, I said sure, fine babe. You do you. Woman power and all that. When she said she was going after art forgers, I said sure, great, even though I was more than a little concerned that they were the same ones who attacked us in Monaco. But, oh no, when she's going after someone who I know to be personally dangerous, I have to stop her. I know her job is important. I know she wants to help us. But I also know what's going to keep her safe. Chasing after the Jamesons, she has to leave that to me."

Amelia shrugged and then stepped into the living room, forcing me to go with her.

"You're serious about this?"

She shrugged. "Yes. Because you're being a twat."

"I am not. What the fuck?"

"Look, I know you care about her. I can see how much she cares about you. The two of you together, it's palpable. And the fact that you would do anything to take care of her, and I mean *anything*, is commendable. I watched you basically jump into enemy hands, just to get her back safely. I know this, but you have to realize that she's not a damsel in distress. I know you need someone to rescue, and Nyla needs rescuing, for sure. *Just not from this.*"

I frowned at her. "What the hell are you talking about?"

"My God, how can someone so pretty and seemingly so smart not get it?"

"I don't know what you're on about."

"Look, Nyla's different. She's this force of nature. You think that nothing can touch her. You think that she walks on water."

"And?"

"There's this other part of her that is just begging for love. A part of her that is begging to be accepted for who she is. And every time you try and stop her from that, every time you try and control her, every time you try to keep her from doing what she *needs* to do, all you're doing is becoming just like every other man in her life who has hurt her."

"I'm not like Denning." My voice was a low warning growl.

"I know that. Relax, handsome. You should know, it's not just Denning; it's her father too. All she's ever wanted is to be like him and to make him proud. She knows that if he had a choice, that maybe he wouldn't have had her."

"That's ridiculous. He's her father."

"He loves her, in his way. But she overheard him and her mother talking one day. It was after Nyla had chased down some bully at school. She made a citizen's arrest, you see."

I blinked in surprise. "Are you kidding me?"

"No. They were living in the States then, and this bully had been harassing kids, stealing money from them, that sort of thing. Nyla cornered him. Full on using every bit of martial arts training she had, she cornered the bully in the gym. She held him there until the principal came for him. Then when the principal came, there was trouble all around. The bully claimed Nyla had kicked him and threatened his balls. Nyla, of course, didn't want to pretend that she didn't know anything about it. The parents were called and all that. But what was really funny was that she made the arrest on the grounds that he'd stolen money from other kids, and he had. He was stacked full of evidence in his pockets. One of the kids even wrote his name on one of the dollar bills he'd taken. So the kid got in trouble. And Nyla was going to get justice. Which was what she wanted. She didn't really care what happened to her. So you see, there is this part of Nyla that is so desperate to follow the rules, to make people proud of her. But then, at the core of it, she's a rebel. So as soon as the bully was handed his arse and his parents were called, when no one was looking, she kicked him in the nuts."

I coughed. "Excuse me?"

"Even though he was about to get justice, Nyla has this streak in her that's rebellious, impulsive, a little bit dangerous to herself and others. She still had to see it being done her way, or it wasn't good enough. And her father, when he found out, he was horrified. He was so angry. Went on and on to her mother, saying if he had to do it over again, he didn't know if he'd make the same decision."

I frowned. "He said that?"

"Yeah. Where she could hear. And you know, I think many a parent has probably felt like that with a child who's a particular handful. But she knew that he would have made different choices because he doubled down with her mother and said, 'I know what I said. She's mine, but sometimes I rethink that choice every single day.' Her mother, of course, was horrified. And Nyla, she took on the burden of his words. So she tries even harder to be just like him, but the thing is, she's not. She is rebellious. There's a part of her that never wants to conform. And there's a part of her that thinks the right thing doesn't always come by following the rules."

"That's fucked up."

"Her father doesn't know she heard this. He couldn't know the impact his words would have on her. But it shaped her. And every rejection he gives her as an adult just reinforces what he said a long time ago. That she's unlovable, that she's difficult, that he would have made a different choice had he known. And so she tries so hard. She just wants to get this right. She wants to be the one to bring in Theroux and to take down Jameson. She knows that it's your thing. Knows that you and your mates have a claim on that. She knows that. She's not dumb. But man, she wants to be the one."

"She's risking too much. I can't be worth it."

"She wants to finally be able to say, 'Look, I did it. I am worthy of your love.' Granted, she's a grown up. But even though she's done all the right things and said all the right things, there will be something hollow about it. She knows, but she wants it anyway."

I sighed. I was forced to plop down on the couch next to Amelia. The clanking sound of the cuffs rang hollow in my ears. "Jesus Christ, I could kill him for that."

"Yeah, me too. Trust me, every time I see him around the office, I really do have the urge to hit him."

"Why go and work for him though?"

"Because Nyla is not self-aware enough to know that she's really torturing herself. In some way, she's still a little girl who wants to make her father proud. And her ex-boyfriend. And her current boyfriend. She wants these people to be proud of her, to acknowledge that she's amazing. The problem is she's always picked knobs who didn't acknowledge how brilliant she is."

"Are you kidding? I always think she's the one who walks on water."

"Then tell her that. Know who she is and *stop trying to fix her*, or change her, or protect her. Stand by her. I know that's hard for you. You probably have some traumatic thing in your background too, something that makes you concerned about safety and protocols and all that good shit."

I opened my mouth to say something, but she interrupted me. "But I don't care. Nyla is my best mate. We had a fight, a pretty major one, a couple of weeks ago, and I said some things that I can't take back, some things I shouldn't take back. And the one thing I realized in all of it is that Nyla, at the core of it, just wants to be loved. And if you fuck with her, I will fuck with you. You might be all powerful and rich, but I swear to God, I will make your life a living hell."

"Noted."

"Excellent. Now, if I unchain you, are you going to behave?"

She dangled the keys. I considered lunging for them, but something told me Amelia would toss them out of the window if I fucked up.

"Yes, I will behave."

"Now, I'm going to actually sit here for another thirty minutes, and you can go to my flat. Please, I'm going to ask that you two don't shag in my bed. I really like my bed. If you must shag, do it on the floor, so I don't have to sanitize any of the furniture."

"Who says we're going to shag?"

She coughed a laugh. "Yeah, okay."

I returned her laugh. "Fair enough."

"Don't hurt her. I swear to God, if you do..."

"Yeah, I know. You already told me. Step off my balls, I get it. I fucked up. Let me fix it."

And then she unlocked the cuffs.

———

East

When I found Nyla, she wasn't alone.

Livy was with her at Amelia's.

Amelia's furniture was oddly boho chic. Not what I pictured for her. Amelia gave a perfunctory no-nonsense vibe in person, but her whole flat was reclaimed wood and colorful vintage items. The overall result was shabby chic but done expertly. Maybe she'd hired a designer?

Livy took one look at me and shook her head. "You fucked up, huh?"

I sighed. "Are you the bodyguard?"

Livy shook her head. "No. Pretty sure Nyla doesn't need one."

I winced at that. "Fine. I deserve that."

Nyla came out of the back room. "Hey, Liv, I—?" Her voice cut off, and she sighed when she saw me. "I'm surprised Amelia was able to wait that long."

"Well, she had me shackled."

"Stop being so melodramatic. You've made your feelings perfectly clear."

Bugger. "Look, I messed up. And I promise it's something that will happen again and again and again. I shouldn't have any expectations that you'll forgive me, but if I could just talk to you for a minute, I would appreciate it."

When I turned around, Livy already had her phone out. "Is it still raining out there?"

Nyla frowned. "Liv, where are we going to have dinner?"

"Sorry. Something came up."

I grinned down at Olivia. "Looking out for me?"

She rolled her eyes. "Someone has to. When my husband texted me with a 911, I knew you'd done something colossally stupid."

"Wow, Ben's a serious mate, isn't he?"

"You're lucky he loves you. Now fix this."

And then she was gone, leaving me alone with Nyla to either love each other or slaughter each other. Nyla crossed her arms over her amazing tits, hiding them from my view. Which was probably for the best because otherwise, I'd be distracted. "Before I say anything else, first let me say I'm sorry."

"East, I don't—"

"No, I will keep saying it again and again. It's not your

ability I question. It's just that there are a lot of psychos out there, and all I want to do is take care of you and keep you safe. The idea that my chance to do that could be taken away scares me. Do you understand how much?"

"Yes, I do, but—"

"I was wrong. You were right. I need to trust in you, but I hold on so tightly to my control because it's the only way I can feel whole again. After not being able to protect my sister all those years ago, I go a little overboard. I just want to take care of you."

"East, I love that you worry about me so much, but could you maybe try to understand that I just want to stand next to you, not behind you?"

"Trust me when I say I want you standing next to me too. I just have a shit way of showing it."

"So are you going to let me protect you as much as you protect me?"

I frowned at that. "Well, yeah. I have to admit that I'm deadly afraid of spiders."

Nyla just rolled her eyes at that.

I shuddered. "They're the worst. Deadly little beasts."

She laughed. "I'm serious."

"You don't seem to understand. You have already changed the course of my entire life. I have never felt like this before. Learning to accommodate someone else, learning to keep someone safe, protect them, and still let them be *them*, is taking some getting used to. But I can figure it out. I'm pretty smart."

"Yeah, humble too."

I took her hands. "Forgive me. I was an idiot, and I shouldn't have said those things."

"You were right. I am impetuous. And it probably did cost me my job."

I cradled her cheeks in my palms. "No. The way you are is

why you're so damn good at your job. Your father and Denning don't see that yet, but they will one day, and you'll already be gone. You don't need them. You don't need to make them happy or work so hard for their approval."

"I don't need your approval either."

"I know. But you have it. I'm sorry. I never want you to doubt yourself. Who you are is exactly perfect and enough, okay?"

Her lashes fluttered as she tried to blink away the tears. "Yeah, I know."

"And I'm an idiot for even suggesting that you can't take care of yourself, because you can. I'm just terrified. My control over this situation's not getting any better. And it makes me worried. But I trust you. As long as you trust me, I trust you."

I could feel the tension ebbing from her shoulders. "I trust you."

"Good." I leaned forward and slid my lips over hers. "Now, how about you let me apologize properly for being a world-class wanker."

"I am eager to see how well you apologize Mr. Hale."

———

Nyla

I HUSTLED INTO THE BUILDING. I was late. Really, really late.

It wasn't my fault, though. I put my tardiness squarely on East. He had been distracting me.

It was the only explanation, because goddammit, I was late.

I had gotten the *Where the fuck are you?* text fifteen minutes ago and started hustling to get to work. After taking the stairs two at a time, wincing with each one because East had gotten inventive when he woke me up and I was sore in places I wasn't even sure I could be sore in.

But dear God, it had been good. So good that, well, now I was late.

Just move your ass.

At the top of the stairs, I made a left, chucking off my coat and slinging it over my shoulder as I swiped my badge. I tried to tuck my hair behind my ears, knowing I probably looked freshly fucked because I hadn't had time to wash it. I'd just spritzed it with some conditioner and water and finger-combed it, enhancing my natural curls.

As I was leaving the penthouse, East had given me that look that said he was ready to drag me back to bed again. His voice when he saw my hair had gone all low and gravelly. "I've never seen your hair like that before."

"I've never been this late before. Usually, I wash it and blow it dry."

"I like it like this. In fact, maybe you could come back to—"

I'd laughed, and then locked myself in the loo so I could put my clothes on.

And somehow, I was *still* late.

Okay, it was because I had allowed him to give me the kind of kiss that curled my toes, and then we'd spent a full minute dry shagging against the door as he tried to fumble my pants open, because I didn't want to leave him any more than he wanted to leave me.

Fucking hell. This was all his fault.

Sure it is.

When I finally made it to the conference room, it was standing room only, and I frowned. Amelia was in the back, and I wove through a couple of people before tapping her on the shoulder. "Thanks for the heads-up."

She leaned back, arms crossed sternly, focusing on Denning as he and my father gave the address to the team.

"You're welcome. What's gotten into you? A little billionaire?"

I coughed to cover my laugh. "A *very big billionaire* actually."

Amelia lifted a brow and turned her head slightly to face me before looking me up and down. "Oh, you don't say. Go, East."

We both had to stifle our giggles then. "What's going on?"

"You didn't miss much. They've been going on about how they need all hands on deck for this new case, But I don't know what it is."

I frowned.

Finally, my father got to the point and switched the projector to a photo of Lord Walter Jameson.

I pinched Amelia's elbow, and she nodded because she couldn't turn around. She had to stay focused.

"We received a call from Lord Jameson. He has good reason to believe that Francois Theroux is going to rob him during his birthday celebration this weekend."

My breath caught. No. There was no way. If that was what Theroux's plan was, he would have called. He would have said something.

Amelia pinched me back.

My father continued up front. "So, we will be going with teams prepared to defend against Theroux and we are planning to capture him. Alive. Have I made myself clear?"

Someone in the front that I couldn't see raised a hand and was called on. "So we're not going with a tactical team?"

My father sighed. "We are, but they've been instructed. Theroux is dangerous, but we are going to do everything in our power to preserve human life. I want him alive. Does everyone understand?"

Everyone murmured their agreement, and the pit of my stomach fell. No. This was not how it was supposed to go. Theroux was mine. Why did Jameson think Theroux was coming for him?

My phone buzzed in my hand, and I glanced down.

Amelia: *After your adventure, Jameson might know what we're up to.*

Nyla: *Fuck.*

Amelia: *Exactly.*

Garreth must have told him that I was nosing around after our interview. Why else call Interpol? I'd tipped my hand. I had fucked up. Mentioning Henry Warlow's name had been a mistake. And now, Jameson was going to thwart our plans.

CHAPTER 27

East

FOR ONCE, Livy, the one who was usually up for anything if it involved keeping Ben safe, stared at us like we had lost our minds. "So what you're telling me is that we are going to go to a party, where your sworn enemy has invited us, and then while we're there, we are going to steal things?"

"Um, how do I explain? Okay, the last time I broke in there, I took files off the computer. We thought that was enough, but we weren't looking for Henry Warlow then. Now that we are, we need to tap into some devices that aren't readily accessible. I've done some research on the property and discovered he's had a server room installed that controls the access to his vaults. I need to be on-site to actually hack into those servers. It's going to take some time."

Livy nodded. "Uh-huh." She then cast a glance at Nyla. "And you're telling us that Lord Jameson has now called for the assistance of Interpol? He's convinced that Francois Theroux is coming for his art, and he would very much like Interpol to investigate?"

I glanced at Nyla, and she met my gaze. Something hot and instant flared in my gut, and she gave a minute shiver before answering. "Right. Something like that. He claims to have received a tip that one of his art pieces is going to be stolen. So, joy of joys, he's also inviting Interpol to that very same party to watch his assets and flush out Theroux."

"So, what you're saying," Livy continued, "is that Jameson knows something is up and that we're coming for him. And he plans to stop us with Interpol. Am I missing something?"

I ran my hands through my hair. "Ben, you got anything to add?" I asked my mate.

He was giving his wife-to-be a sheepish grin. "No, love, you have it all, really."

Livy glanced around the room. "And you're telling me that this seems normal to all of you? That this constant running and fighting is perfectly acceptable."

I winced. "Well, it does keep life entertaining."

Nyla looked at me and shook her head. "Now is not the time."

I laughed. "Okay, fine. It's not ideal."

And then Livy started to laugh. "Not ideal. Great. Of course. We're going to die."

Ben shook his head. "We're not going to die. Everything is going to be okay."

She gave him an exasperated look. "It is not going to be okay. At all. I don't think you know the definition of okay."

Amelia smiled. "Look, I get it. Interpol has probably been up your arse for a while now, and not in a fun kind of way."

Lucas coughed.

Bridge grinned widely. "I'm starting to like her."

Amelia ignored him. "But we have an advantage. I'll be helping to run Interpol's play from the sidelines. I'll know what's going to happen and *when* it's going to happen. My job is only slightly more difficult because I have to make it look like I'm cooperating. Which, in some ways, I will be, while also trying to keep you guys from getting discovered. Or shot. Rest assured that you'll know ahead of time where Interpol agents will be to the letter. But the key is, you *have* to get out when I say it's time to go. No lollygagging, no vengeance schemes." She slid her gaze to me.

I put my hands up. "Oh come on, I'm not the vengeful one." Ben and Bridge both lifted their brows at me. "Oh, thanks a lot, mates."

Drew laughed. "Well, you know she has a point."

I glared at him. "You keep your mouth shut."

Livy laughed again. Sort of a hysterical laughter, actually. "Oh my God, we really are all going to die."

I shook my head. "No, we're not going to die. It's just a little complicated right now."

Nyla stepped to the plate then. "Okay, so you'll all attend the party as guests. Lucas and Bryna, that means you too, but the key is, you two play your parts as royals. We don't need the kind of headache we'd have if someone discovered you were in on this plan."

Lucas laughed. "Yeah, yeah, I hear you."

Nyla's gaze flickered to me. "He's not going to listen, is he?"

I shook my head. "Nope. Chances are he's going to rob everyone in there blind without telling us how he's doing it, and then he'll walk away with a cool mint."

Lucas grinned. "I only steal from the rich, you know. Well, actually, only from rich assholes."

Nyla shook her head. "Oh my God, okay. So you're going to attend the party, and somehow we have to create a distraction. Lucas, if you're the one with the deft hands, you need to either fire an alarm, cause a blackout, something."

He nodded. "I can cause a blackout."

Bryna chirped up then. "Well, that might not be so easy. Looking at East's schematics, it appears the estate has generators. The power will probably come back on quickly because he wants to keep the information he has private."

Nyla nodded. "Right. Then I think our best bet is for Amelia and I to go in early as if Interpol has sent us and get access to the vault that he is most concerned about. East, if you can provide directions that will get us to that server, we will get you the technical information you need. I think that's ideal. And then we'll hand it off to you, and you can use it at the party to get in."

I grinned at her. "Have I told you lately that you're incredible?"

She laughed. "Tell me that when we're not all in jail, yeah?"

Bridge started to gag. "God, are you two done yet?"

Nyla ignored him. "All right, so during the party, East knows what he's supposed to do. Bridge and Ben, you'll act as interference. We have to keep Garreth and his father distracted. But, East, you'll need backup. Amelia and I won't be at the party. Interpol's involvement will be strictly outside the house during the party unless a credible threat is detected, and if I turn up as your date, I'm suspect."

Emma piped up. "This is my chance to shine."

Bridge frowned at that. "And what would you be doing?"

"I'll be the bait."

Bridge's brows furrowed. "What do you mean, bait?"

"What I mean is, I'll be there to keep Garreth occupied."

Bridge's brows only dropped further. "Explain."

I jumped in to her rescue. "Bridge, we know you have a tendency to feel protective toward Emma, but this is for the best."

He only continued to frown. "For whose best?"

Emma cut me off. "Look, you can play caveman all you

want, but let's try and remember that I'm not yours to control. I can do whatever I like. And even though you don't like it, I'm part of the team, so that's the deal."

Bridge glared at me. "Are you fucking kidding me? You know what he's capable of."

I nodded slowly. "Yes, I do know what he's capable of. I also know Emma's pretty capable herself. She's a black belt in jiu-jitsu. She can handle a handsy arsehole on any day."

"You recognize he's capable of killing her, right?"

Ben sat forward. "This is what's happening Bridge. We don't have time to argue with you about it."

I watched as his jaw ticked. "Fucking hell. Fine, since it's all been decided."

Nyla watched us back and forth. "Right. I'm so glad we're in agreement. So maybe now is the time to remind everyone what we've already said. No cowboy antics. No fucking around. No doing things that we don't need to do right now. Get in, get into the server, get the information we need, and pull out."

The love of my life looked pointedly at me, and I threw up my hands. "One time I go off-book, and you never let me live it down."

Everyone laughed. "One time?"

I grumbled. "Fine."

They had a point. Sometimes I was the one who strayed from the playbook, but it was always to ensure the safety of everyone around me. "Fine, I won't go off-book."

Nyla continued. "I mean it. That goes for you too, Bridge. If Emma seems like she's in danger, know that she's not. Besides, Bryna will be there, and she can help out if needed."

Bryna smiled and pulled out what looked like a tube of lipstick but was really a switchblade. "I gave Emma one of these as a present."

Bridge's brows lifted. "Okay, Lucas. I see you have your hands full."

Lucas laughed. "Yup, I sure do. She's my future wife."

Bryna grinned. "One hundred percent."

Emma crossed her arms. "All right with you now, Dad? I can tag along on this little adventure?"

Bridge swore under his breath. "I swear to God, I will tan your behind so fast."

With a chuckle, Nyla stepped forward. "Hey, what you two get up to in your spare time is nobody else's business. But everyone remember... At the party, Amelia and I will be outside, and no matter what, from the moment you step foot in there, we'll be watching and have your back."

We all nodded. Our lives were on the line, and everything relied on our plan going off without a hitch. But I trusted this whole team with my life. I knew that by the end of this we were going to be the last ones standing or we were going to be in jail. And I was definitely too cute for jail.

———

Nyla

MY PALMS WERE SWEATING. Everything hinged on this going exactly right.

As Amelia and I were led into the Jameson mansion, she gave me a tight, reassuring smile and a nod. Unfortunately, we had four of our other team members tagging along as well. Because of who Lord Jameson was, Interpol was making a show, which meant lots of faces. But Amelia had it handled. "Okay, Kyle and Jacinda, I want you going over security footage. Lord Jameson, if you can let your security team know to cooperate with them, that would be helpful."

"Why do you need to look at security footage? Nothing has happened yet."

"Well, yes, but history shows us that people don't usually approach a place cold. They prefer to work a place that they're at least somewhat familiar with. So we want to see if anyone who looked like maintenance men, meter readers, electricians, or any workmen whatsoever have been on the property recently."

"But I wasn't warned of this in advance. I don't need anyone going through my security footage."

Amelia could have backed down, but she wasn't buying his shit. "Sir, if you want us to do our job to the fullest, it's imperative. So it's your call. If you don't agree, we can go now and return when there's been an actual crime reported."

Finally, he nodded. "Fine."

"Thank you, sir." She gave Tony and Ayalla their marching orders as well and instructed them to check all the exterior access points of the estate. Then she turned back to Lord Jameson. "Agent Kincade and I will check the vaults with your most valuable pieces just to make sure they're a hundred percent secure."

He nodded, and I wondered why he wasn't more concerned with us wanting to see his vaults.

Because you are trustworthy. After all, you are Interpol.

That was true. We were the trustworthy ones, yet we planned to copy the security settings of the very high-tech vaults which I would then give to East, who was going to break in later. Completely fine.

"This is it," Lord Jameson said proudly.

After a trip down a lift and a long temperature-controlled hallway, we stood in front of the vault. He waved his hand as if he was showing off something impressive. Inside my pocket, my hand clamped around the device East had given me. I knew that once we were close enough, all I had to do was press a button, and it would check the frequencies of the locking system. Then magically, East would have what he needed to break in later.

"Um, sir, you're going to have to let us in."

He frowned at that. "Why?"

Amelia sighed as if she was much beleaguered by his questions. "Well, because we need to verify what's inside. We would hate to discover later that this room was actually empty and that you'd wasted Interpol's time. And that you'd used this as an alibi for what will later be an attempt at insurance fraud."

His brows lifted. "I would never."

"Well, sir, sorry to say, it has happened before. So if you can let us in, we'll check things out and take a few photographs of what's in here. Then later, a team will need to get in here and verify the full inventory, just as a precaution."

"No one said I would have to do this."

Amelia's back remained straight, and she gave him what appeared to be a beatific smile. But I recognized it as her *Are you kidding me, arsehole?* face. "Sir, when you called Interpol and said that you had a threat against you and your property, and you insisted that Interpol, not Scotland Yard, be the ones to investigate, calling in favors as you did, what did you think was going to happen? Did you think we wouldn't look around and visit your mansion? You have a perfectly accomplished security team, I'm sure. So what exactly did you think was going to happen when you got Interpol involved?"

"I just wasn't told what to expect."

"I recognize that, but we're not in the habit of disclosing everything we're going to do ahead of time. So if you would like us to continue and catch these thieves, to put the people responsible for millions in stolen art behind bars *before* they can steal from you and your family, please, let us do our jobs."

He moved closer to the vault, and we were not even a step

behind him. He glowered as he turned back to us. "Do you really need to see this part?"

Amelia smiled. "Well, we would appreciate a close look at how it works."

He seemed surprised at first, but I could tell he was a little giddy to show off his toys.

"This vault is hermetically sealed and temperature controlled. It stores the most valuable pieces I have. I assume someone will need to catalog these as well."

Amelia nodded. "Once we get our basic assessments of security, I'll have the rest of the team do a full catalog."

He nodded as if finally satisfied. "You recognize, if anything goes missing..."

"I understand, sir, that's why we're here. I need to ascertain that this is, in fact, a credible threat."

"Of course, it's a credible threat."

"Well, I certainly hope not. Where did you say your information came from again?"

"I had an anonymous phone call."

Amelia nodded. "Right. But your very capable security team made a point of showing us all their devices and equipment, and I'm sure they're trying to locate where the original call came from, right?"

"Of course they are, but so far they've been unsuccessful."

"Well, if you don't mind, we'll have our experts take a look."

"Sure, fine."

For a man who was more than likely capable of deflecting any credible threat, using Interpol in this game of cat and mouse seemed rather off.

Maybe because he knew we wouldn't be able to find or trace anything.

Amelia kept him distracted while I appeared to be

photographing his pieces while surreptitiously doing the technical duty East had given me.

When it was done, I breathed a sigh of relief. I turned to Amelia. "All right, the vault is probably ready for a full catalog. I have the initial images we need."

She turned to Lord Jameson. "Thank you so much for your cooperation sir. I'll bring in the rest of the team now."

He nodded. "Actually, now that I think about it, it would probably be wise to have Interpol inside the event."

Amelia blinked. That wasn't the plan.

Her brow lifted, and I knew that to be her slightly panicked face. But then she recovered quickly. "While that's a kind offer, I'm not sure I can secure the man—"

Before she could even get the word *manpower* out, he waved his hand dismissively. "I'll call your boss. It'll be much better talking to the person in charge."

I frowned at that. How many times did she get dismissed in a day?

Even I was rarely dismissed like that. Especially from someone needing our help.

My jaw tensed as I finally saw exactly what she'd been talking and complaining about with my own two eyes. But she ignored it with more poise than Lord Jameson deserved. "Feel free to do that. But, if there is no actual credible threat, having us on-site is overkill. We really don't know how credible the threat is yet."

"In that case, consider it an invitation. One that you shouldn't deny."

I gave Amelia the barest of nods, letting her know that we'd deal with it as it came.

"Fair enough. I'll gather some team members."

"Yes, you do that. Actually, I insist on the two of you being here. Since you seem to be heading up this team, I want you on hand."

My steps faltered. "I'm sorry sir, but I'm not available."

Jameson turned his gaze on me. "Then make yourself available."

Fuck. I wasn't supposed to be anywhere near this. How the fuck were we going to pull this off?

As we were shown out of the vault, Amelia and I exchanged glances, and I knew that she was thinking the exact same thing. Already, our plan was going to shit. We'd be here. Likely, so would several other Interpol agents. Team London Lords was going to be in trouble.

CHAPTER 28

East

My FIRST INKLING that something was wrong was when Amelia came to hand me the device and not Nyla. "Where is she?"

"We have a problem. Jameson wants us at the event tonight. He insisted that since he had a rapport with Nyla, he was sending a car for her. She couldn't do the hand off."

"She's not supposed to be there."

"I know, I know. Look, here it is. I have to get back. I made a point to tell Jameson that I had to coordinate a team so I would not be taking his car service, but he was very insistent about Nyla. I hope that this is what you need, and I hope that you're successful."

I wanted to scream. "She's not supposed to be there. Anything could happen."

"Then make sure something doesn't. She's my best mate. Don't get her killed."

My gut twisted. "Fuck me."

"No thanks, though you're very pretty. I can see why she likes you."

Amelia turned in her dress, all slinky black and sequined. "Where do you keep your gun in that?"

"You probably don't want to know."

"Jesus."

I could hear her laugh ringing out as she hustled out of Lucas and Bryna's townhouse. I turned to my mates. "Christ, are we still doing this?"

Lucas held open his tuxedo. Inside were little sachets filled with lock picking tools and other things that I didn't quite know the purpose of, but I somehow knew people were going to be leaving the event without their jewels. "I'm ready."

I glanced at Bryna, and my brows furrowed. "He's kidding, right?"

She shook her head. "Nope, he's not kidding at all. He's been looking forward to this for two days."

I glanced at Ben and Bridge, and both were ready. I could tell by the set in their jaws.

"Well, let's do it then."

Ben's voice was low when he spoke. "Are you sure?"

"No, not at all. But this is the best chance we're going to get. And Bryna, for the love of God, if you can get Nyla out of there..."

"I'm on it. I like her a lot. I don't want the Jamesons getting their hooks in her."

Jesus Christ, I certainly hoped not. But I knew I had no control over the situation. And that scared me most of all.

Bridge clapped his hands together. "Into the belly of the beast we go."

When we arrived, the party was in full swing. Lots of tuxedos, thigh-high slits, and dazzling jewels. Lucas was probably in heaven.

I, on the other hand, was tense and tight. As soon as we entered, Garreth approached me. "I have an artist for you, mate."

He knew we weren't mates. Part of me wondered if he was doing that on purpose, trying to push, trying to nudge that he knew what we were up to. Did he know what was happening? Maybe, maybe not. I had no idea. But I pressed palms, met people, and talked art like it mattered.

For thirty minutes, I did everything I was supposed to do. I followed all of the rules.

And then it was showtime.

The lights went out and nothing went according to plan.

———

Nyla

NOTHING WAS GOING ACCORDING to plan. I was stuck next to Lord Jameson all night.

For the last hour, I'd had to watch him do little more than sip champagne and bluster.

Amelia though, Amelia got to be in on the plan.

Jameson had stayed close. Every time I had my phone out, he asked me who I was texting, what was happening with the plan to protect his assets.

I couldn't even talk to East.

Across the room, I saw when Lucas entered.

And I knew that somebody was going to come out without a brooch, or a watch, or a phone, or a necklace. He stole with such gleeful abandon.

Next to him, Bryna looked stunning. Her brunette hair was coiled on top of her head. Her elegant black shift gown showed her sun-kissed shoulders and long lean legs. I had worn black too, but my dress was a simple halter with slits up the legs so I could run if necessary.

Also, I kept weapons strapped to my garter.

Yes, I was every action movie cliché.

"Ms. Kinkade you don't look like you're enjoying yourself."

"It's Agent Kincade, and of course I'm enjoying myself, sir. But if you'll just excuse me, I'm going to check in with my team and make sure nothing's amiss."

He put a hand on my elbow and guided me away from the door toward the bar. "No, Agent Kinkade, why don't you have a drink?"

I sighed. "Lord Jameson, is there a reason you don't want me to check on my team?"

"No. It's just that when my son Garreth told me that you were having a look around at the artwork last week, I couldn't help but wonder what you were doing looking around my estate."

"Sir, I'm not sure what your son told you. I got turned around while looking for the loo."

He smiled at me then. "Yes, that's what he said you said. And the cameras around the grounds did point to that, and it didn't seem you were acting particularly suspicious."

"Okay then."

"But I just want to see the mettle of you because Garreth seems quite taken with you, actually. I'd like to get to know you better."

I tried to choose my words carefully so as not to overtly insult his son. "Well, I've only met him twice. I don't know him that well."

"Interesting."

"Just so you know I didn't wander."

"I'm also curious. Did you ever find that man that you were looking for? The one you told me had gone missing in Italy?"

"No. It was just a curiosity."

"Interesting. It's a curiosity no one else has ever brought up. You work for him, don't you?"

My eyes went wide. "I'm sure I don't know what you mean."

"You work for Theroux. I can tell."

"Sir." I glanced down at his hand that was gripping my elbow far too tightly. "Please release me."

"I know he's coming for me."

"I don't know what you're talking about. I'm Agent Nyla Kinkade. I work for Interpol. My father is Roger Kinkade. He is Interpol's Section Chief. I was assigned to his work detail."

He searched my gaze, as if trying to determine if I was being truthful. Then he released me. "Sorry, my dear. You see, when you get to my age, you tend to have a lot of enemies. And my number one enemy is coming after me."

"Uh, who's your enemy sir? I'm very confused."

"A thief."

I played dumb. "Henry Warlow?"

"No, Francois Theroux."

"I don't understand, Lord Jameson. What does Francois Theroux have to do with Henry Warlow?"

His gaze searched mine again, and I kept my mask up, acting confused. It was better that way.

He sighed. "Francois Theroux is the most successful thief in the world. You're telling me you don't know him?"

"Why would I?"

He stepped back a bit. "I'm sorry. It's just at my age, you can get paranoid. Your father shares my concerns though."

"Yes, I am aware of Theroux. My father's been after him a long time."

"Yes. He has. I knew he was the right man for the job tonight."

"Well, if I was with my team, we'd probably be more successful."

"No, you're not joining your team. You're staying right by my side."

"If you say so."

At that instant, the lights went out.

My heart leapt. Jesus Christ, that was East. It was starting.

Someone reached for me, and I assumed it was Jameson, so I deftly avoided him and then rolled to the ground so he couldn't grab me again.

There was pandemonium in the ballroom. People started to scream, glasses were dropped, and the crowd of guests jostled against one another as they waited for the generators to turn on.

I hoped to God Amelia had managed to cut the line, and I prayed to God that East was as fast as he said he was.

I heard Jameson's voice. "Agent Kinkade."

Luckily for me, Denning and the team called for all agents.

"Sorry, Lord Jameson. I must go." The walkie-talkie was loud enough that he heard it.

All agents were being called to the south entrance.

I used my phone's flashlight app like many others in the ballroom had started to do and made my way as quickly as I could and prayed that East had already gotten what he needed.

Please, please, please, please, please, please. On my way to the south entrance, I saw something wrong. A shadow. Was it East? But instead of running out the exit toward the gardens, he was running toward the private quarters.

Jesus Christ, what the hell had gone wrong? There was one office down that way, and the rest were private suites where both of the Jamesons stayed.

Lord Jameson's wife, Tiffany, had been present tonight. She'd only spoken a few words though, seemingly content to let her husband and son have the spotlight.

What was East doing?

I didn't dare call out his name, but I followed him as quickly as I could, taking off my shoes so I could run faster.

In my earpiece, I could hear the team.

Bridge asked, "For the love of God, what has gone wrong?"

Where was East going?

On my walkie, I could hear Denning demanding for everyone to check in.

Then my phone went off and it was Amelia texting. *Where are you? Denning wants to know.*

Nyla: *I'm coming. Jameson held me back.*

Amelia: *Denning suspicious. Wants to know why you aren't where you're supposed to be.*

Nyla: *He knows Jameson had me.*

My phone rang, and Amelia said, "You better get down here."

"Jameson held me up. But East is going the wrong way."

Amelia cursed under her breath. "Get your arse down here."

"I have to make sure he's okay."

"Ny, this isn't the time."

"I know. But you know he wouldn't have broken protocol unless there was a good reason."

"Jesus fuck. Oh God, make it fast. I think Denning's coming your way. He's sending agents to spread out to look for you."

"Oh, fuck me."

"Hurry up and get East the fuck out of there."

"Yeah, I'm on it."

I ran out in the hall, made a left, and followed East into the secondary office. "What the fuck are you doing?"

He whipped around with a gun trained on my chest, and I staggered back. In the moment, even with his mask down, he looked every bit the killer.

"East it's me."

He sighed and pulled his mask up a little. "Jesus, why are you chasing me?"

"You're going the wrong way, and Interpol agents are coming for you right now."

"His laptop wasn't in there. This is a private office, and I thought I might find it in here."

My gut clenched. "Oh my God, we're all going to die."

He laughed. He had his little set of tools out and was already typing something on the keys. And then some little tablet looking thing next to the computer was lit red, red, red and then started glowing green in a circle, lighting up section by section.

"This will just take a minute."

I glanced outside. "Can you get out this way?"

East glanced down. "I have exit routes in every window and door in this place. Don't worry."

"I am worried."

He put his gun away and stalked over to me. "That's going to take a second. But God, can I just say you look beautiful?"

"Thanks. But maybe we don't worry about compliments right now."

He didn't seem to care. He leaned forward and kissed me. Deep. "God, there's something about adrenaline and you and kissing. Want to roll around on the grass with me later?"

I laughed. "No. Focus."

That's when I heard it. A walkie-talkie in the hallway. Fuck me. They were already here.

"You have to go."

With a curse, he planted another quick kiss on my lips and released me. Then he went to the window and opened it. He attached something to the outside. What the hell was that? A grappling hook?

Was he going to rappel down? Jesus. Okay, okay it was only

two stories. He'd be fine. But why did he have that equipment? I had all kinds of questions for him.

The little device on the table turned completely green, and footsteps drew closer.

"East, you have to go *right now*."

He frowned at the door. "If they find you in here, they'll know the laptop was tampered with. I can't just leave you here."

"East, you don't have a choice. I'll just say that we tussled and you escaped."

He frowned. "You don't look like you were in a fight, Nyla."

"Okay." I took a couple pins out of my hair and shook it out. Then I shimmied until part of the strap on my dress tore just a little. "See, I look like I've been in a scuffle. East, come on," I begged him. "You have to go."

He was at the window. Hook ready. And then he did something I didn't expect. He raised his gun. "Ny, I'm sorry."

"What are you doing?"

"Giving you a way out."

And then with a loud crack and searing fire that felt like a red-hot poker, East Hale shot me.

To be continued in ***The Fall of East*** …

———

Thank you for reading EAST BOUND, Book 2 in the HEAR NO EVIL TRILOGY.

East Hale never wanted to shoot the woman he loved. But these things happen when you need to protect the ones you love. With danger closing in all around them, they'll need to work together to bring down their enemies if they're to have their happily ever after.

READ The stunning conclusion in *The Fall of East* now!

You can also read Nathan and Sophie's story right now! Find out what happens when a seductive, jaded playboy with a filthy mouth meets his uptight neighbor and they strike a little ex payback bargain.
One-click MR. DIRTY now!

> *"Mr. Dirty is a **fun and flirty romance** with complex characters and a great storyline."* -
> *Amazon Reviewer*

Can't get enough billionaires? Meet a cocky, billionaire prince that goes undercover in Cheeky Royal! He's a prince with a secret to protect. The last distraction he can afford is his gorgeous as sin new neighbor.
His secrets could get them killed, but still, he can't stay away...
Read Cheeky Royal now!

Turn the page for an excerpt from Cheeky Royal...

UPCOMING BOOKS

The Fall of East
Royal Line
To Catch a Thief

ALSO FROM NANA MALONE
CHEEKY ROYAL

"You make a really good model. I'm sure dozens of artists have volunteered to paint you before."

He shook his head. "Not that I can recall. Why? Are you offering?"

I grinned. "I usually do nudes." Why did I say that? It wasn't true. Because you're hoping he'll volunteer as tribute.

He shrugged then reached behind his back and pulled his shirt up, tugged it free, and tossed it aside. "How is this for nude?"

Fuck. Me. I stared for a moment, mouth open and looking like an idiot. Then, well, I snapped a picture. Okay fine, I snapped several. "Uh, that's a start."

He ran a hand through his hair and tussled it, so I snapped several of that. These were romance-cover gold. Getting into it, he started posing for me, making silly faces. I got closer to him, snapping more close-ups of his face. That incredible face.

*Then suddenly he went deadly serious again, the intensity in his
eyes going harder somehow, sharper. Like a razor. "You look
nervous. I thought you said you were used to nudes."*

*I swallowed around the lump in my throat. "Yeah, at school
whenever we had a model, they were always nude. I got used
to it."*

*He narrowed his gaze. "Are you sure about that?"
Shit. He could tell. "Yeah, I am. It's just a human form. Male.
Female. No big deal."*

*His lopsided grin flashed, and my stomach flipped. Stupid trai-
torous body...and damn him for being so damn good looking. I
tried to keep the lens centered on his face, but I had to get several
of his abs, for you know...research.
But when his hand rubbed over his stomach and then slid to the
button on his jeans, I gasped, "What are you doing?"
"Well, you said you were used doing nudes. Will that make you
more comfortable as a photographer?"*

*I swallowed again, unable to answer, wanting to know what he
was doing, how far he would go. And how far would I go?*

*The button popped, and I swallowed the sawdust in my mouth. I
snapped a picture of his hands.*

*Well yeah, and his abs. So sue me. He popped another button,
giving me a hint of the forbidden thing I couldn't have. I kept
snapping away. We were locked in this odd, intimate game of
chicken. I swung the lens up to capture his face. His gaze was
slightly hooded. His lips parted...turned on. I stepped back a step*

to capture all of him. His jeans loose, his feet bare. Sitting on the stool, leaning back slightly and giving me the sex face, because that's what it was—God's honest truth—the sex face. And I was a total goner.

"You're not taking pictures, Len." His voice was barely above a whisper.

"Oh, sorry." I snapped several in succession. Full body shots, face shots, torso shots. There were several torso shots. I wanted to fully capture what was happening.

He unbuttoned another button, taunting me, tantalizing me. Then he reached into his jeans, and my gaze snapped to meet his. I wanted to say something. Intervene in some way...help maybe... ask him what he was doing. But I couldn't. We were locked in a game that I couldn't break free from. Now I wanted more. I wanted to know just how far he would go.

Would he go nude? Or would he stay in this half-undressed state, teasing me, tempting me to do the thing that I shouldn't do?

I snapped more photos, but this time I was close. I was looking down on him with the camera, angling so I could see his perfectly sculpted abs as they flexed. His hand was inside his jeans. From the bulge, I knew he was touching himself. And then I snapped my gaze up to his face.

Sebastian licked his lip, and I captured the moment that tongue met flesh.

Heat flooded my body, and I pressed my thighs together to abate the ache. At that point, I was just snapping photos, completely in the zone, wanting to see what he might do next.

"Len..."

"Sebastian." *My voice was so breathy I could barely get it past my lips.*

"Do you want to come closer?"

"I--I think maybe I'm close enough?"

His teeth grazed his bottom lip. "Are you sure about that? I have another question for you."

I snapped several more images, ranging from face shots to shoulders, to torso. Yeah, I also went back to the hand-around-his-dick thing because...wow. "Yeah? Go ahead."

"Why didn't you tell me about your boyfriend 'til now?"

Oh shit. "I—I'm not sure. I didn't think it mattered. It sort of feels like we're supposed to be friends." *Lies all lies.*

He stood, his big body crowding me. "Yeah, friends..."

I swallowed hard. I couldn't bloody think with him so close. His scent assaulted me, sandalwood and something that was pure Sebastian wrapped around me, making me weak. Making me tingle as I inhaled his scent. Heat throbbed between my thighs, even as my knees went weak. "Sebastian, wh—what are you doing?"

"

*Proving to you that we're not friends. Will you let me?"

He was asking my permission. I knew what I wanted to say. I understood what was at stake. But then he raised his hand and traced his knuckles over my cheek, and a whimper escaped.

His voice went softer, so low when he spoke, his words were more like a rumble than anything intelligible. "Is that you telling me to stop?"

Seriously, there were supposed to be words. There were. But somehow I couldn't manage them, so like an idiot I shook my head.

His hand slid into my curls as he gently angled my head. When he leaned down, his lips a whisper from mine, he whispered, "This is all I've been thinking about."

Read Cheeky Royal now!

Looking for a few Good Books? Look no Further

FREE
Shameless
Before Sin
Cheeky Royal
Protecting the Heiress

Royals
Royals Undercover

Cheeky Royal
Cheeky King

Royals Undone
Royal Bastard
Bastard Prince

Royals United

Royal Tease
Teasing the Princess

Royal Elite

The Heiress Duet

Protecting the Heiress
Tempting the Heiress

The Prince Duet

Return of the Prince
To Love a Prince

The Bodyguard Duet

Billionaire to the Bodyguard
The Billionaire's Secret

London Royals

London Royal Duet

London Royal
London Soul

Playboy Royal Duet

Royal Playboy
Playboy's Heart

London Lords
See No Evil

Big Ben
The Benefactor
For Her Benefit

Hear No Evil
East End
East Bound
Fall of East

To Catch a Thief

Speak No Evil
London Bridge
Bridge of Lies
Broken Bridge

The Donovans Series
Come Home Again (Nate & Delilah)
Love Reality (Ryan & Mia)
Race For Love (Derek & Kisima)
Love in Plain Sight (Dylan and Serafina)
Eye of the Beholder – (Logan & Jezzie)
Love Struck (Zephyr & Malia)

London Billionaires Standalones
Mr. Trouble (Jarred & Kinsley)
Mr. Big (Zach & Emma)
Mr. Dirty(Nathan & Sophie)

The Shameless World

Shameless
Shameless
Shameful
Unashamed

Force
Enforce

Deep
Deeper

Before Sin
Sin
Sinful

Brazen
Still Brazen

The Player
Bryce

Dax

Echo

Fox

Ransom

Gage

The In Stilettos Series
Sexy in Stilettos (Alec & Jaya)

Sultry in Stilettos (Beckett & Ricca)

Sassy in Stilettos (Caleb & Micha)

Strollers & Stilettos (Alec & Jaya & Alexa)

Seductive in Stilettos (Shane & Tristia)

Stunning in Stilettos (Bryan & Kyra)

~~~

In Stilettos Spin off
Tempting in Stilettos (Serena & Tyson)

Teasing in Stilettos (Cara & Tate)

Tantalizing in Stilettos (Jaggar & Griffin)

Love Match Series
*Game Set Match (Jason & Izzy)
Mismatch (Eli & Jessica)

Don't want to miss a single release? Click here!

Wall Street Journal & USA Today Best Seller, Nana Malone's love of all things romance and adventure started with a tattered romantic suspense she "borrowed" from her cousin.

It was a sultry summer afternoon in Ghana, and Nana was a precocious thirteen. She's been in love with kick butt heroines ever since. With her overactive imagination, and channeling her inner Buffy, it was only a matter a time before she started creating her own characters.

Now she writes about sexy royals and smokin' hot bodyguards when she's not hiding her tiara from Kidlet, chasing a puppy who refuses to shake without a treat, or begging her husband to listen to her latest hair-brained idea.

Printed in Poland
by Amazon Fulfillment
Poland Sp. z o.o., Wrocław

89868703R00179